THE BLACK
OF SIVANIF

KENNETH ANDERSON

The Black Panther of Sivanipalli

The Black Panther of Sivanipalli

KENNETH ANDERSON

Rupa & Co

This reprint in Rupa Paperback 2002
Fifth Impression 2011

Published by
Rupa Publications India Pvt. Ltd.
7/16, Ansari Road, Daryaganj,
New Delhi 110 002

Sales Centres:

Allahabad Bengaluru Chennai
Hyderabad Jaipur Kathmandu
Kolkata Mumbai

Typeset Copyright © Rupa & Co. 2001

Typeset by
Mindways Design
1410 Chiranjiv Tower
43 Nehru Place
New Delhi 110 019

Contents

Introduction

THE FIRST FIVE CHAPTERS OF THIS BOOK ARE DEVOTED TO PANTHERS.
Perhaps you may wonder why I have concentrated on panthers
and not written of the other animals of the jungle too. Well,
for one reason, panthers are still very common in India.
Secondly, they are comparatively easy to find, inasmuch as
to this day they are met within a few miles of some of the
big towns. For a third reason, hunting panthers is fairly
inexpensive and well within the reach of the average person's
pocket. A panther will come for such bait as a dog, a goat
or a donkey; whereas a tiger must be attracted by a buffalo
or a bull, which costs much more.

In return, shooting panthers by the sporting method of
sitting on the ground instead of in the safety of a tree *machan*
offers quite as great a thrill as tiger hunting.

I have also written a chapter about tigers and other animals,
and something more about snakes. Why I have included
snakes is because, although a great deal has been written and
is known about tigers, elephants, lions and big animals in
various parts of the world, not much has been written about

snakes, and most people know very little regarding them, except that in general they should be avoided. I hope I am able to throw some light upon these equally interesting creatures. Nor must the reader think for a moment that tigers, panthers, bears and elephants are the most dangerous creatures to be encountered in an Indian jungle. Far quicker, far less visible, and far more potent is the poisonous snake that lurks in a bush or in the grass.

I have also told the story of a very gallant bison and two adventures with tigers. These last two will give you an idea of the many difficulties, hardships and disappointments involved in trying to shoot a man-eating tiger. In one case I failed completely; in the other I succeeded, but only by pure chance. I have closed with a brief account of a tiger that behaved very strangely. He is alive as I write this—and he is still an engima.

As I record these adventures, the sights and sounds of the present fade way and memories come rushing in. The blackness of the forest night with the star-filled sky above and the twinkling gems of the jungle carpet below, the myriads of fire-flies that glitter together like elfin lamps amidst the dark foliage; and those other, brighter, living lights, the glowing eyes of a tiger, panther or bison, and the green eyes of graceful deer tripping daintily through the undergrowth, reflecting the beams of my torch as I walk beneath the whispering trees.

Come with me for the few hours it may take you to read this book into the domain of the tiger, the panther and the elephant, amidst the stupendous swaying heights and deep shade of the giant trees whose boles form the structure of this marvellous edifice. Forget the false values and ideas of what is called civilization, those imposed rules on the free and simple truths of life. Here in the jungle you will find truth, you will find peace, bliss and happiness; you will find life itself. There is no room, no time at all, for hypocrisy, for make-believe, for that which is artificial and false. You are face to face with the primitive, with that which is real, with that which is most wonderful—which is God.

If I can succeed in spiriting you away for a few moments from all that is mundane in your life, into the marvels of a tropical jungle and its excitements, where your life depends on your senses, your wits, your skill, and in the end on Providence, as you creep on the blood-trail of a wounded man-eater through dense verdure or among piled boulders, then I shall feel myself amply rewarded.

One

A Panther's Way

EVERY PANTHER DIFFERS FROM ANY OTHER PANTHER. SOME PANTHERS are very bold; others are very timid. Some are cunning to the degree of being uncanny; others appear quite foolish. I have met panthers that seemed almost to possess a sixth sense, and acted and behaved as if they could read and anticipate one's very thought. Lastly, but quite rarely, comes the panther that attacks people, and more rarely still, the one that eats them.

A man-eating beast is generally the outcome of some extraordinary circumstance. Maybe someone has wounded it, and it is unable henceforth to hunt its natural prey—other animals—easily. Therefore, through necessity it begins to eat humans, because they offer an easy prey. Or perhaps a panther has eaten a dead human body which was originally buried in a too-shallow grave and later dug up by jackals or a bear. Once having tasted human flesh, the panther often takes a liking to it. Lastly, but very rarely indeed, it may have been the cub of a man-eating mother, who taught it the habit.

Generally a panther is an inoffensive and quite harmless animal that is fearful of human beings and vanishes silently into the undergrowth at the sight or sound of them. When wounded, some show an extraordinary degree of ferocity and bravery. Others again are most cowardly and allow themselves to be followed up, or even chased like curs.

If from a hill-top you could watch a panther stalking his prey, he would offer a most entertaining spectacle. You would see him taking advantage of every bush, of every tree-trunk, and of every stone behind which to take cover. He can flatten himself to the ground in an amazing fashion. His colouration renders him invisible, unless you have the keenest eyesight. I once watched one through a pair of binoculars and was amazed at the really wonderful sense of woodcraft the panther had. Then comes the final rush. In a couple of bounds, and with lightning speed, he reaches his prey.

With unerring aim, he seizes the throat with his powerful fangs from above and behind, so that when the animal falls to earth the panther may be on the side opposite and away from its threshing hooves, which might otherwise cause serious injury. The prey is forced to the ground and that vice-like grip never relaxes till the animal is dead. Even then, the panther retains his vicious hold while sucking the lifeblood of his victim through the deep punctures he has made in its throat.

Imagine, then, the stillness of the jungle and the stealthy coming of the panther as he approaches his kill or stalks the live bait that has been tied out for him. If you want to hunt the panther, watch very carefully: try to penetrate every bush, look into every clump of grass, be careful when you pass a rock or a boulder, gaze into hollows and ravines. For the panther may be behind any of these, or be lying in some hole in the ground. Not only your success, but even your life will depend upon your care, for you have pitted your wits against perhaps the most adept of jungle dwellers and a very dangerous killer.

One of the most difficult and exciting pastimes is to try to hunt the panther on his own terms. This is known as 'still-hunting'.

To still-hunt successfully, you must have a keen sense of the jungle, a soft tread, and an almost panther-like mind; for you are going to try to circumvent this very cunning animal at his own game. You are about to hunt him on your own feet—and remember, he is the most skilful of hunters himself.

The first thing to know is the time of the day he comes out to search for his prey. He is generally a nocturnal animal, and stalks the forest at night. You, being human, cannot see in the dark unless you are aided by a torchlight. But that would not be still-hunting. The next best time would be the late evening just before it grows dark. Then there is a chance of meeting an early panther. It is useless to go out during the day, for at that time he is resting. Besides, he does not like the hot sun.

Secondly, where are, generally speaking, the best places in which to look for him? To answer this, you should know the answer to the next question—on what does a panther normally prey in the jungle? The reply to that question is not going to be very helpful, for a panther will eat anything that is alive, provided it is not too large to be tackled. Jungle fowl, peafowl, rabbits, monkeys, wild pigs, and any of the deer family, excepting the very large stags. Near villages, domestic pigs, dogs, goats, sheep, donkeys and average-sized cattle are his staple diet. Even a stray village cat will fill the bill, provided it is foolish enough to stray too far from the huts.

Let us suppose for the moment that we are in a jungle where the panther hunts his natural food. How does the panther go about his hunting? Remember, he has marvellous sight and acute hearing, but hardly any sense of smell. What would you do, if you were in the panther's place?

Obviously, one of two things. You would either move around silently in localities where the food is to be found, or you would hide yourself near some spot where your food is likely to come. The panther does just that.

He moves about stealthily, on padded feet, in places where he thinks the birds and animals he is seeking are likely to be, or he lies in wait for them near some water hole or salt lick that they generally visit.

If he is stalking and wants to be silent, he cannot always move in the undergrowth, or among dead leaves, for they will crackle or rustle. So he walks stealthily along footpaths, game-trails, a forest fire-line, or in the shelter of the banks of a *nullah* or a stream. Alternatively, he hides at the approaches to water, or a salt lick, where he can pounce upon his quarry as it passes by. It is in such places that you must look for him.

Further, movement on your part will attract his attention. Therefore, take a walk around the jungle in the daytime and see if you can discover pug-marks—not just a stray set of pugs, but a series of marks, old and new. When you have found them, you will know you have hit upon a well-used panther trail. Try to select a point where two or more such trails meet or cross, or a spot where such a trail or a fire-line crosses a stream.

When you have found it, return the same evening and hide yourself behind a convenient tree-trunk or bush; and then, whatever you do, sit perfectly still while keeping a sharp lookout along the *paths* or sections of fire-line or streambed that are in view. If you are lucky, you may see a hunting panther walking along one of these, perhaps looking up now and again into the trees in search of a monkey or one of the larger jungle birds. It goes without saying, of course, that in such vigils you might also spot a tiger, an elephant, or one of the several deer species.

But let us continue to suppose for the moment that you are only after a panther. If you can locate a jungle pool or a salt lick, it would be convenient to lie down under some cover beside it, or behind an ant-hill, if available. You will derive much entertainment in observing the various denizens of the forest as they visit such a rendezvous. Don't be too surprised if, after a time, you notice a panther or tiger taking up a somewhat similar position to your own, although I may warn you that it will be very hard for you to become aware of them, so silently do they move. As I have already said, such places are favoured by carnivora when lying in wait for their natural food.

I remember that I was once lying in the grass behind the trunk of a tree overlooking a salt lick formed in a corner of a shallow ravine. Earlier examination had shown that spotted deer and sambar visited this salt lick in large numbers. It was growing dusk when the faintest of rustles a little behind me caused me to turn my head slowly and glance back. There I saw a panther regarding me with very evident surprise. Seeing he was discovered, he stood up and half-turned around with the intention of getting away. Then he looked back at me once again, as much as to say, 'Can't you get the hell out of here?' Finally he moved off.

It is fascinating to watch one of these animals with her cubs, or a tigress with hers. The solicitude of the mother is very noticeable. Carnivora do not bring their cubs out of the cave where they are born until old enough to walk stably and understand the rudiments of hunting. Till such time, they are sheltered carefully in the cave. When very young, they are fed entirely on milk. When they grow a little older, the mother begins to feed them on raw meat which first she herself eats and partially digests, and then vomits out for the cubs to feed on. As the cubs themselves become able to digest stronger meat, the mother brings her kills to the cave— perhaps a jungle fowl or peafowl, and as time passes, small animals, increasing to the leg of deer, or perhaps a deer itself.

Cubs are very greedy and if left to themselves will overeat and make themselves ill. I have kept a number of panther and tiger cubs, and have found the former particularly prone to gastritis. They will stuff themselves by gobbling chunks of raw meat, and will drink bowls of blood, till almost unable to move. Once they are attacked by gastritis, the malady proves practically incurable, and they die in three or four days in great agony. This complaint seems to affect them until they are about eight months old, and I have lost quite a few by it.

In the wild state, a mother appears to know this instinctively and gives her young just enough to eat, supplementing raw meat with natural milk till the cubs are quite big and start to bite and scratch her while she is suckling them.

If danger threatens the cave, in the form of intruding human beings or the male of the species, which is rather fond of eating his young, she will move them to a safer abode. This she does by carrying them in her mouth by the scruff of the neck, one at a time.

When the cubs are old enough to walk, the mother takes them out for education in the art of stalking and killing for themselves. This is quite a lengthy process. She begins by killing the prey herself, while the cubs hide in the undergrowth. Then she calls them with a series of guttural mewing-like sounds, allowing them to romp over the dead animal, bite it and get the taste of a fresh kill and warm blood. The ferocious sounds emitted by the cubs when doing this are quite amusing to hear. They bolster up their courage and lash themselves into a fury, growling and snapping at each other and even at their mother.

The next lesson starts when she only half-kills the prey, or hamstrings it, allowing the youngsters to finish the task as best they can. This they begin doing by attacking the throat and biting the animal to death—a very cruel process.

Education in the art of killing goes much farther in the case of tiger cubs than in that of panthers. Panthers choke their victims to death by gripping the throat and hanging on, whereas the tiger very scientifically breaks the neck. Hence tiger cubs take much longer to teach, and it is a common occurrence for a tigress to kill four or five cattle in a herd while teaching her young which, equally often if left to themselves, make a mess of the job by merely biting or mauling an animal, which eventually escapes.

I have mentioned that a tiger is a very scientific and neat killer. He generally leaps half across the back of his quarry, bending over and seizing the throat on its other side, while hanging on with his forepaws in a powerful shoulder-grip. Then he wrenches upwards and backwards in a swift, violent jerk which topples the animal over. It is the combined weights of the quarry and the tiger, coupled with the sudden mighty twist of the neck, that breaks the victim's neck.

When a mother tiger or panther comes out on the hunting trail with her young, they follow behind, copying every action of the parent and sinking to the ground or behind the cover exactly as she does. At such times it is dangerous to be too near a tigress. She is liable to attack you in defence of her young. A pantheress is less likely to attack, although she will demonstrate by growling ferociously. Even so, one never can tell, and it is wise to have your rifle ready when a family procession comes into view.

But whatever you do, and unless utterly unavoidable and in self-defence, please do not shoot the mother, be it panther or tiger, for if you do the cubs will invariably escape into the jungle where they may starve to death, or if they are big enough they may develop into man-eaters. You should remember they have not yet learned properly the art of killing their natural food, other animals. If you interrupt their education at this stage they may, by force of circumstances which you have created, turn to killing human beings to appease their hunger. Bear in mind always that a human being is much easier to stalk, attack and kill than any of the larger animals.

An interesting period to indulge in this pastime of stalking is during the Indian winter—that is, the months of November, December and January—for then is the mating season of both these species of carnivora.

Of course, you should remember that these animals are mostly active during the night, and that there is only an off-chance of hearing or seeing them towards dusk. It is thrilling to listen to the sound of a tigress calling her mate, and one can almost detect the note of impatience in her summons. I should warn you, however, that tigers are definitely dangerous during this season, particularly when courting the female, or in the act of mating. Their method is exceedingly rough, both the tiger and tigress often biting and scratching each other freely.

You may have observed the strange behaviour of domestic cats during mating. Multiply this many, many times, and you will have some idea of the savagery of tigers when making love. They lash themselves into a frenzy and a fury, and woe betide a human who intrudes upon their privacy at this time of sexual excitement. The tigress has the reputation of being even more excitable and consequently more dangerous than the tiger at this period. A tigress on heat, calling lustily, has often stopped forest operations and bullock-cart traffic through the jungle over large areas.

Panthers are much the same in this respect, but generally lack the courage to attack a human intruder, although they will demonstrate in no uncertain manner.

A panther resembles a cat more closely than does a tiger. The scratching up of sand or dead leaves by the side of a game-track reveals where a panther has answered the call of nature and then covered up the excreta, exactly in the same way as a domestic cat. A tiger, however, will not bother to do this, but leaves it exposed in the manner of a dog. The excreta, in both cases, consists mostly of the undigested hair of the last kill.

The hyaena, which is a carrion eater, swallows bones and all complete. So the droppings of this animal are easily recognisable as hard, white lumps of semi-digested bones. The track of a hyaena is identifiable in the great difference between the size of the fore and hind-paws; the forepaws are much larger.

Panthers, like tigers, retract their claws when walking, so that the difference between a panther's pug-marks and those of a hyaena, which are about the same in size, is that the 'ball' of the panther's pug is much larger than the hyaena's, while the points of the claws do not show at all. The hyaena, being unable to retract its claws, leaves their imprint clearly on the ground.

In the past there has been much controversy between those sportsmen who have claimed that the panther and the leopard are two entirely different species of animal and those who have said that they are one and the same. This argument has died out with modern times, when it has been recognized that they are indeed one and the same. Difference in environment and diet has caused some animals to grow to a much larger size than others. The forest-dwelling panther, with his richer diet of game-animals, generally grow, much bigger and has a darker and thicker coat than the panther that lives near villages, where his food is restricted to dogs and goats. Also, living among rocks and boulders as the latter generally does, his coat is paler, and the hair short and coarse. Incidentally, the darker coat of the forest-dwelling panther helps to camoulflage him very effectively against the dense vegetation of the jungle, while the paler coat of the 'village panther', as he is sometimes called, makes it very difficult to detect him among the rocks where he lives.

Very occasionally, however, there are exceptions in both cases, and Nature appears unaccountably to break her own rule. I have shot some very large panthers living near villages and far from the regular jungle, possessing dark rich coats of hair, and some quite small ones within the forest with pale coats.

Much the same applies to tigers. Those that have accustomed themselves to eating cattle become heavy and fat, while the true game-killers are sleek and muscular, carrying no fat at all, for they have a far more strenuous time hunting wild game than does the cattle-lifter, which procures its prey with little or no effort. Strenuous exercise reduces fat, not only in human beings, but in tigers also.

Man-eaters of both species are distinct anomalies and the products of unnatural circumstances, some of which have been mentioned already.

Panthers can climb quite well and they sometimes ascend trees after monkeys, or to escape when pursued by wild dogs. Tigers do not, although I have known one in the Mysore Zoological Gardens that has accustomed itself to climbing quite high and lying on a platform that had been specially built for it on a tree within its enclosure. This is an instance of the fact that tigers, like human beings, as individuals differ from one another.

Both panthers and tigers hunt monkeys by a quite unique method. Jungle monkeys are very vigilant and keep a sharp lookout for carnivora, which are their natural enemies. At the sound or sight of any of these animals they climb to the topmost branches, where they are safe. Knowing this, panthers and tigers charge at the foot of the tree up which the monkeys have climbed, uttering a series of terrific growls and roars. These fearsome sounds quite unnerve the poor monkeys, which, instead of remaining on their perches where they are safe, attempt to leap to the next tree; or, if that is too far away, jump to the ground from enormous heights with the intention of making a run to climb another tree. In this process some of them injure themselves or are stunned, and fall easy victims to the clever hunter.

One of the most intelligent animals, if not the most intelligent, in the Indian jungle is the wild dog. *Shikaris* of earlier days have variously given this place to the wild elephant, tiger and panther, but if you have studied the habits of the wild dog you may be inclined to disagree with them. When hunting deer they send out 'flankers', which run ahead of the quarry and ambush it later. In large packs of thirty or more, these animals are fearless hunters, and will ring, attack and kill any tiger or panther by literally tearing it to bits, despite the number of casualties they may suffer in the process.

Particularly in the forests of Chittoor district, in the former Presidency of Madras, they have earned quite a reputation for this, and I know of at least three instances where a very gory battle had been waged, resulting eventually in the tiger being torn to shreds, but not before he had killed a half-dozen of the dogs and maimed many others. I have never come across a panther destroyed in this fashion because, as I have said before, of their ability to escape by climbing trees.

The tiger takes to water and will swim across large rivers freely. Especially in hot weather, he is very fond, during the midday hours, of taking his siesta by the banks of a shady stream or pool, sometimes lying in the water itself. He hunts freely on rainy days, and his pug-marks are often seen in the morning after a night of pouring rain. This is not so with the panther. A true cat in every respect, he detests water, abhors rain, and is not given to swimming, although he can do so in emergencies, such as to escape from a pack of wild dogs.

The tiger was originally an immigrant into India from the colder regions of Mongolia. Hence his liking for cool spots in which to shelter from the heat. The panther is a true native of India and of the tropics.

Tigers very occasionally mimic the calls of sambar, obviously to attract and ambush them. Such mimicry is heard very rarely and only in forests where deer are plentiful. Panthers, however, do not follow this practice but rely entirely on their silent stalking, their ability to flatten themselves to the ground and hide in incredibly small places, and their final quick rush upon their quarry.

It was often said by the sportsmen of the past that the tiger is a 'gentleman' while the panther is a 'bounder'. I think these sayings have gained popularity from the experiences some of those hardy, old stalwarts have gained while following wounded animals of both species with their old-fashioned guns, frequently muzzle-loaders. Hats off to them, indeed. Ill-armed and awkwardly clad in the fashions of those days, wearing heavy boots and cumbersomely thick solar topees, they followed a wounded animal fearlessly on foot. How different from the modern 'hunter' who shoots at night from the safety of a motorcar, the lights of which dazzle the poor animal and give it not the ghost of a chance!

A wounded tiger generally betrays his whereabouts by growling as his pursuer approaches, but a wounded panther often lies silent and concealed, and attacks the hunter from behind, when he has passed. Hence there seems to be some justification for those who labelled the panther a 'bounder'. Actually, a tiger is generally far braver and certainly much more formidable, and when he attacks to kill he finishes that job very thoroughly. A panther, however—unless he is a man-eater—will maul his pursuer and then escape rather than kill him outright.

Panthers gnaw at the bones of their kills, even when they are in a very far advanced state of decomposition. As a rule, tigers do not visit their kills after the second day. For one thing, they eat much more and so have finished all there is to eat, after two or three meals. Also, on the whole, they are cleaner feeders. Decomposed flesh becomes embedded beneath the claws of both species. This breeds dangerous germs, and it is the scratches inflicted by these animals, more than their bites, that lead to blood-poisoning. Tigers are very conscious of this foreign matter under their claws, and clean them, in addition to sharpening them, by scratching upon the soft bark of certain trees. Panthers do this very rarely, so that their claws are generally more infected. Trees bearing such claw-marks at the height of six or seven feet, where a tiger has reared up on his hind legs and cleaned the claws of his forepaws, are a happy sign to the hunter of the presence of his quarry.

In other ways also, the tiger is a much cleaner feeder. Whereas a panther starts his meal by burrowing into his kill from the stomach end, and soon has the stomach, entrails, offal and so on, all mixed up with the meat of his kill, the tiger makes a vent near the anus into which he inserts his paw and removes the intestines and stomach, dragging them about ten feet away before he begins to eat a clean meal. To facilitate this procedure, he often removes the tail of the animal by biting it off near the root. The larger type of panthers found in forests occasionally do the same thing, but never the normal and smaller beasts, which soon get themselves mixed up in a repast in which the guts and excreta are all included.

The cave or den of a tigress and her cubs is very cleanly kept compared with that occupied by a family of panthers, and seems conspicuously free of bones and other waste matter which is almost always present where panthers live.

Apart from the mating season, tigers advertise their presence in a jungle much more than panthers do. The tribes of aborigines living in the forests of India will confirm this and will tell you the rough direction of the trails generally followed by tigers while out hunting. Their melodious, deep-throated and long-drawn moaning call, terminating in that never-to-be-forgotten 'oo-oo-ongh' that reverberates down the aisles of the valleys and across the wooded glens of the jungle in the stygian darkness beneath the giant forest trees, or in the phosphorescent moonlight, is music to the jungle-lover's ears. The harsher but less distance-carrying call of the panther, very closely resembling a man sawing wood, that occasionally penetrates the still darkness of the jungle night, is much less frequently heard.

Another habit peculiar to the tiger is his way of following a particular beat on his hunting expeditions. This may extend for miles and miles, maybe a hundred miles; but it invariably follows the same course; perhaps the bed of a certain dry *nullah,* along the banks of a river or stream, through some wooded valley or the shoulder of a hill. On a favourite trail you may find the pug-marks of the hunting tiger, imprinted in the powdery dust; and, once having found them, be sure you will find them again. Some days may pass, extending into weeks, a month, or perhaps longer, depending on the distance covered by his beat; but you may be almost certain that the tiger will pass that way again. He rarely returns by the route he has gone, but works around in an enormous circle, coming back to the place where you found his pug-marks and going on in the same direction once more.

While on his beat, if he is successful in killing an animal, the tiger will remain in the vicinity for a couple of days till he demolishes it, when he will resume his itinerary.

It is important to bear this peculiar habit in mind when trying to anticipate the movements of a man-eater, for he will always return to the same locality within a roughly calculable number of days, depending upon the stretch of territory covered by his beat. You may come to know the number of days and the line of his beat approximately by plotting on a map the human kills he has made, and the dates on which he has made them, followed by some very elementary mental arithmetic.

A panther never seems to follow any such pattern, but is here, there and everywhere. Like looking for the 'elusive Pimpernel', this habit of appearing anywhere and disappearing just as abruptly, makes the movements of a man-eating panther almost impossible to anticipate or forecast. He will turn up quite unexpectedly to claim his human victim, at a time and place very far from that predicted by the most experienced and astute of *shikaris*.

In this chapter I have tried to give you some hints on 'still-hunting', as well as telling you about some of the habits and peculiarities of the larger carnivora. I have deliberately abstained from recounting instances of animals shot by me on such occasions, as I feel they may not interest you much.

After all, the fun of the game lies in pitting your skill, woodcraft, endurance and cunning against that of these animals and in beating them at their own game, rather than in merely killing them. In fact, I would very strongly advocate that you carry a camera along with you, and I would ask you to confine yourself to taking photographs of these very beautiful creatures in preference to shooting them. Take your rifle with you by all means, as a protection in emergencies; but try to abstain from needless killing if you can resist the temptation.

Remember always that a good, cleverly-taken photograph is a far more meritorious and commendable achievement than any stuffed trophy hanging on the wall or decorating the floor of your drawing-room. With the first you can view the animal as often as you wish in all the beauty of its living grace and strength; whereas a stuffed trophy, like a cast cocoon or broken eggshell, is just the husk of a once-beautiful animal which sooner or later will deteriorate and be destroyed by time and insects.

Two

The Man-eating Panther of the Yellagiri Hills

IT WAS MID-AFTERNOON. THE TROPICAL SUN BLAZED OVERHEAD, A veritable ball of fire. The jungle lay still and silent under its scorching spell. Even the birds and monkeys that had chattered all morning were now quiet, lulled to sleep in the torpid air.

Beneath the dark shadows of the forest trees some relief was to be found from the golden glare, even though the shadows themselves throbbed and pulsated in that temperature. Not the least movement of the air stirred the fallen leaves that thickly carpeted the jungle floor, forming Nature's own luscious blanket of crisp yellow-brown tints. When the monsoons set in, these same crisp leaves would be converted into mouldering manure, which in course of time would serve to feed other forest trees, long after the jungle giants from which they have fallen had themselves crashed to earth.

The heavy stillness was occasionally broken by a hollow sound from the wooden bells hanging from the necks of a herd of cattle that had been driven into the jungle for grazing. These wooden bells serve two purposes. The first and main object is to enable the herdsmen to locate in the thick underbrush the whereabouts of the animals that wear them. The second object is to frighten off any carnivora that becomes disposed to attack the wearers. Quite often the second purpose is successfully achieved, as tigers and panthers are suspicious animals and hesitate to attack a prey from whose neck is suspended a strange wooden object emitting queer sounds. But sometimes again the ruse does not succeed, depending upon the nature of the particular tiger or panther concerned, and even more on its hunger at the given moment.

This particular afternoon was to witness one such exception. A fat and brown young bull was browsing on the outskirts of the herd, munching mouthfuls of grass beneath the shade of a clump of ficus trees. With each mouthful that it tore from the ground it would raise its head a little to gaze in idle speculation at the surrounding jungle, while its jaws worked steadily, munching the grass. Nothing seemed to stir and the brown bull was at peace with itself and the world.

It would not have felt so complacent, however, if it had gazed behind. Not a rustle rose as a tuft of grass parted to show two malevolent green eyes that stared with concentrated longing at the fat brown bull. The eyes were those of a large male panther of the big forest variety, and his heavy body, nearly equalling that of a tigress in dimensions, was pressed low to the ground, the colouring of his rosettes merging naturally with the various tints of the grasses.

Slowly and noiselessly the panther drew his hind legs to a crouching position. His muscles quivered and vibrated with

18

tenseness. His whole form swayed gently, to gain balance for the death-charge that was to follow.

Then, as a bolt from the blue, that charge took place. As a streak of yellow and black spots, the heavy body of the panther hurtled through the air and, before the brown bull was aware that anything was happening, the cruel yellow fangs buried themselves in its jugular. For a moment the bull struggled to maintain its equilibrium with its forefeet apart, hoping to gallop into the midst of the grazing herd. But with its air supply cut off, and its lifeblood jetting from the torn throat, its resistance was but momentary. It crashed to earth with a thud all four feet lashing out desperately in an attempt to kick off the attacker. The panther adroitly squirmed his body out of reach of the lashing hooves, but never released his merciless grip on the bull's throat. A snorting gurgle burst from the gaping mouth of the stricken animal, the feet kicked less vigorously, and then its terror-stricken eyes slowly took on a glazed and lifeless expression as death came within a few minutes of the attack.

Thus did Nathan, the herdsman, lose one of his best beasts, as the rest of the herd, alarmed by the noise made by the dying bull, galloped through the jungle for safety to the forest-line that eventually led to the village, a couple of miles away.

But this was not to be Nathan's only loss. In the next three months he lost four more of his cattle, while the other two herdsmen who lived in the same village each lost a couple. On the other hand, the panther responsible for these attacks concluded, and no doubt quite justifiably, that he had found a locality where food was plentiful and easy to get. He decided to live nearby in preference to moving through the forest in his normal hunt for game, which was far more arduous anyhow.

The monsoons then came and with the heavy rains pasture grew up everywhere and it became unnecessary to drive the herds of cattle into the jungle for grazing. Grass sprang up near the village itself, and in the few adjacent fields, and the herds were kept close to the village where they could be more carefully watched.

This change, of course, was not relished by the panther, and he became bolder, as he was forced by circumstances to stalk the herds in the new pastures.

The forest thinned out in the vicinity of the village, while the fields themselves were completely tree-less. This made the panther's approach more and more difficult, and often enough the herdsmen saw him as he tried to creep towards their charges. On such occasions they would shout, throw stones at him and brandish the staves they carried. These demonstrations would frighten him away.

Then his hunger increased, he found that he must choose between abandoning the village herds altogether as prey and go back to stalking the wild animals of the forests, or adopting a more belligerent policy towards the herdsmen.

The panther decided to adopt the latter policy.

One evening he crept as far as possible under cover and then dashed openly towards the nearest cow. Two herdsmen, standing quite near, saw him coming. They shouted and waved their sticks, but his charge never faltered till he had buried his fangs in the cow's throat. The herdsmen stood transfixed for the few minutes it took for the cow to die. Then they began to hurl stones and invectives at the spotted aggressor while he lay with heaving flanks across the still-quivering carcass of his prey.

When the stones thudded around, the panther let go his grip on the cow and with blood-smeared snout growled hideously at the men, his evil countenance contorted and his eyes blazing with hatred. Faced with that hideous visage and those bloodcurdling growls the herdsmen ran away.

At this stage of affairs the villagers requested the local forester to do something to help them; otherwise to enlist help from some other quarter. The forester, whose name was Ramu, had done a bit of shooting himself and owned a single-barrelled twelve-bore breech-loading gun. Although it was part of his duties as the representative of the government to check poachers, he himself was accustomed to indulge in a little poaching over water holes and salt licks, his quarry being the various kinds of deer that visited such spots, or an occasional jungle pig. As often as was possible he avoided letting his subordinates, the forest guards, know of these surreptitious activities, but when that was not possible he made sure of the guards' silence by giving them a succulent leg from the animal he had shot, together with a string of dire threats of what he would do to them if a word about it was breathed to the range officer. Despite all these precautions, however, the range officer had come to know of Ramu's favourite pastime. He was a conscientious young officer, keen to uphold the government's policy of game preservation, and tried to catch his subordinate in the act. But that worthy had so far succeeded in keeping a clean official slate. Perhaps he was too wily, or his threats to the guards so fearsome that the Range Officer (R.O.) had not yet succeeded.

So far Ramu had not tried his weapon against any of the larger carnivora, and when the villagers approached him for help to shoot the panther he was not over-keen to tackle the proposition. But the villagers persisted in their requests, and soon it was made very evident to Ramu that his honour was at stake, for he could not delay indefinitely with vague excuses of being too busy to come to the village, or of having run out of stock of ammunition, and so forth.

21

Therefore Ramu arrived at the village one morning carrying his weapon. He was hailed as the would-be saviour of the situation and immediately took full advantage of the fact by settling down to a very hearty meal provided by the villagers. After washing this down with a lota (tumbler) of coffee, he belched contentedly and announced his intention of indulging in a nap for an hour before tackling the business for which he had come.

Ramu awoke a couple of hours later, by which time it was past midday. He then demanded of the headman that a goat should be provided as bait. This was done and Ramu set out for the jungle, accompanied by five or six villagers.

Being the forester in charge of the section he was well-acquainted with the locality and had already selected, in his mind, the tree on which to build his *machan*. This was a large banyan, growing conveniently at the point where the track from the village and the forest fire-line met. It also happened that a *nullah* intersected the fire-line near the same spot. The panther was known to traverse all three of these approaches as had been evidenced by his frequent pug-marks, so that Ramu's choice was indeed a wise one; for if the panther walked along the fire-line or came up the *nullah* he could not help spotting his goat, while he himself, in the *machan*, could see up and down both these approaches as well as part of the track leading to the village.

On this tree, then, Ramu instructed the villagers who had accompanied him to build a *machan* twenty feet or so off the ground, and being well-skilled in the art of making hide-outs himself, contrived to conceal it cleverly with leaves, so that it would be quite unnoticeable to the panther.

It was past four o'clock that evening before the work was completed. Ramu climbed into the *machan* and the goat was then tethered by a rope round its neck to a stake that had been driven into the ground.

When the villagers left, the goat, finding itself alone, gazed in the direction of the village *path* and bleated lustily. Conditions were as perfect as could be, and the panther heard the goat and pounced upon it at about six, while the light was still good. Ramu had loaded his gun with an L.G. cartridge which he fired at the panther while the latter was holding the goat to the ground by its throat. There was a loud cough; and the panther somersaulted before dashing off into the undergrowth. The goat, which was already dying from suffocation and the wound inflicted in its throat, was killed outright by a pellet that passed through its ear into the brain.

Ramu waited awhile, then descended the banyan tree and hastily retreated to the village, where he told the people that he was sure he had hit the panther and had no doubt that they would find him dead the next morning.

With daylight a large party of men assembled and, headed by Ramu, went down to the banyan tree. There they found that the goat had been completely eaten during the night by a hyaena. Ramu pointed out the direction in which the panther had leaped and the whole party of men searched in close formation. It was not long before they came upon a blood-trail on the leaves of the bushes and lantana, indicating that in truth he had scored a hit. But of the panther there was no sign, although the party followed the trail for over a mile before it eventually petered out.

For two months after this no fresh attacks on cattle or goats were recorded, and everyone, including Ramu, was sure that the panther had gone away into some thicket and died.

Then one evening a lad of about 16 years was returning to the village along the same forest line. He was alone. Coming around a bend he saw a panther squatting on his haunches about twenty yards away, looking directly at him. ·He halted in his tracks, expecting the panther to make off as an ordinary panther would do. But this panther did nothing of the kind. Instead, he changed his position to a crouch and began to snarl viciously.

The boy turned around and ran the way he had come, and the panther pursued him. Luckily, at the place he overtook the boy, a piece of rotting wood happened to be lying across the forest line. As the panther jumped on his back and bit through his shoulder near the neck, the boy was borne to earth by the weight, and in falling saw the piece of rotting wood. Terror and desperation lent strength to his hands and an unusual quickness to his mind. Grasping the wood, he rolled sideways and jammed the end into the panther's mouth. This caused the panther to release his hold, but not before he had severely scratched the boy's arm and thighs with his claws. Springing to his feet, the boy lashed out at him again; this unexpected retaliation by his victim caused the panther to lose courage and he leaped into the bushes. Still grasping the wood that had saved his life, and with blood streaming down his chest, back, arms and legs, the boy made a staggering run for the village.

That was the first attack made upon a human being. The next followed some three weeks later, and this time the panther did not run away. It happened that a goat-herd was returning with his animals when a panther attacked them and seized upon one. The herdsman was poor and the herd represented all his worldly wealth. So he tried to save his goat by screaming at the panther as he ran towards him, whirling his staff. It was a brave but silly thing to have done, knowing that a panther was in the vicinity that had recently attacked a human being without provocation. He paid for his foolish bravery with his life, for the panther left the goat and leapt upon him to clamp his jaws firmly in his throat.

The goats ran back to the village. Seeing no herdsman returning with them, some of the villagers wondered what had occurred, but for the moment did not attach any significance to what they had noticed. It transpired that this herdsman was alone and had no relatives, so that it was nearly an hour later and growing dusk before his absence was really accepted as a fact, and it became evident that something had happened to him. It was too late by then to do anything.

Next morning the villagers gathered in a party of about thirty persons, armed with clubs and staves, and left the village to try to find the goatherd. They went down the track leading from the village to the jungle. The hoof-marks of the herd of goats as they had run back to the village the previous evening were clearly visible along the trail. They proceeded a little further and there they came upon the spot where the panther had made the attack. Clearly impressed in the dusty earth were the pug-marks of the large spotted cat. There was also a distinct drag-mark where the panther had hauled his victim away. Scattered at intervals were a few drops of blood from the throat of the man that had trickled to the ground. But the earth away from the track was sun-baked and hard and had absorbed the blood, and it was difficult to locate, though the drag-mark was quite clear.

The panther had taken his victim off the track along which the man had been driving his goats, and had hauled the body into the jungle. But he had not gone very far from where he had originally made his kill, and within about a hundred yards the group of villagers discovered the body of the victim. The chest and a small portion of one thigh had been eaten. Thus the maneater of the Yellagiris came into existence.

The Yellagiris are a crescent-shaped formation of hills lying immediately to the east of Jalarpet Junction railway station on the Southern Railway. The opening of the crescent faces away from the Junction, while its apex, so to speak, rises abruptly some three thousand feet above sea level about two miles from the station. A very rough zigzag *path* winds up the steep incline, and in places one has to clamber from boulder to boulder.

Many years ago—in 1941 in fact—I had purchased a farm of small acreage at the top of this ridge. I had intended keeping this farm, which is about ninety-five miles from Bangalore, as a weekend resort, but had not found the time to visit it regularly. As a result, the open land was quickly being encroached upon by the ever-prolific lantana shrub.

I had decided to visit this place for about three days to supervise the removal of the lantana, and when I made this visit I happened to arrive a few days after the death of the goatherd. The coolies I had engaged for the work told me about the panther, of which no news had been published in any of the newspapers. They assured me that it continued to haunt the precincts of the village, for they had again seen its pug-marks only the previous day.

The news interested me and I thought I might as well make an attempt to bag the animal. I had brought neither of my rifles with me, but only my twelve-bore shotgun, as the Yellagiris abound in jungle fowl and during the few visits I had made there I had always shot a couple each time for the pot. Further, with this object in view, I had brought along with me only two L.G. cartridges for emergencies, the rest being number six shot for the jungle fowl. Therefore I would have to make sure of the panther with the only two L.G. shells available.

I stopped work on the lantana about midday and went back with the labourers to reconnoitre the ground. It was much as I had expected. The jungle fell away into a narrow belt of lantana which ceased only at the few fields that bordered the village. Clearly visible on a footpath at the end of one of these fields was the trail of a panther—a fairly large adult male, judging from his pugs. He had passed that way only the night before.

I went to the village and introduced myself to the *Patel*, or headman, whom I had never met before, and told him how I came to be there. He expressed great pleasure at my presence and was most enthusiastic in his promises of every cooperation. We held a discussion and I told the *Patel* that I would like to buy a goat to tie up as a bait in the initial stage of my operations against the panther.

And here was where the *Patel's* cooperation was needed, as no goats were available in his village. It was only with much difficulty and considerable delay that he was able to procure one for me from a neighbouring hamlet, a kid that was small enough in size to ensure that it would bleat when tied up. The *Patel* himself accompanied me, and four other men, one of them leading the goat, the rest carrying hatchets with which to construct a *machan*.

They led me back along the track to the place where the herdsman had been attacked, and finally to the spot at which they had found his remains. It was densely overgrown with small bushes of the Inga dulcis plant, known as the 'Madras thorn' or 'Korkapulli' tree. It was out of the question to sit on the ground there, as the thorns grew so close together as to prevent one from seeing any animal beyond the distance of a couple of yards. So we were compelled to retrace our steps along the track for about a quarter of a mile.

There we came upon quite a large and leafy jack-fruit tree which, with its thick leaves growing in profusion, seemed to provide the ideal setting for the construction of a *machan*. At about a height of eight feet the first branch led off the main stem of the tree. The third branch after that extended over the track itself and bifurcated conveniently at about fifteen feet from the ground.

When the villagers left, the goat, finding itself alone, gazed in the direction of the village *path* and bleated lustily. Conditions were as perfect as could be, and the panther heard the goat and pounced upon it at about six, while the light was still good. Ramu had loaded his gun with an L.G. cartridge which he fired at the panther while the latter was holding the goat to the ground by its throat. There was a loud cough; and the panther somersaulted before dashing off into the undergrowth. The goat, which was already dying from suffocation and the wound inflicted in its throat, was killed outright by a pellet that passed through its ear into the brain.

Ramu waited awhile, then descended the banyan tree and hastily retreated to the village, where he told the people that he was sure he had hit the panther and had no doubt that they would find him dead the next morning.

With daylight a large party of men assembled and, headed by Ramu, went down to the banyan tree. There they found that the goat had been completely eaten during the night by a hyaena. Ramu pointed out the direction in which the panther had leaped and the whole party of men searched in close formation. It was not long before they came upon a blood-trail on the leaves of the bushes and lantana, indicating that in truth he had scored a hit. But of the panther there was no sign, although the party followed the trail for over a mile before it eventually petered out.

For two months after this no fresh attacks on cattle or goats were recorded, and everyone, including Ramu, was sure that the panther had gone away into some thicket and died.

Then one evening a lad of about 16 years was returning to the village along the same forest line. He was alone. Coming around a bend he saw a panther squatting on his haunches about twenty yards away, looking directly at him. He halted in his tracks, expecting the panther to make off as an ordinary panther would do. But this panther did nothing of the kind. Instead, he changed his position to a crouch and began to snarl viciously.

The boy turned around and ran the way he had come, and the panther pursued him. Luckily, at the place he overtook the boy, a piece of rotting wood happened to be lying across the forest line. As the panther jumped on his back and bit through his shoulder near the neck, the boy was borne to earth by the weight, and in falling saw the piece of rotting wood. Terror and desperation lent strength to his hands and an unusual quickness to his mind. Grasping the wood, he rolled sideways and jammed the end into the panther's mouth. This caused the panther to release his hold, but not before he had severely scratched the boy's arm and thighs with his claws. Springing to his feet, the boy lashed out at him again; this unexpected retaliation by his victim caused the panther to lose courage and he leaped into the bushes. Still grasping the wood that had saved his life, and with blood streaming down his chest, back, arms and legs, the boy made a staggering run for the village.

That was the first attack made upon a human being. The next followed some three weeks later, and this time the panther did not run away. It happened that a goat-herd was returning with his animals when a panther attacked them and seized upon one. The herdsman was poor and the herd represented all his worldly wealth. So he tried to save his goat by screaming at the panther as he ran towards him, whirling his staff. It was a brave but silly thing to have done, knowing that a panther was in the vicinity that had recently attacked a human being without provocation. He paid for his foolish bravery with his life, for the panther left the goat and leapt upon him to clamp his jaws firmly in his throat.

The goats ran back to the village. Seeing no herdsman returning with them, some of the villagers wondered what

29

had occurred, but for the moment did not attach any significance to what they had noticed. It transpired that this herdsman was alone and had no relatives, so that it was nearly an hour later and growing dusk before his absence was really accepted as a fact, and it became evident that something had happened to him. It was too late by then to do anything.

Next morning the villagers gathered in a party of about thirty persons, armed with clubs and staves, and left the village to try to find the goatherd. They went down the track leading from the village to the jungle. The hoof-marks of the herd of goats as they had run back to the village the previous evening were clearly visible along the trail. They proceeded a little further and there they came upon the spot where the panther had made the attack. Clearly impressed in the dusty earth were the pug-marks of the large spotted cat. There was also a distinct drag-mark where the panther had hauled his victim away. Scattered at intervals were a few drops of blood from the throat of the man that had trickled to the ground. But the earth away from the track was sun-baked and hard and had absorbed the blood, and it was difficult to locate, though the drag-mark was quite clear.

The panther had taken his victim off the track along which the man had been driving his goats, and had hauled the body into the jungle. But he had not gone very far from where he had originally made his kill, and within about a hundred yards the group of villagers discovered the body of the victim. The chest and a small portion of one thigh had been eaten. Thus the maneater of the Yellagiris came into existence.

The Yellagiris are a crescent-shaped formation of hills lying immediately to the east of Jalarpet Junction railway station on the Southern Railway. The opening of the crescent faces away from the Junction, while its apex, so to speak, rises abruptly some three thousand feet above sea level about two miles from the station. A very rough zigzag *path* winds up the steep incline, and in places one has to clamber from boulder to boulder.

Many years ago—in 1941 in fact—I had purchased a farm of small acreage at the top of this ridge. I had intended keeping this farm, which is about ninety-five miles from Bangalore, as a weekend resort, but had not found the time to visit it regularly. As a result, the open land was quickly being encroached upon by the ever-prolific lantana shrub.

I had decided to visit this place for about three days to supervise the removal of the lantana, and when I made this visit I happened to arrive a few days after the death of the goatherd. The coolies I had engaged for the work told me about the panther, of which no news had been published in any of the newspapers. They assured me that it continued to haunt the precincts of the village, for they had again seen its pug-marks only the previous day.

The news interested me and I thought I might as well make an attempt to bag the animal. I had brought neither of my rifles with me, but only my twelve-bore shotgun, as the Yellagiris abound in jungle fowl and during the few visits I had made there I had always shot a couple each time for the pot. Further, with this object in view, I had brought along with me only two L.G. cartridges for emergencies, the rest being number six shot for the jungle fowl. Therefore I would have to make sure of the panther with the only two L.G. shells available.

I stopped work on the lantana about midday and went back with the labourers to reconnoitre the ground. It was much as I had expected. The jungle fell away into a narrow belt of lantana which ceased only at the few fields that bordered the village. Clearly visible on a footpath at the end of one of these fields was the trail of a panther—a fairly large adult rough and steep boulder-covered track by night with a man-eating panther in the vicinity, but I knew that it would be quite safe as long as I had the petromax burning. My 405-rifle and haversack of equipment strapped to my back, plus the light hanging from my left hand, made quite a sizeable and uncomfortable load up that steep track, and I was drenched in perspiration by the time I reached the top of the hill. The village was still a mile away, and a cold breeze chilled my damp clothes as they dried on my back while I walked along.

I awoke the *Patel,* who in turn awoke most of the village, so that a concourse of a hundred dusky faces and gleaming white teeth surrounded me in the light of the petromax.

The *Patel* offered me food, which I politely declined, but I told him I would be grateful for some hot tea. This was soon prepared, and while sipping it from a large brass utensil belonging to the *Patel,* I heard the story he had to tell me.

Actually there was nothing much to tell. After my last visit everybody had been very careful when moving about in the day, particularly in the vicinity of the forest. At night they had remained indoors. Then as the weeks had passed without any further signs of the panther, as always happened vigilance was correspondingly relaxed.

The mail-carrier used to ascend the hill early in the morning, leaving Jalarpet at about 6 a.m. from the small post office situated adjacent to the railway station. All the mail trains passed during the night, from Bangalore as well as from Madras on the east coast and Calicut on the west coast. Postal traffic to the Yellagiris was comparatively small, and the few letters or articles that were destined for the hill-top were placed in individual bags by the sorters on the various mail trains and unloaded at Jalarpet Station. The mail-carrier, who was to ascend the hill, would open these bags in order to place all their contents into the one bag he carried up, slung across his shoulders or sometimes balanced on his head.

His one protection—which was intended not so much as a weapon of protection as an emblem and badge of office, as well as a sound-device to frighten away snakes—was a short spear, on the shaft of which were fitted a number of iron rings. This spear he would carry in his hand, striking the base of it against the ground at every few paces. The rings would jangle against the iron shaft and against each other, making the loud jingling-jangling noise that has been known to the mail-carriers for almost a hundred years throughout the length and breadth of India.

On that fateful day the mail-carrier had as usual set out from the small post office at Jalarpet at about six o'clock in the morning. But he never reached the top of the hill. The villagers had become accustomed to hearing him and seeing him as he jingled and jangled his daily route through the main street of the village. But that morning they had not heard the familiar sound. With the indifference and apathy peculiar to the East, nobody worried or thought anything about it.

After the midday meal, a party of men had started to descend the hill, bound for Jalarpet. About a quarter of the way down, they noticed the rusty colour of dried blood splashed on the rocks that formed a trail. They had stopped to wonder about it, when the sharp eyes of one individual had noticed the mail-carrier's spear lying away from the track and near a bush. Guessing what had happened, the whole party turned tail and hurried back to the village. There they had gathered reinforcements, including the *Patel,* and returned eventually to find the partly eaten corpse of the unfortunate mail-carrier.

The *Patel* had written out the telegram and sent it by the same party of men to be despatched to me from Jalarpet

Station. With all the confusion it had not reached me till after three the following evening, a delay of some twenty-four hours, although Jalarpet is just eighty-nine miles from Bangalore. I was also informed that the police authorities at Jalarpet had removed the body for inquest and cremation.

By the time all this conversation was over and I had elicited all the information I required, or perhaps it would be more correct to say all the information that the *Patel* and the villagers knew about the panther, it was past four in the morning. The *Patel* lent me a rope cot which I carried to the outskirts of the village, where I lay down upon it for a brief sleep of two hours till dawn, when I awoke, not to the familiar calls of the forest, but to the loud yapping of a couple of curs who were regarding me on the rope cot with very evident suspicion and distaste.

As I have said, the Yellagiri Hills do not hold a great deal of regular forest, and there is therefore a complete absence of aboriginal jungle-folk of any kind. I realised that I would have to rely upon the villagers and myself to try to discover ways and means of locating the panther.

One of the questions I had asked earlier that morning concerned the panther's possible hide-out. No definite reply had been given to this, but a couple of cattle-grazers had stated that they had on three or four occasions during the past few weeks observed a panther sunning himself in the afternoon on a rocky ledge of a hill named 'Periamalai' or 'Big Hill', to give it its English translation. The Yellagiris themselves form a plateau at the top, and this Periamalai is the one and only hill rising above the level of the plateau and forms the highest peak of the crescent-shaped Yellagiri range. It is nearly 4,500 feet above mean sea level.

I went to the *Patel's* house and found him still asleep, but he soon woke up and offered me a large 'chumbo', which is a round brass vessel like a miniature water-pot, of hot milk to drink. I then asked him to call the cattle-tenders who had seen the panther on Periamalai and to ask them to accompany me to the hill and point out the particular ledge which the panther was said to frequent.

It took some time before these two individuals could be persuaded to go with me. They were most unwilling and I could see that they were definitely scared. However, the *Patel* used his own methods of persuasion, which included threats of retribution if they refused, so eventually I was able to set out accompanied by them.

Periamalai is situated about three miles to the east of the village and in the opposite direction to the *path* from Jalarpet, which ascends to the west. In all, about five miles lay between this hill and the spot where the unfortunate mailman had been killed. In addition, practically all the land between was cultivated. The jungle covering Periamalai itself receded down the slopes of the Yellagiri range in the direction of that portion of the crescent that faces north. I was not happy about this as I felt that the cattle-grazers might have seen another panther entirely, and not the one that had killed the postman.

Arriving at the base of Periamalai, my two companions pointed to a ledge of rock that jutted out some 300 feet above, and stated that that was the spot where they had seen the panther sunning himself on several afternoons. Thick lantana scrub grew from the foot of the hill right up to the base of the ledge and to about halfway up Periamalai, where the regular forest began. I could see that, as was happening with so many of the smaller forest tracks in southern India, the lantana pest was slowly but surely encroaching on the jungle proper and smothering the original trees. Like the Yellagiri range itself, Periamalai is a rocky hill consisting of piles of boulders and to look for a panther in that sea of lantana and among those rocks would be a hopeless task, as the former was impenetrable.

So I marked out a place under a tree growing at the foot of the hill and told the men that we would return to the village and procure a bait, and that they should come back with it and tie it at the spot I had selected.

Accordingly we went back and the *Patel* procured for me a donkey. A goat would have been of no use in this case as I did not intend to sit up with it. Should it be killed, the panther would devour it at one meal and there would be nothing left to justify his return the following night, whereas the donkey was big enough to warrant the panther coming back for what remained after the first meal. Against this was the disadvantage that a goat would more readily and quickly attract the panther by its bleating, whereas a donkey would be silent.

But I relied on the fact that if the panther lived anywhere on the hill, from his elevated position he would be able to see the donkey tied on the lower ground. So I borrowed some stout rope and instructed the cattlemen to take the donkey up and tether it at the spot I had already pointed out to them.

This done, the *Patel* himself and three or four villagers came along with me to point out the place where the mail-carrier had been done to death. It turned out to be at a spot about a mile and a half from the village, just where the track from Jalarpet passed through a belt of lantana and rocky boulders. I had, of course, passed the place myself the previous night when ascending the hill with the lantern, but had not noticed the blood in the lantern-light. No doubt this had been just as well or my tranquillity would have been greatly perturbed.

We came upon a few dried splashes of blood on the trail, and my companions pointed out me a spot nearby to where the unfortunate man had been dragged and partly eaten. As I have already said, his remains had been removed to Jalarpet for cremation, so that there was nothing to be gained by remaining there any longer.

A cashew-nut tree stood beside the trail about three hundred yards higher up, and beneath this tree I asked the Patel to tie another donkey.

Then we walked back to the village, and I suggested that a third donkey be tied at some place where the scrub jungle came closest to the village. The Patel once more used his influence to procure two more donkeys and sent them out by different parties of men to be tied as I had instructed.

It was past one in the afternoon by the time all this had been done, and I realized that there was nothing more for me to do but await events. I could only hope the panther would kill one of three donkeys that night, provided of course he chanced to come upon it. Since the panther had made but only a few human kills thus far, it was clear that he was mainly existing upon other meat.

The Patel set a hot meal before me, consisting of rice and dhal curry, mixed with brinjals and onions grown on his land and made tremendously hot with red chillies which had been liberally added. I must say I enjoyed that meal, though the sweat poured down my face in rivulets as a result of the chillies. My host was highly amused at this sight and began to apologise, but I stopped him with the assurance that I did enjoy such a meal. Copious draughts of coffee followed, and when I finally arose I was a very contented person.

To pass the time I went down to my small farm and pottered about for the rest of that evening. You may be interested to know that this farm of mine consists of only one and a half acres of land, but it is a very compact farm at that. There is a 'marking-nut' tree, from the nut of which a black fluid is extracted for making a marking-ink generally used by launderers and dhobis for writing the initials of the owners on the corner of each article they send to the wash. Once marked, this 'ink' cannot be washed out. Three 'jack' trees, which are of a grafted variety, produce fruit weighing from two to twelve pounds each or even more. There are a few guava trees, some peaches and a vegetable garden. The two existing buildings, or *kottais* as they are called are mud-walled affairs with thick thatched roofs made from a mixture of jungle grass and the stalks of '*cholam*' grain. A small rose and croton garden fronts them. At that time I had about three dozen fowls, including leghorns, rhodes and black minorcas, and a few ducks. My drinking-water comes from a small well into which I introduced some fish, which I had originally brought from Bangalore to keep the water clean. A small stream in front forms one of my boundaries, and bamboo trees line the other three sides. Although such a small place, it is extremely 'cosy', and an ideal retreat for a quiet Sunday visit from Bangalore.

About half the land is low-lying and borders the stream I have just mentioned. I have tapped some water from this rivulet and grown a variety of black rice, known as 'Pegu rice' and originally imported from Burma. To my knowledge, my farm was one of the very few spots in southern India where this black Burma-rice then grew. I knew it had been sown in many places, but its cultivation had proved a failure for one reason or another.

An interesting feature about this farm was a story that one of the two *kottais* was haunted by the ghost of the brother of the Anglo-Indian lady from whom I had purchased it in 1941, lock, stock and barrel, poultry included, for the sum of Rs. 500/-; about £35 in English money. This man had died of a reputedly mysterious disease which I was told occurred in sudden attacks of excruciating pain in his left arm and chest—probably angina pectoris. He had been very much attached to the small farm and was said to have spent over twenty-five years there after purchasing it as waste land. Then he gave it to his sister, as he had no family of his own. However, as the story went, after his death, passing villagers had frequently seen him standing before his *kottai* in the evenings just as dusk was falling. Thereafter, needless to say, the villagers avoided the place.

His sister told me nothing about the alleged haunting till the day after I had purchased the farm and paid the cash before the sub-registrar when I had registered the sale deed, probably thinking the 'ghost' would put me off the transaction. Then she told me that her dead brother would sometimes roam about the two *kottais* at night, and also that she had clearly seen him many times in the moonlight attending the rose trees which had been his special hobby. She hastened to add that the 'spirit' was quite harmless, made no sound or troublesome manifestation, and just faded away if approached.

I have failed to mention that some very ancient furniture came to me with the *kottais*: a bed in each building, a broken-down dressing table, two almirahs and some three or four rather rickety chairs. The beds were of the old-fashioned sort, having battens.

I well remember the first night I slept in one of the *kottais* (incidentally the one in which the brother had died), for it was a rainy night and the roof of the other *kottai* was leaking. I had spread my bedroll, without mattress, on the battened cot and had lain down to sleep. The hard battens, however, were irksome and pressed against my shoulder blades and back. After failing to woo slumber for some time, I had decided that the floor would be far more comfortable. Of course, there were no electric lights, so I had lighted a candle to enable me to remove the bedroll and place it on the floor, when I had extinguished the candle and lain down to sleep. This time I was successful and had fallen asleep immediately.

I do not know when I awoke. It was pitch dark. Something heavy and cold and clammy moved and rested against my throat, and what seemed like two icy wet fingers extended across either side of my neck.

Now I am not an imaginative person. I am not afraid of the dark. Nor am I superstitious. But in a rush of memory I recollected the dead brother and his ghost, the fact that I had left my torch on the windowsill some feet away, and also that I did not know where I had left the matchbox. These thoughts came simultaneously, while the cold clammy wet thing distinctly moved and seemed to press its two extended fingers even more tightly on either side of my throat. I could feel my hair rising. To lie there any longer was impossible. With what seemed superhuman energy I scrambled to my feet and dashed towards the unfamiliar windowsill where I had left my torch. Probing wildly in the dark, I at last found that elusive torch. I pressed the button, expecting to see the ghost and its clammy hands, cold from the grave, before me! Instead, there on the floor was quite the largest toad I had ever seen in my life. A huge, black, slimy fellow, almost a foot long. He had come into the *kottai* because of the rain.

This just goes to show what human nerves can do. Hardly a few seconds earlier I had been scared stiff by the thought of the supernatural and the unknown. Now I laughed to myself as I guided the toad with the toe of my slippered foot to the door of the *kottai,* and then out into the rain.

Next morning all three donkey baits were alive, and so I spent the day on my land. No one had any news to give about the panther. Another night passed and the following morning found all three of the donkeys still in the land of the living. This time there was a little news. After the death of the mail-carrier the post was conveyed up the hill by three men instead of one, the party consisting of the relief mail-carrier who had replaced the poor fellow that had been killed, together with two *chowkidars*—literally, 'watchmen'—who had been pressed into service to accompany him as bodyguards. They were armed with crude spears in addition to the 'emblem of office' spear which had once been the equipment of the deceased mail-carrier and now automatically fell to his successor.

These three men excitedly reported at the village that they had seen a panther sunning himself on the ledge of a rock about a quarter of a mile downhill from the place where the previous mail-carrier had been done to death.

Upon hearing this news the *Patel* had despatched a villager to run and tell me. Taking my rifle, I accompanied him back to the village, where both the *chowkidars* offered to come along with me to point out the rock. We covered the distance of a little over two miles in good time. But only the bare rock-ledge stared us in the face. The panther that had been lying there, man-eater or otherwise, had gone, and it was too hot, too rocky and too hopeless to search for him among the piles of boulders. However, the news was encouraging, as it indicated the panther was still in the vicinity. Before returning to the village and my small farm, I once again examined the bait under the cashew tree and mentally selected the branch on which I would fix my *machan* if occasion arose.

That night brought good luck, though bad for the donkey beneath the cashew-nut tree, for the panther killed and ate about half of him during the hours of darkness.

Early next morning this fact was discovered by the party of men whom I had delegated to inspect, feed and water each one of the three baits in turn. They came back and told me, after having taken the precaution to cover the remains of the donkey with branches to protect it from being devoured to the bones by vultures.

I finished an early lunch and with my greatcoat, torch and flask of tea and some biscuit, proceeded to the village, where I readily obtained the loan of a *charpoy* from the *Patel*. Four willing helpers carried this to the cashew-nut tree, where it was slung up and secured with the ropes we had brought along with us. I personally supervised the camouflaging of the *charpoy* with small branches and leaves, till it was invisible from every direction, as well as from below. That this job should be done very thoroughly was, I knew, most essential when dealing with man-eating carnivora. The slightest carelessness might make all the difference between success and failure. A leaf turned the other way, with its under-surface showing uppermost, or any portion of the *charpoy* being visible from any angle, a remnant of twigs or fallen leaves at the base of the tree, any of these would be sufficient to arouse the suspicion of a man-eater, which is always extremely cautious in returning to its kill.

All arrangements were eventually completed to my satisfaction, and the only fault that I could find was that the *machan* was rather low, not more than ten feet from the ground. Also that the cashew-nut tree was easy to climb. It was about two-thirty in the afternoon when the party of men who had accompanied me left, after I had instructed them to return at dawn in case I did not go back to the village myself during the night.

I sat back on the *machan* and made myself as comfortable as possible.

It was a sweltering afternoon, the heat being reflected by the boulders that were piled around in all directions. The tree itself afforded little protection from the afternoon sun that beat down upon me. Indeed, I was glad when evening approached and the sun began sinking towards the Mysore plateau to the west. Far below me I could see Jalarpet railway station on the plains, and the puffs of cream-coloured smoke from the shunting-engines in the yard. At intervals a train would arrive or leave, and the whistles of the locomotives could be clearly heard. All else was silent.

Towards dusk a single peacock wailed in the distance and a couple of nightjars flitted around the tree. Except for them there were no signs of any other animals or birds.

Then the shadows of night descended. Sitting on the slope of the hill facing the west, I could see the plains grow dark as if covered by a black mantle, while yet the last vestiges of daylight lingered on the hilltop above me. The lights of Jalarpet began to twinkle one by one, prominent among them being the blue-tinted neon lamps of the station platforms and shunting yards. Here and there I could make out the red and green lights of the railway signals. From the north a train rolled towards Jalarpet, the bright headlamp of the engine cutting a swath of light before it. Then the train encountered an incline and the engine began to labour under its load. 'If she can do it ... I can do it ... if she can do it ... I can do it.' Her puffs as she struggled to top the rise formed the words in my imagination, and I listened to the clanking of her worn big-end bearings. All these sounds seemed so close to me—and yet they were so far; they were over five miles away at least, as the crow flies.

Darkness fell around me. It was a moonless night. The heavy clouds scuttled across the sky, some of them merging with the tops of the Yellagiri range. No friendly stars shone down, and the darkness became intense. I would have to rely on my sense of hearing.

Insects were conspicuous by their absence, and even the friendly chirp of the wood-cricket was not to be heard. I sat still on the cot. Now and then a passing mosquito buzzed around my head, to settle on some part of my face or hands. Then came the faint sharp sting of pain as it imbedded its needle-pointed proboscis into my skin. I would move my fingers or hand a little, or noiselessly blow against my own face by slightly protruding my lower lip. This would disturb the mosquito, which would either go on its way or fly around in a further effort to take another bite at me.

I am accustomed to sitting up in the jungle on *machans* or in hide-outs and so lost count of the time, for in any case it served no purpose to keep looking at my wristwatch unnecessarily. I could not anyway make time pass quicker.

Thoughts of all kinds creep into a man's mind on such occasions, some pleasant, some otherwise, and some reminiscent. I remember that, that evening, for some unaccountable reason, I began thinking of some way of inventing a new sort of bicycle, something that one could propel fast and for long distances with the minimum of effort. Is it not strange what the human mind may think of when it is forced to be idle?

My reveries concerning this bicycle were disturbed by what seemed like a faint sigh. I knew the panther had arrived and was standing over the dead donkey. The muffled sound I had heard had been made by his expelled breath as he slightly opened his mouth.

I reasoned that to switch on my torch and fire at this juncture might be premature. Better to let him settle down to his meal. I wish I hadn't, for in doing so I lost what might have been a successful shot, and caused the death of another human being.

I waited expectantly for the sound of the meat being torn, and bones being crunched, which would have assured me that the panther was tucking in at the donkey, but instead I heard nothing. The moments slipped by and then I became uncomfortably suspicious that something had gone wrong.

I know from experience how noiseless any of the carnivora can be when they want to; particularly a panther which can come and go not only soundlessly, but also without being seen, and that too in broad daylight. Under the present conditions of intense darkness this animal might have been a yard away, or a mile away, for all the difference it made in that gloom.

I glanced down at the luminous dial of my watch, which showed that it was twenty minutes to nine. I waited without moving. Nine o'clock came and passed, and then, from a section of boulders to my right, I heard a deep growl, followed in a few seconds by another.

Somehow the panther had become aware of my presence. He could not have smelt me, as panthers have little or no sense of smell. He could not have heard me, for I had made no sound. Therefore, he had either looked up inadvertently and become aware of the *machan*, or some intuition had warned him. In either case, he now knew a human being was there. He might then have tried climbing up into the tree to pull me down, but as likely as not his sense of self-preservation had warned him that this particular human being was dangerous to him and not of the same sort as the men he had killed.

Of course, this panther might not be a man-eater, although in the light of his present conduct this seemed the less reasonable explanation.

The growls were initially intended as a warning. As they increased they were also clearly meant to bolster up the animal's own courage. Perhaps he would lash himself into a fury after a sufficient number of growls to attack the tree on which I was sitting and try to climb up. As I have had occasion to remark before, panthers frequently do this with monkeys, whom they terrify with a series of loud growls before rushing at the trunk of the tree. Then the monkeys generally fall off or jump down in sheer terror. As likely as not he expected the noise he was making to have the same demoralising effect on me.

Very soon the growls increased both in volume and tempo. The panther was now making a terrific noise. As I had just thought, he was either trying to frighten me away completely or off my perch; alternatively, he was building up his own courage to rush the tree. I prepared for the latter eventuality.

Some more minutes of this sort of thing went on and then out he came with the peculiar coughing roar made by every charging panther. As he reached the base of the cashew-nut tree I leaned over the edge of the cot, pushing aside the camouflaging twigs to point the rifle downwards while depressing the switch of my torch. I knew I had to be quick because, as I have told you, the *machan* was only about ten feet off the ground and, the tree being easy to climb, the panther would reach me in no time.

As bad luck would have it, one of the camouflaging branches fell down upon the panther. No doubt this served to delay, if not actually to deter, his progress up the tree. But it also served to screen him completely from the light of the torch. As I looked downwards I just saw the branch shaking violently and guessed that it covered the panther.

At that moment I did a foolish thing. Instead of waiting till the animal could break clear of the offending branch, I quickly aimed at the spot where I felt his body would be and pressed the trigger. The report of the shot was followed by the sound of a falling body as the panther went hurtling backwards to the ground. For a second I thought I had succeeded in killing him, but that thought lasted only for a second, for no sooner did he touch the ground than he jumped clear of the branch in which he had become entangled, and I caught a momentary glimpse of his yellow form leaping into the undergrowth before I had a chance to work the underlever that would reload my rifle.

I shone the torch at the spot where he had disappeared, but neither sight nor sound of him or his further progress came to me. Silence reigned supreme. He might be lying dead in the bushes, or he might be wounded there, or he might have disappeared and be a long way off. There was no way of knowing.

I continued to shine the torch around for some time and then decided to sit in darkness in the hope of hearing some sound of movement. But there was absolutely nothing. I waited for another hour and then made up my mind to fire a shot into the bushes in the direction in which he had gone, hoping it would elicit some reaction if he were lying there wounded. So, switching on the torch, I fired the rifle at the approximate spot where he had vanished. The crash of the report reverberated and echoed against the hillside, but there was no sound or response from the panther.

A goods train started from Jalarpet and began to climb the gradient to Mulanur on the ghat section that led to Bangalore. The banking engine at the rear, whose duty it was to help by pushing till the top of the gradient was reached, began to push vigorously and its puffing and clanking eclipsed the sounds made by the engine at the front, whose driver was perhaps taking it easy because of the ready help behind him.

I waited until 11.30 p.m. The loud whistling from the engine of the incoming Madras-Cochin Express decided me to come down from the tree and go back to my *kottai* for a comfortable night's sleep. I felt quite safe in doing this as, had the panther been wounded and in the vicinity, he would have responded to the noise of my last shot. Either he was

47

dead or far away. Even if he had been lying in wait, that last shot would have frightened him off.

I came down from the cashew-nut tree and by the light of my torch made my way back to the village, where, before going on to my *kottai,* I related all that had happened to the *Patel* and the excited villagers.

Early next morning I came back to the village, where at least twenty willing men assembled and offered to help me. They in turn, under my advice and directions, gathered half-a-dozen village curs. Thus, safe and strong in numbers, we proceeded to the cashew-nut tree and the site of the previous night's occurrences.

The remains of the donkey had been untouched. A hole in the ground, directly below the tree, showed where my bullet had buried itself in the earth, nor was a speck of blood to be seen anywhere. We thoroughly searched among the bushes into which the panther had disappeared and into which I had fired my second shot, as well as the surrounding boulders and bushes for quite a wide area, but it was clear that I had missed entirely and that my bullet of the night before had failed to score the lucky hit I had hoped for. The panther had got completely away.

Ill-tempered and disgusted with myself, I returned with the men to the village, where I told the *Patel* that my time was up and that I would have to return to Bangalore. However, I asked him to send me another telegram should there be further developments. Then I went to the *kottai,* gathered my belongings and packed them in my haversack, and soon was repassing the cashew-nut tree on my descent to Jalarpet, where I caught the evening express from Madras that got me home by eight-fifteen the same night.

That was the end of the first round of my encounter with the Yellagiri man-eating panther.

Contrary to expectations, I heard nothing more from the *Patel*. When two months had elapsed I wrote him a letter and received a reply within a few days stating that there had been no further news of the animal. This made me think that it may have relinquished its man-eating habits or have crossed over to the Javadi range of hills which lay scarcely fifteen miles south of the Yellagiris. On the other hand, had the latter been the case I would still have heard through the Press or by government notification if any people had been killed on the Javadi Hills. I was therefore inclined to the former theory and felt that the panther had given up his tendency to attack human beings. Of course, my chance shot might have found its mark, and the animal may have crept away to die in some secluded place. But this last theory was hardly tenable.

Nine more weeks passed before the next news arrived in the form of a telegram from the *Patel*, despatched from Jalarpet railway station, stating that the panther had reappeared and once again killed a human being. The telegram asked me to come at once, and with two hours to spare I caught the next train.

This happened to be a slow train which brought me in to Jalarpet station at about half-past eight that night. There was no purpose in my climbing the hill immediately, for there was nothing I could do just then; so I decided to take a few hours' sleep in the waiting-room and make the ascent at dawn. This plan did not prove very successful, however. To begin with, the noise of the passing trains disturbed me each time I fell asleep, being a light sleeper. Secondly, the attacks of mosquitoes and bedbugs, with which the chair seemed to abound, impelled me to walk about the platform, which I did till five in the morning, when I set off for the foot of the Yellagiris about two miles away. It was dawn as I began the climb and I reached the *Patel's* village by 7.15 am.

My friend the *Patel* greeted me with his usual hospitality and brass 'chumbo' of heavily milked, hot coffee. Then he told me that the panther had attacked and killed a young woman three mornings previously, when she had gone to draw water from a stream running past the base of Periyamalai hill. He also informed me that the people of the village to which the girl had belonged had arrived shortly afterwards and recovered the remains of the victim for cremation. Apparently the panther had eaten but little of the unfortunate woman, perhaps because it had been disturbed by the party of men searching for her and had not had time to settle down to his meal.

This time I decided to tie a live bait in the form of a goat and sit up over it, as my stay on the Yellagiris could not exceed four days, as I had only that much leave. So the *Patel* offered to procure one for me from the same neighbouring village where he had got them the last time, but said that it would cost a tidy sum of money—about twenty rupees—as not only were goats scarce on the Yellagiris but their owners in that village, which was about three miles away, had become aware of the demand and had raised their prices accordingly. I agreed and handed over the money, and in the time that it would take for the goat to be brought, went down to my farm to see how things were getting along.

At noon, after consuming the cold lunch I had brought with me from Bangalore, I returned to the *Patel's* village only to find that the goat had not yet arrived.

It was two in the afternoon before the man who had been sent to fetch the animal returned with a black goat that was rather old, in the sense that it was past the stage where it would bleat for a long time when left alone, and so help to attract the panther. Secondly, as I have said, it was a black goat. Black or white goats occasionally cause suspicion among certain panthers. A brown bait, whether goat, dog or bull, is generally the best to use, in that they resemble in colour the wild animals that form the panther's natural food. However, there was no time now to change the goat and I would have to make the best of circumstances.

The *Patel* and four or five men accompanied me, the latter carrying axes, ropes and the same *charpoy* I had used on the last occasion. We reached the village to which the girl had belonged in a little under an hour. There another couple of men joined my party, who offered to point out the exact spot at which the young woman had been killed.

It was perhaps three-quarters of a mile from the village. A stream, bearing a trickle of water, ran from west to east and skirted the base of Periamalai Hill perhaps a half-mile away. This stream was sandy and bordered by a thick outcrop of mixed lantana and wait-a-bit thorns. At the spot where the girl had been attacked a shallow hole had been dug by the villagers to form a pool for watering their cattle when the weather became dry and the rest of the stream ceased to flow. It was to this place that the girl had come for water when she had been killed the previous day. The lantana grew quite close to the pool, and it was evident that the man-eater had stalked her under cover of this thicket, and from there had made his final pounce.

As matters stood, this panther had again confirmed that he was most unusual in his habits, even for a man-eater. He had repeatedly attacked his human victim in broad daylight. Only tigers do this, as man-eating panthers, being inherent cowards at heart, usually confine their activities to the hours of darkness. I was inclined to think that this animal was perhaps already lying up in the thicket before the girl arrived and could not resist the temptation of a meal so readily offered.

With this idea in mind, I went down on hands and knees and began a close examination of the lantana bushes and the ground in the vicinity, where I shortly found confirmation of my theory, for one of the bushes provided ample shelter for a regular lie-up. Beneath it the carpet of dried lantana leaves rendered impossible the chance of finding any visible track, but a faintly prevailing odour of wild animal inclined me to confirm my guess as correct, and that the panther used this place now and then to lie up, as it offered ideal proximity for attack on any prey that might approach the pool to drink.

This was encouraging for, if the panther had used it before, there was every likelihood that he would use it again. Further, as I have already told you, Periamalai Hill lay about half a mile away. The panther might have his regular den among the rocks and caves higher up the hill and would find this lantana lair a most convenient place in which to await the coming of an unsuspecting victim.

As I studied these conditions an idea suddenly came to me. I would create a scene as close as possible to what the panther might expect it to be. I would tether the goat to a stake beside the pool to make it appear like an animal that had come there to drink. And I would forestall the panther's arrival by hiding myself beneath that very same lantana bush. Should he hear the goat, or catch a glimpse of it from higher up the hill, from where it would be clearly visible, he would make straight for this point of attack and would find me waiting for him.

I explained my idea to the *Patel* and the men who had acompanied me. They thought it clever, but the *Patel* decided it was foolish, in that it entailed too great a risk. I convinced him that there was really little danger as, due to the denseness of the surrounding lantana and the thickness of the bush itself, the panther would have difficulty in getting at me from any of the sides or rear, and could only reach me through the entrance to this under-cover shelter, while I would be expecting him to arrive from that direction and would be ready. Further, his attention would be concentrated on the goat and he would scarcely suspect an enemy would await him in his own lair.

The stake which we had brought along was accordingly hammered deep into the sand with the aid of a stone from the streambed. I crept under the bush and took my time in making myself quite comfortable for the night. I also clamped the torch to the barrel of my rifle, and tested it to see that it was in good order. This torch I had lately purchased. It was a three-cell arrangement of the fixed-focus type. Finally, I took a long drink of tea from my water-bottle before ordering the men to tether the goat to the stake by its hind legs.

While all these preliminaries were going on the goat had been kept some distance away, so that it should not come to know that a human being was sheltering in the bushes so close by; for once it knew that, there was very little chance of it bleating from a sense of loneliness. On the other hand, if the goat really felt it had been left alone, there was much more reason why it should cry out.

While the goat was being tied I remained perfectly silent. After finishing their job, the *Patel* and his men went away and I was left by myself to await what might happen.

It was hot and still beneath the lantana, and long before sunset it was quite dark where I was sitting. The goat had bleated a few times at the beginning and then had stopped. I could only hope that it would begin calling again when darkness fell. But I was sorely disappointed. Occasionally I had heard the sounds made by the goat as it kicked and struggled against the tethering rope, but these had now lapsed into silence and I came to the inevitable conclusion that the damned animal had gone to sleep.

Of necessity, in my position I had to keep wide awake and alert the whole night and could not share the goat's slumbers. I envied that blasted goat.

Mosquitoes worried me, and insects of all kinds ran over my body. Bush mice, which are even smaller than the domestic variety, rustled the leaves and crept along the stems of the lantana. Once something long and soft slithered through the dry leaves and along the sides of the bush. It was a snake. Whether harmless or poisonous I could not know. I sat absolutely motionless in spite of the mosquitoes and insects, and the slithering died away.

The panther did not come. No sounds penetrated the silence under the bush, not even the calls of a night-bird. Time moved on its long and tedious course. The luminous hands of my wristwatch very slowly clocked the passing hours. I felt drowsy but dared not give in to my inclination to close my eyes even for a few fitful seconds. I tried to think of other things and other events to get my mind off the panther. The only thing I could think of was to damn the goat.

The greying light of a new day gradually filtered in, not even heralded by the call of a jungle fowl, peafowl, or any other bird. I came out of that bush the most disgusted man in the whole of India. The goat, which had been lying curled up and fast asleep by the stake, lazily got to its feet, stretched leisurely, wagged its stumpy tail and regarded me in a quizzical fashion as much as to say, 'Come now, who is the real goat, you or me?' Knowing the answer, I refrained from a spoken confession.

Instead, I untethered that wretched animal, which followed me back to the village where the *Patel* lived. That worthy, with the same party of men who had accompanied us the day before, was just about to set forth to see how I had fared. Telling him to return the black goat, I said that I would snatch a few hours' sleep and then go myself to find a more satisfactory bait. I went to my *kottai* and slept till noon.

I was feeling hungry when I awoke, so I opened a tin of salmon, which I ate with some bread I had brought with me from Bangalore. The bread had become rather dry, but was improved by the tinned butter I spread thickly upon it. This served to fill me for lunch. I had already set my portable Primus stove to boil water for tea and the beverage was indeed refreshing. While eating my lunch I brewed a second kettle of tea to put into my water-bottle. Gathering the necessary equipment for another night's vigil, I returned to the *Patel's* village. Fortunately the weather was warm as the previous night, so that an overcoat was unnecessary.

I took the *Patel* along with me to add force to my argument, and walked to the village where the goats were available. There, after some picking and choosing, followed by some red-hot bargaining, I was able to select a half-grown animal that was more likely to bleat. It was past 3.30 p.m. when we set out for the place where I had sat up the night before, but really there was no hurry, as the spot had already been selected and there was no *machan* to fix.

Before five o'clock I had crept into the bush, the new goat was tethered and the men were on their way back.

Hardly were they out of sight and earshot than the goat began to bleat, and he kept this up incessantly. I silently congratulated myself on my selection.

With evening it again became quite dark beneath the lantana, the goat called loudly and I waited expectantly for the panther. An hour passed. Then I heard an almost imperceptible rustle, the faintest sound of a dry twig being trodden upon, and I sensed the panther was coming. The crucial moment had almost arrived. Now I had to be careful not to shine the torch before the panther was fully in view. If I did so, I knew he would disappear. On the other hand, if I delayed too long, he might see me first and perhaps make a charge, or even vanish.

With all my senses at full stretch, I waited. There were no fresh rustlings or other sounds. Then I heard a faint hiss.

Instinctively I knew the panther had seen or sensed me. He had curled back his lips in a snarl, preparatory to the growl that would most likely follow. That curling of his lips had occasioned the slight hissing sound I had heard. It was now or never. My thumb went down on the switch-button of the torch. Its beam sprang right into the twin reddish-white eyes of the panther. I could clearly see his face and chest perhaps ten feet away. Aiming quickly at the throat I pressed the trigger of the Winchester. The panther appeared to come forward a pace. Then he reared up on his hind legs, but not before my second bullet took him full in the chest. He fell over backwards out of sight and threshed the bushes for a few seconds. Next came the unmistakable gurgling sounds of a dying animal; then silence.

I waited another half-hour before deciding to take the risk of leaving the bush. I thought it reasonably safe to do so, as I was almost sure the panther was dead. Holding the cocked rifle before me, I crawled out of cover and stood beside the goat. My first impulse was to cut it loose and take it in tow along with me. Then the thought came to my mind that the panther I had fired at might not have been the man-eater after all, but just an ordinary animal. If that were so, I would need to exercise every precaution in returning to the *Patel's* village in the darkness and could not afford to hamper myself by leading a goat that would necessarily distract my attention. So I left it where it was and set out for the *Patel's* abode, where I arrived after slow and cautious walking. The people were still awake and I told them what had happened. Then I went to my *kottai* for a sound night's sleep.

Next morning we found the panther where he had fallen. An old male, with a somewhat craggy and pale coat, he showed every sign of being the man-eater for his canine teeth were worn down with old age and his claws were blunt and frayed.

But only time would tell whether I had bagged the real culprit.

By noon I was on my way down the hill with his pelt.

Many years have elapsed since that incident took place, but no more people have been killed on either the Yellagiri or Javadi ranges, and so I am reasonably sure I succeeded that night in bringing the man-eater to bag.

Three

_____

Old Munuswamy and the
Panther of Magadi

THE TOWN OF BANGALORE, WHERE I LIVE, LIES PRACTICALLY IN THE
centre of a straight line drawn from the city of Madras, on
the east coast of India bordering the Bay of Bengal, to the
town of Mangalore, on the west coast bordering the Arabian
Sea. Bangalore is on a plateau just over three thousand feet
above mean sea level. Nobody who has lived there can ever
forget its; unique climate—neither too hot nor too cold, and
neither too rainy nor too dry—with lovely misty mornings
in the cold weather, from November to the middle of
February, and with bracing cool mornings even in summer.
The name, Bangalore, is an Anglicised version of the Kanarese
words 'bengal uru' meaning 'bean town' as translated literally,
whence it has become known as the 'city of beans'; and
nobody who has eaten them can ever forget Bangalore's

luscious fruits and vegetables of both tropical and European varieties.

Bangalore was far from being a city until the end of the Second World War, when its strategic military position, its great potential to grow into a large industrial city, and all its other assets have joined together to make it the most popular place in India. Following a wide influx of refugees both during and after the war, it has trebled its population, has become highly industrialised and is now a fast-growing city.

But this is not going to be a description of the merits of Bangalore; it was merely to say that I live in a very beautiful city. Bangalore is built on a number of hills, and if you stand on any one of them and look around, you will see three very high hills on the horizon, respectively to the north, the north-west and the west. They are all within a radius of thirty-five miles and each is above four thousand feet in height. The hill to the north is the highest. It is really not one but three hills, consisting of three peaks together which make up the Nundydroog group. 'Droog' means 'hill fortress', and the easternmost of these three peaks is crowned by the remains of an old fort, still in a good state of repair, built by that redoubtable Mahommedan warrior Tippoo Sultan, the 'Tiger of Mysore'. It embraces a point overlooking a sheer drop of some 600 feet. This is known as 'Tipoo's Drop', because it was here that this hoary soldier dispensed with those who annoyed him by making them walk, blindfolded, on a narrow swaying plank out over the abyss. If they could walk to the end of the plank and return, they were spared. There seems to be no record of anyone accomplishing this feat. Perhaps the plank swayed too much— or maybe it was made to sway too much. Who knows? Historians are not very clear on this point.

To the northwest of Bangalore is the hill called Sivanaganga. It has a temple at the summit and is a place of pilgrimage for Hindus. It also has a well at the top that is said to be so deep that it is bottomless. Another version is that this well is the beginning of a secret underground passage running all the thirty-five miles to Bangalore.

The third hill to the west is known as Magadi Hill. Viewed from the rising ground in Bangalore it appears to be sugar-loaded in shape; but when you get there you find it has two humps like a dromedary. Between them is a heavily-wooded valley difficult to enter, for the approaches are slippery; if you should slip, you will not end much better off than did those blindfolded prisoners with whom Tippoo amused himself on Nundydroog.

This is the valley that brings me to the beginning of the story, for it was here that the panther that terrorized Magadi was said to have his cave.

Magadi hill is surrounded by gorgeously wooded and hilly country. To the south lies a stretch of reserved forest, covering a series of hills, extending southwards for over seventy miles to the Cauvery river, near a place called Sangam. Not all of this area is reserved forest, but a large part is, while the rest is thickly covered with scrub jungle. About midway down this line of hills, and between the towns of Closepet and Kankanhalli, the peaks cluster particularly high and closely, and the area swarms with panthers. This hunting ground is my son, Donald's, particular paradise. He has shot forty panthers there and over a dozen bear, I think, and he is little more than twenty-three years old.

To the west of Magadi hill are plains of low scrub. Black-buck, hare, peafowl, partridge and quail abound. The hills continue to the north, but there they are much lower. To the east lies more hilly country, and Bangalore, about thirty-five miles away. The Arkravarthy river, a comparatively small stream, crosses the road to Bangalore near the twenty-three milestone, and it has been dammed just there. The catchment area is big enough to ensure an ample supply of water to Bangalore throughout the driest year. This dam is known as Tippagondahalli, and huge pumps send the water the remaining twenty-three miles to Bangalore.

There you have the full setting of the country where this leopard first appeared. It must not be thought that there is anything special about this animal because I have used the name 'leopard'. A leopard and a panther are one and the same creature. For no good reason that I know of, in India we more often call them panthers.

The events that I am going to relate took place before the last war.

This panther killed some goats and a village cur or two at some of the few scattered hamlets that lie at the foot of Magadi hill. Nobody took much notice of him, for panthers had been doing that sort of thing in that part of the country for generations and generations of panthers and the people have grown up with them.

Time passed and he grew more confident of himself. He killed some young bulls—and some cows too.

Now the bull is a sacred animal in India and no Hindu will touch his flesh. Nevertheless, the bull does all the hard work. He ploughs the fields and he draws the bullock-carts. He even turns the huge stone wheels that grind *chunam* or limestone. But with all his many uses and considerable value, people do not begrudge a panther eating one of their bulls now and again—provided he does not become too greedy. But when he goes in for killing cows—which supply milk and butter, from whence comes 'ghee', which is melted butter and a cooking medium used throughout the length and breadth of the country and of much value—he commits an unpardonable offence and it is high time something is done.

In Bangalore there lives—and I use the present tense because he is still there—an individual named 'Munuswamy', who claims to be a professional 'gentleman's *shikari*' guide. He is also a rogue. He brings in items of *shikar* news to town and passes them on to novices and greenhorns in the game. 'Master, there is herd of forty wild pigs can shoot near Whitefield, only twelve miles away.' Or, 'Master, on tenth mile on Magadi Road and eighteenth mile on road to Mysore City there plenty herds of black bucks got, fifty animals in each, which master very easily can shoot.' He demands a reasonable advance of money for the information, and should he turn up on the day appointed to accompany the novice to the place, the latter generally wonders what has become of those many wild pigs and blackbuck that were said to abound. But do not underestimate Munuswamy for a moment. He is quick-witted and a ready liar. 'See, master,' he will say, 'I told you come soon long time back. You no come. Only yesterday big crowd military officer *sahibs* come in car. Them shoot two pigs. All run away now. Master come again another day, eh?'

Wild pigs and blackbuck are only 'chicken feed' to Munuswamy. To see him at his best is to watch him bringing news of a panther to some unfortunate greenhorn who is about to learn the lesson of his life. He will present himself at the gate of the bungalow, or accost the *sahib* on the road, with somethihg like this: 'Sar, me big gentleman-*shikari*-guide. Me show master blackbucks, wild pigs, peacocks, hares, partridge and green pigeons. Or master like snipes and wild ducks? Them come plenty, plenty in December month— Kistmiss time got. Master like shoot very very big panther? Him large one got. Only fifteen miles from here, Kankanhalli road. Master give fifteen chips advance, me tie live donkey. Panther kill donkey, me come tell Master. Me also build *machan* very fine. Master shoot panther very easy.'

The novice is astounded. Only fifteen rupees for a live-bait? A panther only fifteen miles away? Who said hunting was an expensive or difficult hobby?

So the fifteen rupees are handed over to Munuswamy, who then remembers that master must give him another two rupees towards his food and three rupees for bus charge, when he brings master news of the kill. The greenhorn thinks this is very reasonable and forks out another five rupees. Munuswamy goes away most contented.

His first call is at one of the many local toddy-shops. He drinks only 'toddy' and eschews spirits in the form of *'arrack'*, which he says is too strong for him anyhow. But he drinks three bottles of toddy. This is the fermented juice of the coconut palm. Then old Munuswamy goes into a deep sleep.

The next day he wakes up and sets about the business of baiting the 'panther' in right earnest.

In Bangalore there are two animal 'pounds' for stray cattle, dogs and donkeys. The official charge for reclaiming your donkey, if it has been so impounded, is one rupee. After an interval of about ten days, unclaimed animals are sold by public auction to repay part of the expenses incurred in feeding them during those ten days. These auctions take place about twice a week, and it is a very simple matter for Munuswamy to attend one of them and purchase a donkey for about two rupees. Or he may even wrongfully pose as the owner of one of the impounded animals and claim possession of it. After all, one donkey looks much alike another, and there is no means by which the official in charge can test the truth of Munuswamy's claim, particularly if he sends a friend or agent to make it.

So Munuswamy gets the donkey, for which the *sahib* paid him fifteen rupees, for only two rupees, thereby making a profit of thirteen rupees, representing a potential 650 per cent on his initial outlay. A good beginning indeed.

Then he sets out on a long walk of some miles to wherever he has told the *sahib* the panther is to be found and ties the donkey there for a couple of days. Early in the morning of the third day or so he kills the donkey himself. This is how he does it. He has one of those huge penknives that incorporate about a dozen appurtenances, among them a round sharp-pointed instrument originally intended to be used, I believe, for removing stones from horses' hooves. At least this is what I am told, but I am not quite sure myself. With this crude instrument, he stabs the unfortunate animal in its jugular vein, and when it falls down, he stabs it again, making four wounds in all, two on each side of the throat. With the blade end of the same pen-knife he cuts open the belly, scatters the entrails about and tears off some chunks of flesh from the outer skin. Then he covers the carcass with branches. Lastly, he removes from a dirty bag he has brought with him a mysterious object. Can you guess what it is? This is Munuswamy's ace trick. It is a panther's paw, crudely stuffed with straw. With this he makes a series of 'pug-marks' here and there.

With the scene set to his expert satisfaction, for a few annas Munuswamy thumbs a lift to town in a lorry, and in great excitement summons the *sahib*. The greenhorn becomes excited too. In frantic haste he makes the 'missus' prepare sandwiches for him and tea for his thermos flask, while he himself cleans his rifle, assembles rounds, torchlight, batteries and a number of other odds and ends—most of which he never uses and are quite useless anyhow. Then away he drives with Munuswamy at high speed to the place where, the 'panther' has 'killed'.

Munuswamy points out the 'pug-marks' on the ground and the panther's 'teeth-marks' on the donkey's throat, and the *sahib* is convinced. He also arranges a *machan* to be tied, using two coolies to do so, for whose services he charges two rupees each, though he pays ~~them~~ only twelve annas. Finally, before the *sahib* ascends, he strikes a bargain. If master shoots the panther, he must give Munuswamy twenty rupees *baksheesh*. If master misses—that is master's own fault—he must give his faithful retainer ten rupes. If the panther does not turn up—master should not forget that panthers are very, very cunning animals and sometimes don't return to a kill—well, he, Munuswamy has worked very hard in the hot sun for master's sake and must get five rupees. The bargain is struck.

Strangely enough, Munuswamy trusts master, just as much as he expects master to trust him.

Well, the panther doesn't come—for the best of reasons: there is no panther. Munuswamy takes care to pocket his five rupees first, then consoles master by reminding him that panthers are unpredictable creatures and that this one might come next time. He offers to tie another donkey. And so the story goes on and on, till the greenhorn abandons the idea even of seeing one of these most elusive creatures and decides to confine his attention to wild duck or partridge. Even here, Munuswamy is still useful.

You may ask me: 'How do you know all this about Munuswamy?' I was such a greenhorn once and he 'had' me no less than four times. One day an accident occurred—for Munuswamy. He was pointing out the 'pug-marks' to me. A stray cur had been watching us interestedly and suddenly darted into a bush and came out carrying a cloth bag. Munuswamy, in great consternation, gave chase. The dog ran and something spotted dropped out of the bag. Munuswamy rushed for it and so did I. It was a panther's stuffed foot. Then, at the threat of the most violent death—even more violent than the donkey's—he related his *modus operandi* to me in detail, much as I have told you.

I am a long-suffering individual and believe in the adage to 'live and let live'. If there are greenhorns as foolish as I was, just waiting to be 'plucked'—well, why should Munuswamy not pluck them? So, I have never spoilt his game and Munuswamy rather likes me.

Don't think that, by telling you this, I am spoiling his game now, for Munuswamy assumes a different name each time he presents himself to a new recruit to the band of hunters that abound in Bangalore. He may be Ramiah, *Poojah*, Pooniah, or have a hundred aliases. But in case you should come to Bangalore at any time and aspire to join our ranks, I will give you one hint about him—a casual description. If an English-speaking 'gentleman's *shikari*-guide' presents himself to you—a lean, tall, oldish, very black man, with long hair drawn to the back of his head and tied in a knot, and large protruding eyes, whether he is wearing a turban or cap, *dhoti, lungothi* or baggy trousers or shorts, and even if he says his name is Jack Johnson, keep far from him and lock your purse up safely in a drawer. As likely as not it is my old friend Munuswamy, the happy-go-lucky 'crooked' guide.

In talking about this individual, I am aware that you may think I have strayed very far from my story. But really I have not, because he plays quite a prominent part at the beginning and at the end of it. And I am sure you have enjoyed making the acquaintance of this quite unusual and unique character, anyway.

This Munuswamy had come to hear about the activities of the panther that had begun killing bulls and cows in the Magady Hill area. Do not imagine that, although Munuswamy invariably manufactured his own panthers, he did not know anything about real ones. He did. In years gone by, when he was younger and times were not so hard, he had been a genuine *shikari* himself and knew a good deal about these animals. So when the information reached him, he went to Magadi by bus and made a first-hand investigation, during which he came to understand the panther had been killing goats and cattle rather frequently.

You will appreciate that because of his methods and the strange fact that nobody who went out shooting with Munuswamy ever saw a panther, and very rarely saw anything else, his reputation as a guide was getting somewhat tarnished. More than half the homes of gentlemen *shikaris,* both European and Indian, whether experienced or novices, were fast closed to him. This was a very deplorable state of affairs for Munuswamy and reacted directly on his exchequer and consequently upon his stomach. The time had come to remedy it and vindicate himself.

The fact that the panther was killing boldly and frequently should make him easy to bag, and it awoke Munuswamy's latent hunting instincts. He decided that he would shoot the animal and then advertise the fact in town by a procession, in which the panther would be taken around the streets of Bangalore on a bullock-cart to the tune of tom-toms. Even better than that, Munuswamy would have his photograph taken with the panther and present copies to such of his clients as were still on speaking terms. To those who were not he would post copies. On the back of each he would have a short statement to the effect that *shikari* Munuswamy had shot this panther on such and such a day, at such and such a place, because the *sahibs* who had come with him had been unable to do so, in spite of all the help he had given them.

The more he thought of it, the more old Munuswamy thrilled to the idea. That would give them something to think about. And it would give a tremendous fillip to his waning reputation.

Having sold his own gun long ago, he somehow contrived to borrow an old hammer-model .12 bore double-barrelled weapon. Then he revisited the scene and told the villagers that he, Munuswamy the old *shikari,* who had once served with generals and viceroys, had come to shoot the animal that was causing them such loss. He said he intended to live in the village of Magadi, which is situated about four miles northwest of the hill from which it takes its name, and told them to bring him news immediately if any of their animals were killed.

Two days later the news came that the panther had killed another cow. Taking the solitary ball cartridge, and the three others containing L.G. shot that he had borrowed with the gun, Munuswamy repaired to the spot, tied his *machan* and shot the panther high up in the shoulder with the ball cartridge. The L.G. in the other barrel—for he had fired both barrels together to make certain—helped to pepper him too, but the panther got away nevertheless. Reviewing the situation later, Munuswamy decided he was too advanced in years to follow wounded panthers. Moreover, the advantages he might get out of the 'propaganda stunt' that had fired his imagination did not now appear to weigh sufficiently against the dangers of following up the blood trail left by the panther. So he decided to call it a day and returned to Bangalore.

Weeks passed, and then the old story, which invariably begins the same way, took its usual course. A panther began to attack dogs and goats outside some of the villages situated beside the twenty-two miles of roadway that stretches outwards from Magadi to Closepet. In two instances the people in charge of the herds had tried to save their goats and had been attacked. A man and a boy had been mauled in this way.

Then a *jutka*-man and his pony entered the picture. Three persons had detrained one night at Closepet railway station from the night train from Mysore. As there was no bus service at that hour, these three men had decided to travel to their destination, a village ten miles from Closepet, by *jutka*. A *jutka*, for those of you who are unfamiliar with the word, is a two-wheeled vehicle covered by an elliptical roof of matting reinforced with bamboos, and is drawn by a small breed of pony especially reared for the purpose. *Jutka* ponies resemble the ordinary village 'tat', except that they have shorter manes and shorter tails.

The *jutka* arrived at its destination and unloaded its passengers. The driver decided to sleep in the village and return to Closepet the next morning. He unharnessed his pony and fed it with some of the dried grass he carried in a gunny-bag, slung just below the floor of the vehicle. Then he went to sleep.

The pony evidently finished the grass and began to stray along the village street, hoping to find some more growing there. In this way it came to the outskirts of the village, which was after all a tiny place.

From the back of the last hut along the street something sprang up suddenly against its side, and began to tear at its throat. Neighing shrilly, the pony galloped back up the street. The something that had attacked it had tried to hold on, but had lost its grip on the pony's throat and fallen off, but not before it had inflicted a nasty wound. That something had been the panther.

The sounds made by the terror-stricken pony and the growls of the panther awoke the jutka-owner, who saw his animal rushing towards him. It halted, quivering with fright, blood pouring from its throat. He raised an immediate alarm.

The pony could not haul the *jutka*; so next day the owner walked it back to Closepet, where he reported the matter to the police. News spread and it became known that the area was threatened by a panther that might any day become a man-eater.

Shortly afterwards a man was pounced upon within two miles of Magadi village itself and badly mauled. Villagers, tending their fields some distance away, rushed to the rescue and found him on the ground, severely bitten and raked by the animal's sharp claws. They carried him into Magadi, and to the Local Fund Hospital there, for attention. A police report was made, and the local police *daffedar*, whose rank is about equivalent to that of a sergeant, being the most senior officer in the village and in charge of the police *chowki* or station, set out to make an on-the-spot examination of the evidence given, accompanied by a constable with a bicycle.

He was taken to the place at which the ryots had picked up the injured man. While he was looking at the blood marks and pug-tracks, and perhaps making copious notes in the way that policemen do, somebody looked up and said they could see the panther lying on a rocky outcrop at the top of a small hillock, hardly two furlongs away. The *daffedar* saw him, borrowed his constable's bicycle, and pedalled furiously back to the village for one of the three service-rifles that formed the entire police armoury there.

Though he pedalled furiously back, by the time he reached the place, his constable and one or two villagers who had remained, said the panther had disappeared over the top of the hill. The villagers told the *daffedar* that if he cared to make a detour around the hillock—the distance wasn't very great—he might yet be able to cut the panther off on the other side.

The *daffedar* was nothing if not keen and brave, and, taking one of the villagers along to indicate the short cut, hastened around the hill, loading a single 303 round into the weapon he carried. The constabulary in India are armed with rifles of the same type as the military, with the only difference that the magazines are generally removed, so that only one shell at a time can be fired, thus preventing a trigger-happy copper from using his weapon overenthusiastically at a time of riot of local disturbance. For this reason, the *daffedar* had only one round to fire with, and two or three others in his pocket.

They came to the other side of the hill, but they found no signs of the panther. Many boulders were scattered about, and the villager suggested they ascend the hill a little, as the panther was probably around somewhere. This they did, and from between or from behind some rocks the panther emerged. The *daffedar* was taken by surprise and fired from his hip, missing completely. The next second saw him on the ground with the panther on top, biting and clawing at his chest and arms. His companion was in full flight down the hill.

After the few seconds during which it had vented its rage, the panther, which had not yet become a man-eater, left the wounded policeman and sprang back to the shelter of the rocks whence he had come. The badly hurt *daffedar* lay where the beast had left him.

Meanwhile the fleeing villager ran back to the constable and the other villagers and told them what had happened. The constable leaped upon his bicycle and made for the police station in the village, where he summoned the other three members of the local force and told them their *daffedar* had probably been killed.

Taking the remaining two rifles from their racks, and two 'lathis' in addition, the four representatives of the law hastened back to the hill, being reinforced as they went along with more and more villagers. A party of over ten people finally picked up the *daffedar,* who was in a bad way, and carried him back to the Local Fund Hospital. The next day an ambulance was sent for from Bangalore, which conveyed him to the Victoria Hospital in the city.

The reports of the panther's various attacks had all been registered, but when he attacked one of their own force— and a *daffedar* at that—the police really got busy. It did not take them very long to find out who had been the root of all this trouble, and at this stage, old Munuswamy, the rascally *shikari* guide, re-entered the scene.

The police caught him. Witnesses had testified that he had built a *machan* and sat up for the panther. They also said he had wounded it. To have done that he must have used a firearm. Did he have one? Did he possess an Arms Licence? Was he hiding an unlicensed weapon? Did he borrow it? Who from? Why? When? Where? Did the owner have a licence? How many cartridges did he take?

There were a hundred-and-one questions to answer. Altogether, poor Munuswamy could see he was in for a bad time. The number of charges against him, culminating with the statement that if the *daffedar* died from his wounds he might be charged with 'potential manslaughter',—filled a page and would undoubtedly send him to jail for a long, long time.

Then Munuswamy's inborn initiative came to his rescue and he made his greatest bargain. He undertook to shoot the panther within four days and lay the body at the feet of the district Superintendent of Police (D.S.P.). If he failed, the police could do as they liked with him. If he succeeded, the charges should be forgotten.

The D.S.P., being a practical officer, was more interested in having the panther shot than in prosecuting Munuswamy. For it was obvious that this animal was well on the way to becoming a man-eater; whereas Munuswamy, with all his rascally ways, was unlikely to rise to such heights of evil fame. So the D.S.P. gave him just four days and let him out of the lock-up.

The same afternoon I heard a voice persistently calling, 'sar, sar', at my front door. It was Munuswamy. With tears rolling down his cheeks—how he got them to flow so instantaneously is a secret which he has not yet confided to me—he related his whole tale of woe from beginning to end, and all the information that he knew or had been able to gather about this panther, much as I have told the story here.

He had just four days in which to shoot the panther, he insisted, failing which he would go to 'big, big jail' as he termed it. Laughingly I asked him why he did not run away. The idea had occurred to him, he admitted, but where else throughout the length and breadth of India would he be able to find such sporting *sahibs* who gave him money so freely; such obliging auctions where he could pick up live donkeys for as little as two rupees; and, oh! the many other advantages which come with living in Bangalore. The old man broke down at these thoughts and his tears flowed faster than ever. I would not have been surprised to learn that a few of them were genuine.

Would I please help him by shooting this panther? I would be saving him, and oh! so many other people that it might yet kill.

I conceded the latter point, but I told Munuswamy frankly that I wasn't too interested in the former. He was not offended. I said I would help him on one condition: that, as he had undoubtedly been the root of all the trouble, he would have to be beside me and not run away when the panther was shot.

The old boy actually smiled as he agreed. Strangely, his tears had vanished entirely.

That very evening I took him down to the house of the D.S.P., to whom I laughingly recounted the circumstances under which Munuswamy had presented himself. I told the police officer that I did not know if he had really been serious in allowing Munuswamy a reprieve of four days in which to kill the panther, but I pointed out that if this was so, such a time-limit was an encumbrance, as I wanted the old rogue with me to assist, and it would be a nuisance if the police butted in on the fifth day and took him away.

The D.S.P. replied that he had really meant to give him only four days in which to fulfil his undertaking, but in view of what I said he would not interfere so long as I went ahead and tried to bag this animal. He also helped by handing me a letter, calling upon all police officials to whom I might show it to render me every assistance.

Of course I did not tell this to Munuswamy. That would have made him relax his efforts. Instead, I mentioned that the D.S.P. *sahib* was beginning to regret having allowed him as long as four days and wanted to cut them down to three, but that I had interceded on his behalf and saved the situation in the nick of time.

This made Munuswamy more grateful to me than ever, and as impatient to be off on our trip. In the Studebaker we reached Magadi Hill early the next morning and started making inquiries at the various hamlets at its foot, including the place at which Munuswamy had wounded the panther. Asking questions as we went along, we worked our way right up to Magadi village itself, where I spoke to the police constables who had rescued their *daffedar*. Thence we set off in the car along the road to Closepet, stopping at each wayside village to ask questions. In this way we came to the village where the panther had attacked the pony, and eventually to Closepet town itself, where the Sub-Inspector of Police, to whom I showed the note given me by the D.S.P., immediately sent for the *jutka*-man. I interrogated him and he told me what had happened to his pony.

It took until late that evening to ask all these questions, but in spite of them I had found nobody who appeared to know where the panther was likely to be living, or his particular

74

habits. Of course, I knew there was no hurry, but Munuswamy's dark countenance was even more haggard when he realised that one out of his four days of grace had passed already with no substantial results.

We came back to Magadi village that night and slept in the travellers' bungalow.

Early next morning a skinny-looking individual presented himself and stated that he earned a living gathering honey from the hives on the surrounding hills, by collecting herbs and other medicinal roots, and by snaring hare, partridge and quail when he got the opportunity. He said he had been told the night before that I had been around with Munuswamy, seeking information about the panther, and he had come to report that he was almost certain the animal lived in a cave in the recesses of the cleft between the two hummocks of Magadi Hill.

I asked him what made him so certain of this. He replied that some weeks earlier he had been there to collect herbs and had observed that an animal, dripping blood, had crossed some rocks, leaving a distinct trail. Following cautiously, he had found panther pug-marks where the animal had left the rocks. He had then stopped following. Later, he came to know that on the previous day someone had wounded a panther not far away. That somebody had been Munuswamy.

He knew of the cave, having taken honey from beehive in its vicinity many times in the past. A couple of days previously, just after the *daffedar* had been atacked but before my informant had come to hear of it himself through having been away for a week at Closepet, he had approached the cave to see if the bees had begun to build again. He was some distance away from it when an animal had growled at him. Remembering at once the blood-trail he had found weeks earlier, he had left the valley as fast as he could.

This was news indeed.

I started asking questions, and he undertook to lead me to the cave, provided that I was prepared to creep on hands and knees for a furlong or so through the dense lantana that led to the valley and the cave.

I agreed and told Munuswamy that the time had come for him to fulfil his part of the bargain, which was to accompany me and be in at the killing of the panther, to atone for his sin in having wounded it in the first place.

If I had expected him to show fear, I was mistaken. The police had so terrified him that he was more afraid of the remaining three days running out without bagging our quarry than of facing any panther.

I waited for the sun to become hot, while I ate a leisurely 'chota hazri'. This was in order to allow the panther time to fall asleep for the day within his cave. If I arrived there too early, he might hear me coming and beat a retreat.

We left the bungalow by car at exactly ten o'clock and in less than fifteen minutes reached a point on the road almost opposite the valley between the two hummocks of the hill. The lean man, who had given his name as Allimuthu, indicated that we should have to get out. I parked the car in the shade of a tree just off the road and the three of us got down. I worked the under-lever of my rifle, just to check that it was moving freely. Then Allimuthu, Munuswamy and I set off for the cave.

The hill is about two miles from the road. We reached the base and started climbing towards the valley, which was no longer visible, because of the trees around us. Over their tops I could just see the summits of the two hillocks above, and to the right and left of us.

We climbed for an hour and it was a stiff ascent. Then we came to a veritable sea of lantana bushes which had entirely enveloped the trees and the lesser jungle. This was the place.

Alimuthu indicated, where we would have to crawl through and under the lantana for some distance.

I can assure you that covering the next furlong or so of ground was a strenuous effort. We were perspiring and scratched by thorns already as it was. Allimuthu crawled ahead; I followed closely, and Munuswamy was even closer behind. By the time we negotiated that lantana-belt we were dripping with sweat and my khaki shirt and pants were torn in many places. I am sure I left small portions of my face, neck and hands hanging from many of the barbed hooks that serrate each branch of lantana shrub.

We eventually broke free of the belt and entered the valley between the hummocks. It was strewn with boulders everywhere, covered to half their height by spear-grass. Allimuthu whispered that the cave was to the left and about three-fourths of the distance along the valley. It was an impossible place in which to spot a panther, even at a short distance. A dozen tigers would have been equally invisible there.

I took the lead now, with Allimuthu behind and Munuswamy immediately behind him. I kept to the right and skirted the foot of the right-hand hummock, so that if the panther charged from the cave, or any cover to our left, I should have a chance to see it coming. We drew opposite the cave. There was an overhanging cleft in the rock above it. I noticed that this rock was pitted with barnacles of wax that had been the sites of old honeycombs, although there appeared to be no fresh ones. The inside of the cavern was hidden by the long grass and piles of rocks that lay scattered outside it, many of which had apparently rolled down the hillside from above.

Then we heard it. An unmistakable growl. Allimuthu reached out to touch my shoulder to stop me, but I had already caught the sound.

It might have been made by a panther—or it might have been made by a bear.

I stopped to think. There were two courses open to me. There was no doubt that the sound had come from in front: from the cave or some place very close to it. I could throw stones or advance a little closer. I felt afraid to follow the latter course. The creature, whatever it was, could rush down upon me from the higher level of the cavern. If I failed to see it coming between the grass and rocks, or missed it with my first shot, I could expect real trouble.

Discretion got the better of valour and I whispered to Allimuthu and Munuswamy to hurl stones in that direction. They did so.

Nothing happened.

With my rifle cocked and ready, I watched for the slightest movement in the scene before me.

They hurled more stones, but still nothing happened.

Then I noticed a slight movement of the long grass away to the right, leading up the hill, beyond the side of the cavern where it adjoined the sloping ground behind.

That movement might have been caused by the breeze or by some animal slinking through the grass. Of one thing I was certain, it was definitely not a bear. Bruin is black in southern India, and I would easily have picked out such a black object against the brown grass. Nor for that matter could Bruin sneak about in such fashion—not even if he tried. He is a blundering type, who either bursts upon a scene or bursts away from it.

I strained my eyes and then saw part of the spotted shape as it drew level with the height of the rock that overhung the cavern.

The animal had stopped moving now and was undoubtedly looking back at us, although I could not make out its head or face in the grass. A couple of seconds more and it might be gone.

I covered that spotted patch in my sights and gently pressed the trigger.

The panther shot up and out of the grass, bent up double like a prawn, and then rolled backwards down the slope and was hidden from view in the grass. Scrambling upon a boulder, I tried to look down and see him. There was nothing to be seen.

I waited for ten minutes; then I crept forward, after motioning to Allimuthu and Munuswamy to take cover. Every now and then I leaped on to a boulder to see if I could catch a glimpse of the animal.

Eventually I did, and all my caution was unnecessary, for the panther was quite dead. That snap shot of mine had been a lucky one. The .405 bullet had passed through the back of his neck and into his skull.

Examination showed where the ball from Munuswamy's gun had travelled clean through the animal's back, high up and behind the shoulder-blades. It had made a big hole in leaving and had caused a nasty open wound in which maggots were crawling. Two L.G. pellets were embedded in the skin, but the wounds caused by them appeared to be healing. The main wound, however, would eventually have caused the animal's death, if it had not made him a man-eater before then. This was a middle-aged male, just under seven feet in length.

We had a lot of trouble lugging his body through that infernal lantana thicket, but we made it after more toil and sweat.

That evening we laid the body before the D.S.P's feet. Exactly forty-eight hours had passed since I had asked him to extend the time limit of four days. But Munuswamy and I had accomplished the task in half that time. The D.S.P. was all smiles.

Four

The Black Panther of Sivanipalli

SIVANIPALLI HAS ALWAYS BEEN A FAVOURITE HAUNT OF MINE BECAUSE of its proximity to Bangalore and the fact that it lends itself so conveniently to a weekend excursion or even a visit of a few hours on a moonlit night. All you have to do is to motor from Bangalore to Denkanikotta, a distance of forty-one miles, proceed another four miles by car, and then leave the car and walk along a footpath for five miles, which brings you to Sivanipalli. The hamlet itself stands at the edge of the Reserved Forest.

Nearly three miles to the west of this small hamlet the land drops for about three hundred feet, down to a stream running along the decline. To the south of the hamlet another stream flows from the east to west, descending rapidly in a number of cascades to converge with the first stream that runs along the foot of the western valley. To the east of Sivanipalli itself the jungle stretches to a forest lodge, Gulhatti Bungalow,

80

situated nearly five hundred feet up on a hillside. East of Gulhatti itself, and about four and a half miles away as the crow flies, is another forest bungalow at a place called Aiyur. Four miles northeast again there is a Forestry department shed located near a rocky hill named Kuchuvadi. This is a sandalwood area, and the shed houses an ancient huge pair of scales which are used for weighing the cut pieces of sandalwood as they are brought in from the jungle, before being despatched to the Forestry department's godowns at the block headquarters at Denkanikotta.

Northwards of Sivanipalli, thick scrub jungle extends right up to and beyond the road, five miles away, where you have to leave the car, before setting out for the hamlet on foot.

Sivanipalli itself consists of barely half-a-dozen thatched huts and is hardly big enough to be called even a hamlet. A considerably larger village named Salivaram is found three miles to the north, just a little more than halfway along the footpath leading to the main road.

Fire-lines of the Forestry department surround Sivanipalli on all four sides, demarcating the commencement of the surrounding reserved forest at distances varying from half a mile to a mile from the hamlet. There is a water hole almost at the point where two of these fire-lines converge at the southeastern corner. The two streams that meet the west of the village at the foot of the three-hundred-foot drop wind on through jungle in the direction of another larger village named Anchetty, about eight miles southwestward of Sivanipalli itself.

I have given this rather detailed description of the topography of the surrounding region to enable you to have in mind a picture of the area in which occurred the adventure I am about to relate.

It is an ideal locality for a panther's activities, with small rocky hills in all directions, scrub jungle, heavy forest and two streams—apart from the water hole—to ensure a steady water supply, not only for the panthers themselves, but for the game on which they prey. Because of this regular supply of water, a fairly large herd of cattle is quartered at Sivanipalli, which is an added attraction, of course, so far as these felines are concerned!

As a result, quite a number of panthers are more or less in permanent residence around the area. That is the main reason why I was attracted to Sivanipalli the first day I visited it in 1929.

The jungle varies in type from the heavy bamboo that grows in the vicinity of the water hole to the thick forest on the southern and western sides, with much thinner jungle and scrub, interspersed with sandalwood trees, to the east and north.

The countryside itself is extremely beautiful, with a lovely view of the hills stretching away to a hazy and serrated blue line on the western horizon. Banks of mist float up from the jungle early in the morning and completely hide the base of these hills, exposing their tops like rugged islands in a sea of fleecy wool. On a cloudy day, the opposite effect is seen, for when storm clouds settle themselves along the tops of the hills, entirely hiding them from view, only the lower portions of their slopes are visible, giving the impression of almost flat country.

I have spent many a moonlit night 'ghooming'—derived, from the Urdu verb 'ghoom', meaning 'to wander about'— the jungles around little Sivanipalli. They hold game of every description, with the exception of bison, in moderate numbers. There is always the chance of encountering an elephant, hearing the soughing moan of a tiger, the grating sawing of a panther, or the crash of an alarmed sambar as it flees at your approach while you wander about the moonlit forest.

You will not be able to see them—except perhaps the elephant, for both species of carnivora, and the sambar as well, are far too cunning and have long ago seen or heard you coming.

You may stumble upon a bear digging vigorously in the ground for white ants or tuber-roots, or sniffing and snuffling loudly as he ambles along. You will undoubtedly hear him, long before you see him as a black blob in the confused and hazy background of vegetation, looking grey and ghostly in the moonlight.

As far back as 1934 Sivanipalli sprang a surprise. A black panther had been seen drinking at the water hole by a herdsman returning with his cattle from the forest where he had taken them for the day to graze. It was shortly after five o'clock in the evening, which is the usual time for the cattle to be driven back to the pens in the village to be kraaled for the night. It is the custom to drive them out in the mornings to the jungle for the day's grazing at about nine, or even later, and to bring them back fairly early in the evening, the apparently late exodus and early return being to allow time for the cows to be milked twice a day.

Thus it was only a little after five and still quite light when the herdsman saw this black panther standing beside a bush that grew close to the water's edge, calmly lapping from the pool. He swore that it was jet black and I had no reason to disbelieve him, for there seemed no real point in a deliberate lie. When the herd approached, the panther had gazed up at the cattle; but when the herdsman appeared amidst his beasts it just melted away into the undergrowth.

Now the black panther is not a separate or special species. It is simply an instance of melanism. A black cub sometimes, but very rarely, appears in a litter, the other cubs being of normal size and colour. Black panthers are said to occur more in the thick evergreen forests of Malaya, Burma, Assam and similar localities than around this district. They have also been seen and shot very occasionally in the Western Ghats of India. I have every reason to believe the view that they prevail in these heavy evergreen forests, for then their dark colour would afford considerably better concealment. At the same time, as they are simple instances of melanism, they should occur anywhere and everywhere that panthers exist, regardless of the type of the jungle prevailing. I have only seen one other black panther in its wild state, and that was when it leapt across the road on the ghat section between Pennagram and Muttur near the Cauvery river, at about six one evening. They are one of Nature's—or rather the jungle's—mysteries that has never been quite satisfactorily solved.

If you look closely at a black panther in a zoo, you will discover that the rosette markings of the normal panther are still visible through the black hair, although of course they cannot be seen very distinctly.

When the herdsman saw this black panther, he came to the village and told the people all about it. A black panther had never before been seen or heard of in this area and his tale was generally disbelieved. Having seen the animal with his own eyes, of course, he had no doubts, although he sincerely believed that it had not been a normal or living animal he had laid eyes upon but Satan in just one of the numerous forms he often adopts in the jungle to frighten poor villagers like himself.

Some weeks passed and no one saw or heard of the black panther again. The herdsman's story was forgotten.

One day, some months later, in mid-afternoon, with the sun shining brightly overhead, another herd of cattle was taking its siesta, squatting with closed eyes or lazily munching the grass in the shade of neighbouring trees. The beasts lay in little groups of two to half-a-dozen. The two herdsmen had finished their midday meal of *ragi* balls and curry, which they had brought along with them, tied up in a dirty piece of cloth, and were fast asleep, lying side by side in the shade of another tree.

It was indeed a peaceful scene, as from an azure sky the tropical sun sent down its fiery rays that were reflected from the earth in waves of shimmering heat. The herd of cattle was relaxed, drowsy and unwatchful when the black panther of Sivanipalli took his first toll.

Appearing unexpectedly, the panther fastened his fangs in the throat of a half-grown brown and white cow, but not before she had time to bellow with pain and leap to her feet, lifting her assailant off the ground with his teeth locked in her throat.

The cow's agonized cry awakened one of the sleeping herdsmen, who was astounded by what he saw. He awoke his companion to look upon the Devil himself in an unexpected black form, and they watched as the stricken cow dropped to earth to ebb out her life, kicking wildly. The black panther maintained his grip. Thus she died. The men had leapt to their feet.

Ordinarily, in the event of an attack by a panther on one of their cattle, they would have rushed to its rescue, brandishing their staves and shouting at he tops of their voices, if not actually to save the life of the victim, at least to drive off the attacker before he could drag away the kill.

In this case neither of them found the nerve to do so. They just stood rooted to the spot and gazed in astonishment. As they did so, the panther released his hold on the throat of the dead cow and looked in their direction. Although he was some fifty yards away they could clearly see the crimson blood gushing from the cow's torn throat and dyeing the muzzle of the panther a deep scarlet against the black background of fur.

They turned tail and fled.

When the few villagers of Sivanipalli heard this account, they were very reluctant to go out and bring back the carcase before it was wholly eaten. This they would most certainly have done had the killer been a normal panther, but the presence of this unheard-of black monstrosity completely unnerved them. They had been told of a panther described as being jet black by the herdsman who had first seen him at the water hole. Being villagers themselves, they had allowed a wide margin for exaggeration in that case, but here were two more herdsmen, both saying the same thing. Could it be really true?

After that day, the black marauder began to exact a regular toll of animals from Sivanipalli. He was seen on several occasions, so that there was no more doubt in the minds of any of the villagers as to his actual existence and colour.

When the people came to know of his presence in the jungle, forcibly brought home to them by these frequent attacks on their animals, even their usual lethargy and apathy was shaken and they became more and more careful. Eventually a stage was reached when the cattle were not driven out to graze beyond a radius of about a quarter of a mile from the village.

Finding that his food supply was being cut off, the black panther started to extend his field of operation. He killed and ate animals that belonged to herds coming from Anchetty to the southwest and from Gulhatti and Aiyur to the east. He even carried off a large donkey from Salivaram which, as I have said, lay to the north of Sivanipalli and well outside of the forest reserve proper.

Just about this time I happened to pay a visit to Sivanipalli accompanied by a friend. We had gone there after lunch on a Sunday, intending to take an evening stroll in the forest and perhaps get a jungle fowl, or a couple of green pigeon for the pot. The story of the advent and activities of the black panther greatly interested me. Only once before had I seen one of its kind outside a zoo, and I was therefore determined to bag this specimen if possible.

I offered to pay the villagers the price of the next animal killed by this panther if they would leave it undisturbed and inform me. They must go by bus to the small town of Hosur Cattle Farm, which was the closest place to a telegraph office, where a message could be sent to me at Bangalore. I also asked them to spread the same information to all persons living at places where the panther had already struck. Finally, as a further incentive and attraction, I said that I would not only pay for the dead animal, but give a cash *baksheesh* of fifty rupees to him who carried out my instructions carefully.

Anticipating a call within the next few days I kept my portable *charpoy-machan* and other equipment ready at Bangalore to leave within a few minutes of receiving the telegram. But it was over a fortnight before that call eventually came. Moreover it arrived late! That is to say, it reached me just before four o'clock in the evening. I was on my way by four-fifteen, but it was about seven-fifteen and quite dark by the time I reached Sivanipalli.

I noticed that the telegram had been handed in at Hosur Cattle Farm at about one-thirty that afternoon, which was far too late, apart from the additional delay that had taken place at the Bangalore end because it had been classed as an ordinary message, instead of an express telegram, as I had specified.

There was a man named Rangaswamy living at Sivanipalli, who had assisted me as *shikari* on two or three previous occasions, and it was this man who had sent the telegram from Hosur Cattle Farm to say that the panther had made a kill at ten that very morning, shortly after the cattle had left the village for grazing. The herdsman in charge, who like the rest had been told of my offer to pay for the animal that had been killed, with a cash bonus as well, had very wisely not touched the carcase but had run back to Sivanipalli with the news which he had given to Rangaswamy, who in turn had made a great effort to reach Denkanikotta in time to catch the twelve-fifteen bus. This he had just managed to do, reaching the Hosur Cattle Farm telegraph office by one o'clock.

Commending Rangaswamy and the herdsman for their prompt action in sending me the news, I now had to decide between trying to stalk the panther on his kill with the aid of torchlight or waiting at Sivanipalli until the following evening to sit up for him. The former plan was a complete gamble as there was no certainty whatever that the panther would be on the kill, or anywhere near it, when I got there. At the same time I could not find any very convincing excuse to justify spending the next twenty-four hours cooped up in the hamlet doing nothing.

I enquired where the kill had taken place and was informed that it was hardly half a mile to the west of the village, where the land began its steep descent to the bed of the stream about three miles away. It seemed too temptingly close and this decided me to tell Rangaswamy and the herdsman that I would endeavour to bag the panther that very night while he was eating the kill, if they would lead me to a quarter of a mile from the spot and indicate the direction in which the kill lay. I felt I could trust my own sense of hearing and judgement to guide me from there on.

They were both against this plan and very strongly advocated waiting till the following evening, but I said that I would like to try it anyhow.

By the time all this talk was finished it was ten minutes to eight and there was no time to be lost, as the panther would probably be eating at that very moment. I clamped my three-cell, fixed-focus electric torch which was painted black to render it inconspicuous, to my rifle and dropped three spare cells into my pocket together with five spare rounds of ammunition. Four more rounds I loaded into the rifle, keeping three in the magazine and one in the breech. Although the 405 Winchester is designed to carry four rounds in the magazine and one 'up the spout', I always load one less in the magazine to prevent a jam, which may occur should the under-lever be worked very fast in reloading. Lastly, I changed the boots I had been wearing for a pair of light rubber-soled brown 'khed' shoes. These would to a great extent help me to tread lightly and soundlessly. I was wearing khaki pants and shirt at the time, and I changed into the black shirt I generally wear when sitting up in a *machan*.

Rangaswamy and the herdsman came along with me up to a dry rivulet. Then the latter told me that this rivulet ran almost directly westwards with just two bends in its course to the spot where the panther had killed. He said the dead cow had later been dragged about two hundred yards inside the jungle roughly northwards of the place where the rivulet completed the second bend.

Their instructions were clear enough and I was grateful for the two bends in the stream which enabled them to be so specific. Telling the men to go back, as I would eventually be able to find my own way to Sivanipalli, I started out on my attempt.

I considered the wisest and most silent approach would be along the bed of this dry stream rather than along the top of either of its banks. Any slight sounds I might inadvertently make would then be muffled and less audible to the panther. Secondly, by walking along the bed of the stream I could easily follow its course without having to shine my torch to see

89

where I was going, which I might have to do if I were to walk along the bank where the vegetation would impede me, the more so because it was very dark indeed and the sky very overcast, the clouds completely hiding the stars and whatever pale light they might have cast.

Accordingly I moved forward very carefully and soon felt the stream making its first curve, which was in a south-westerly direction. After a while the stream started to turn northwards again, and then straightened out to resume its westerly course. I had passed the first of the two bends the herdsman had mentioned.

Not long afterwards it curved into its second bend, but this time in a northerly direction. I moved as carefully as possible to avoid tripping upon any loose stone or boulder that might make a noise. Although from the information I had been given I knew the kill was still about three hundred yards away, panthers have very acute hearing, and if my quarry were anywhere in the immediate vicinity, if not actually eating on the kill, he would hear me and, as like as not, make off again.

Fortunately the rivulet was more or less clear of boulders and bushes along this part of its course and this helped me to edge along silently. A little later it had completed its northward turn and it began to curve southwards. After a few yards it straightened out once more and resumed its main westerly direction.

I halted. I had reached the place at which the panther had killed the cow and from where he had dragged the kill into the jungle for about two hundred yards to the north. I knew that I must now leave the rivulet and strike off into the undergrowth to try and locate the carcass and the killer, whom I hoped to surprise in the act of eating. In the deep gloom I had only my sense of hearing to guide me.

I tiptoed towards the northern bank of the stream which was, at that spot, only breast-high. With my feet still on the sandy bed, I gently laid the rifle on the bank and, folding my arms across my chest, leaned against it, listening intently.

Five minutes passed, but there was no sound of any kind to disturb the silence. Perhaps the kill was too far away to allow me to hear the panther eating; that is, if he was on the kill and if he was eating.

Putting my weight on my hands, I gently drew myself up to the top of the bank, making no sound as I did so. I then picked up the rifle and started to move forward very, very slowly. The darkness was intense. At the same time I knew I had really little, if anything, to fear from the panther should he discover me, as he was not a man-eater and had shown no inclination at any time to molest human beings. Nevertheless, this was my first experience with a black panther and I had heard several of the usual stories about them being exceptionally dangerous and aggressive. That made me quite nervous, I can honestly tell you.

Inching forward, I stopped every few yards to listen for sounds that would indicate that the panther was busy eating. Only they could guide me, as it was hopeless to expect to see anything without the aid of my torch, which could only be used when I was close enough to fire. The slightest flicker of the beam now would drive the panther away should he happen to see the light.

I went along in this fashion, taking what seemed an interminable time. Perhaps I had progressed seventy-five yards or more when, during one of the many stops I made to listen, I thought I heard a faint sound coming from in front and a little to the right. I listened again for some time, but it was not repeated.

Bushes and trees were now growing thickly around me, and my body, in pushing through the undergrowth, was making some noise in spite of the utmost care I was taking to prevent this. So were my feet as I put them down at each tread. I tried pushing them forward by just raising them off the ground and sliding them along, but I was still not altogether silent. I did this not only to try and eliminate noise, but to disguise my human footfalls should the panther hear me. He would certainly not associate any sliding and slithering sounds with a human being, but ascribe them to some small nocturnal creature moving about in the grass and bushes; whereas the sound of an ordinary footfall would immediately convey the fact that there was a man in the vicinity. An uncomfortable thought came into my mind that I might tread on a poisonous snake in the dark, and the rubber shoes I was wearing did not protect my ankles. I dispelled that thought and tried walking around the bushes and shrubs that arose before me. This caused me to deviate to some extent from the northerly course towards the dead cow I had been instructed to follow.

I stopped every now and then to listen, but the sound I had last heard was not repeated. It was some time later that I concluded that I had far exceeded the distance of two hundred yards from the rivulet at which the kill was said to be lying and also that I had hopelessly lost all sense of direction, enveloped as I was amongst the trees and scrub, under an overcast sky.

Then suddenly. I heard the sound I had so long been hoping to hear—the unmistakable sound of tearing flesh and crunching bones.

I had been lucky indeed. The panther was on his kill at that moment and, what was more, was actually engrossed in feeding. Now all I had to do was to try to creep sufficiently close to enable me to switch on my torch and take a shot.

But that was all very well in theory. The idea was far easier than its execution.

To begin with, the sounds did not come from the direction in which I was moving, but to my left and some distance behind me, indicating that I had not steered a straight course in the darkness. I had veered to the right, bypassing the kill. Perhaps the reason I had not heard the sound of feeding earlier was because the panther had only just returned. Or—and it was a most discomforting thought that came into my mind—maybe he had heard me in the darkness as I passed and deliberately stayed quiet.

I paused for a few moments and listened so as to make quite sure of the direction from which the sounds were coming. In the darkness I guessed the panther to be anything from fifty to a hundred yards away.

I now started to slide my feet forward very slowly and very cautiously towards the noise.

If the panther had dragged his kill into or behind a bush it would be impossible for me to get the shot I hoped for. On the other hand, all the advantages would be with the panther were I to fire and wound him, and if he attacked—the proposition was altogether a most unpleasant one.

At the same time, I tried to encourage myself by remembering that never before had this panther molested a human being, and that the light from my torch, when eventually I flashed it would fill him with fear and keep him from attacking me, if it did not drive the animal off entirely.

It is difficult to describe truthfully the minutes that ensued, or to recount what I actually did. My mind and senses were so alert and intense, that I negotiated all obstacles in the way of trees and undergrowth automatically. I knew that as long as I could hear the sounds made by the panther as he feasted I could be certain that he was fully engaged on the task at hand and was unaware of my approach. It was only when these sounds ceased that I would have to look out, for then the panther had heard me and had stopped his feeding to listen.

The sounds continued and so did I, creeping forward cautiously, never putting my foot down till I had tested each step with my toe. When I heard or sensed a leaf rustle beneath me, I groped for a place where I could tread more silently. All the while I kept my eyes strained upon the darkness before me and my ears pricked for the sounds of feeding.

Then suddenly those sounds stopped, and an absolute, awful silence engulfed me.

Had the panther stopped eating for a while of his own accord? Had he finished and gone away? Was he just going away? Or had he heard my stealthy approach and was even at that moment preparing to attack? The alternatives raced through my mind and I came to a halt too.

I remained thus, silent and stationary, for some time. Just how long I have no idea, but I remember that I was thinking what I should do next. To move forward, now that he had stopped eating, would certainly betray my approach to the panther—that is, if he was not already aware of my presence. However careful I might be, it would be impossible for a human being to move silently enough in the darkness to be inaudible to the acute hearing of such an animal. On the other hand, if I stayed put and kept quiet, there was a chance that I might hear the panther, should he approach, although panthers are well known to move noiselessly.

Of the two courses of action, I decided on the latter, so just stood still. As events were shortly to prove, it was lucky that I did so.

For a few moments later a very faint rustling came to my straining ears. It stopped and then began again. Something was moving. It could have been anything. It was a continuous sort of noise, such as a snake would make as it slithered through the grass and undergrowth. But a panther could just as easily cause it by creeping towards me on his belly. I can assure you that it was a very frightening thought.

One thing was certain. The sound did not come from a rat or a frog, or some small jungle creature or night-bird. Had such been the case, the faint noise would have been in fits and starts; in jerks, as it were, each time the creature moved. But this was a continuous sort of noise, a steady slithering or creeping forward, indicating slow but continuous progress. It was now certain beyond all doubt that the sound was being made by one of the two things: a snake or the panther.

I have taken some time in trying to describe to you my innermost thoughts as they raced through my mind. In fact, they raced through so fast that I had made up my mind within a few seconds of hearing that ominous, stealthy, creeping approach.

Another few seconds longer and I had decided that the panther was certainly creeping towards me, but as long as I could hear him I knew I was safe from any attack. Then abruptly the noise ceased.

Next came the well-known hissing sound comparable to that made by an angry cobra when it exhales the air from its body in a sudden puff. The panther was beginning to snarl. Very shortly he would snarl audibly, probably growl, and then would come the charge. I had heard the same sequence of noises often enough before and knew what to expect. Quickly raising the rifle to my shoulder, I pressed the switch of the torch.

Two baleful reddish-white eyes stared back at me, but I could make out nothing of the animal itself till I remembered I was dealing with a black panther, which would be practically invisible at night.

Perhaps it had at first no vicious intentions in approaching me, but had just sneaked forward to investigate what it had heard moving about in the vicinity of its kill. But having identified the source as a hated human being, that hissing start to the snarl showed that the black panther had definitely decided to be aggressive. His eyes stared back at the light of my torch without wavering.

I had plenty of time in which to take careful aim. Then I fired.

Instead of collapsing as I hoped and expected, or at least biting and struggling in its death-throes, the panther sprang away with a series of guttural roars. Had I missed entirely, or had I wounded the beast?

I felt certain that I could not have missed, but that was a question that could only be settled by daylight. I turned to retrace my steps.

This time, of course, I was free to use my torch, and with its aid I walked back roughly in the direction I had come.

I had thought wrong, however, and floundered about for half an hour without being able to regain the rivulet up which I had approached.

I looked at the sky. It was still cloudy and I could not pick out a single star that would help set me, even roughly, in the right direction to Sivanipalli village. Then I remembered that the land sloped gently westwards from the hamlet towards the ravine formed by the two rivers to the west. Therefore, if I walked in a direction that led slightly uphill I could not go wrong and would surely come out somewhere near the village.

I started walking uphill.

But I did not reach Sivanipalli or anywhere near it. To cut a long story short, it was past eleven-thirty that night when I landed, not at Sivanipalli or its precincts as I had expected, but more than halfway up the track leading northwards to

Salivaram. After that, of course, I knew where I was and within half-an-hour had reached the village.

There I awoke Rangaswamy and related what had happened. There was nothing more to do then than bed down for the night.

I have told you already that Sivanipalli was a small place boasting scarcely half-a-dozen huts. Rangaswamy himself was a much-married man with a large household of women and children and I could not expect him to invite me into his hut. So I lay down in a hayrick that stood a little off the main *path* and pulled the straw, already damp with dew, over me to try and keep warm.

If you should ever wish to undergo the lively experience of being half-eaten alive by the tiny grass ticks that abound in and round forest areas in southern India, I would recommend you to spend a night in a hayrick at Sivanipalli. You will assuredly not be disappointed. The grass tick is a minute creature which is normally no larger than the head of a pin. After it has gorged itself on your blood it becomes considerably larger. But it is a most ungrateful feeder. Not only does it suck your blood, but it leaves a tiny wound which rapidly develops into a suppurating sore. This increases in size in direct proportion to the amount of scratching you do to appease the intolerable itch and eventually turns into quite a nasty sore with a brown crust-like scab, and a watery interior. Moreover, should many of these creatures favour you with their attention at the same time, you will surely get a fever in addition to the sores.

I hardly slept at all during the rest of that confounded night, but spent the remaining hours of darkness scratching myself all over. Dawn found me a very tired, a very disgruntled and a very sore individual, who had most certainly had the worst of that night's encounter with the enemy—in this case the almost microscopical little grass tick.

The first thing to do, obviously, was to make some hot tea to raise my morale, which was at a decidedly low ebb, and with this in view I went to Rangaswamy's hut, only to find the door closed fast. It was evident that the inmates intended making a late morning. This did not fit in with my plans at all, so I pounded on the solid wooden structure and called aloud repeatedly. After quite a time I heard sounds of movement from within. Eventually the wooden bar that fastened the door on the inside was withdrawn, and a very tousled-headed, sleepy Rangaswamy emerged.

I instructed him to light a fire, which he started to do on the opposite side of the village road by placing three stones on the ground at the three points of a triangle, and in the middle making a smoky fire with damp sticks and straw. I had not brought any receptacle with me for boiling water, so I had to borrow one of his household earthenware pots, which he assured me was absolutely clean, a statement which I myself was not quite prepared to believe from its appearance.

However, the water eventually boiled. I had put some tea leaves into my water bottle, after emptying it of its contents, poured in the boiling water, re-corked it and shook it in lieu of stirring. In the meantime the inmates of the other huts had come to life. They watched me interestedly. Some offered little milk, and someone else contributed some jaggery, or brown sugar, for which I was very grateful, having also forgotten to bring sugar. We boiled the milk and put some lumps of jaggery into my mug, adding tea and boiling milk. Believe it or not, it brewed a mixture that did have some resemblance to tea.

Breakfast consisted of some eggs which I purchased and hard-boiled over the same fire. By about seven I had restored enough interest in myself and events, after my dreadful encounter of the previous night with those obnoxious little ticks, to think of doing something about the panther.

I asked Rangaswamy to get the herdsman who had accompanied us the previous night and who had not put it an appearance so far that morning, or one of his companions, to collect a herd of buffaloes if they were obtainable and drive them into the thick undergrowth to dislodge the panther, as I felt confident that I had not missed the brute entirely with my one shot.

All present answered that there were no buffaloes in Sivanipalli; and no one was willing to risk his cattle being injured in a possible encounter with the panther. Just then my missing companion of the night before—the herdsman who had accompanied me—turned up. He said that he had a friend at Salivaram who owned a muzzle-loading gun. He had wanted to borrow the gun so as to come along and assist me, and with that in view he had set out to Salivaram early that morning while it was yet dark. Unfortunately, his friend was away with his gun and so he had been unable to borrow it. He had returned empty-handed.

I thanked him for his thoughtful intention to assist me, but inwardly I was more than thankful that he had been unsuccessful in borrowing the muzzle-loader. With an inexperienced user, a muzzle-loader can become mighty deadly weapon and I confess I would have felt most nervous with him and that gun behind me.

Having failed to obtain the use of buffaloes, I then tried to enlist the cooperation of the owners of such village curs as there were at Sivanipalli. After some humming and hawing, one solitary cur was produced. She was a lanky bitch, with ears cut off at their base, entirely brown in colour, with a tremendously long curved tail. The typical example of village 'pariah dog', as they are called, whose ears had been amputated when a puppy because of the ticks which would in later life have become lodged on and inside them. With villagers, it is a simple process of reasoning to come to the conclusion that it takes less effort, and far less time, to cut off the ears of their dogs when they are puppies than periodically to remove scores of ticks in later life.

By a strange coincidence, this bitch was named 'Kush', which reminded me of the name of the dog 'Kush Kush Kariya' owned by my old friend of jungle days,* Byra the poojaree. I don't know if this name is a favourite among the dog owners of the forest areas of Salem district, or whether it just lends itself to a natural sound emitted to attract the attention of any dog. Personally I am inclined to the latter idea. Whatever it may be, I did not know then that this bitch Kush would conduct herself every bit as precociously as her namesake, the animal owned by Byra.

Finally, accompanied by Rangaswamy, the herdsman, Kush and her owner, we set off to try and find out what had become of the panther.

We retraced our steps of the night before to the spot where my companions had left me, then followed in my own footsteps along the two bends in the rivulet and finally climbed its northern bank at the place I had chosen the previous night.

Thereafter I led the way with cocked rifle, Kush running between me and her owner, who came last in file. Between us came Rangaswamy, with the herdsman behind him.

As I had already discovered the night before, the undergrowth was dense, so that there was no means of tracing the exact course I had followed only twelve hours previously; nor, being daylight, was I able to pick out any of the trees

---

* See *Nine Man-eaters and One Rogue* (Allen & Unwin, London).

100

or bushes I had negotiated in the darkness, although I knew roughly the direction in which I had gone.

The herdsman, of course, knew where the kill lay, but I did not want to go directly to it, my idea being to find, if possible, the place where I had fired at the panther. I did not succeed. Those who have been in jungles will understand how very different in size, shape and location just a small bush appears in daylight compared with its appearance at night. Darkness greatly magnifies the size of objects in the forest, distorts their shape and misleads as regards direction.

To help me find what I was looking for, I got the herdsman to lead us to the dead cow, which he found without difficulty. Incidentally, it had been half-eaten, although of course there was no means of knowing just then whether the panther had fed before my encounter with it, or whether I had entirely missed him and he had returned to feed after I had left. Panthers sometimes return to their kill if they are missed, although such behaviour, in my experience at least, is not very common.

Having reached the kill, I now tried to recollect and recast the direction from which I had come, so as to try and follow my own footsteps from there and eventually come to the spot where I had fired. Unfortunately I had no means of knowing exactly how far the panther had crept towards me, but had to rely entirely on my own judgement as to how far away he had been when I first heard him feeding. Sounds in jungle at night, when both the hearer and the origin of the sound are enveloped by the surrounding undergrowth, can be very deceptive, and the distance they may travel is hard to guess for that very reason. I felt that to the best of my knowledge, I could have been standing anything from fifteen to fifty yards from the dead cow.

Deciding approximately on the distance where I might have been standing, I paced off those fifteen yards and got one of the men to mark the spot by bending down a small branch. Then I paced another thirty-five yards to attain the maximum distance of fifty yards, which I judged would be about the greatest that could have separated me from the feeding panther I had heard the night before. Here we bent another branch.

Somewhere in between these two markers, and very approximately in the same direction as I was walking, I knew I should find some sign of whether my bullet had struck the panther. If I did not find anything then I would have to conclude that I had completely missed him.

By this time I was also sure that the panther, if he had been wounded, was not lurking anywhere in the immediate vicinity, for had that been the case he would undoubtedly have given some sign by now, hearing us walking about and talking. That sign would have been in the form of a growl, or perhaps even a sudden charge. The absence of any such reaction and the complete silence led me to conclude that even if I had hit him, the wound was not severe enough to prevent him from getting away from the spot.

I instructed my three companions to cast round in a circle, and search carefully for a possible blood-trail. I joined them, and it was not very long before Kush, sniffing at something, attracted her owner's attention. He called out that he had found what we were looking for. Gathering around him and the bitch we saw an elongated smear of dried blood on a blade of lemon grass.

My spirits rose considerably. Here was proof that I had not missed. The height of the blood mark from the ground indicated that I had wounded my quarry somewhere in the upper part of his body, and as I knew I had fired between his eyes as they had reflected my torchlight, my bullet must have grazed his head. Alternatively, if he had happened to be crouching down with raised hindquarters at that time (a rather unlikely position for a panther to adopt when creeping forward), my bullet might be embedded itself somewhere in the rear part of his back.

This was where Kush showed her merit. She was a totally untrained cur, but she instinctively appeared to sense what was required of her. For a little while she sniffed around wildly and at random, then started to whine and run ahead of us.

We followed and found more bloodsmears on leaves and blades of grass where the panther had passed. Between the bushes and clumps of high grass there were spots of blood on the ground too. This was an encouraging find, as it showed that the animal had been bleeding freely, clear evidence that the wound was not just a superficial graze.

The blood itself had mostly dried, except in some very sheltered places. There it was moist enough to be rubbed off by the fingers. However, it was neither thick nor dark enough to suggest that my bullet had penetrated a vital organ, such as a lung.

Kush set out very rapidly in a westerly direction, and it was quite obvious she was following a trail that would eventually bring us to the sharp decline in the land, down to the bed of the stream flowing from north to south before it joined the other stream lower down and turned westwards. This stream, before its confluence, is known as the Anekal Vanka. The combined streams are called Dodda Halla, which in the Kanarese language literally means the 'Big Gorge'. It has this name because so many sections flow through ravines and gorges as they twist and twine a torturous *path* past the village of Anchetty. There the river changes its course abruptly and turns southwards, past Gundalam, to its eventual junction with the Cauvery river. It is this same stream, the Dodda Halla, that was once the haunt of the man-eating tiger of Jowlagiri,* but that is another story. I have explored every section of it, right up to the place where it joins the Cauvery, and have nicknamed it the 'Secret river', partly because of the fact that due to the many miles of rough walking entailed in following its course, few people come that way, and it is delightfully lonely and far away from the sight and sound of human beings; also because I have discovered secrets of geological interest along its banks. I hesitate to divulge them, for with their publicity must automatically follow the next necessary evil, the violation of the sanctity of one of the most delightfully isolated jungle localities in Salem district.

Returning to events as they occurred that morning. The undergrowth was very dense, but to the unerring instinct of Kush this appeared to offer no obstacle. In fact, the trouble lay in keeping up with her. Her small and lithe brown body dodged in and out between bushes and outcrops of 'wait-a-bit' thorn. Our legs, hands and arms were severely lacerated by these thorns because we were moving at a foolish speed in order to keep the bitch in sight, taking no precautions whatever against a sudden attack by the wounded panther if he happened to lie immediately ahead of us. At times the brambles and other obstructions slowed us down, and Kush would get far ahead and disappear. It then became necessary to whistle her back, and when she did so, which was only after some minutes, she appeared to experience some difficulty in picking up the trail again.

We had no rope with us, so I borrowed the herdsman's turban and knotted one end of the cloth around Kush's neck, giving the other end to her owner. But it was a small turban

---

* See *Nine Man-eaters and One Rogue* (Allen & Unwin, London).

and the cloth too short. The man had to stoop down to retain his hold, while Kush strained, spluttered and coughed in her anxiety to forge ahead.

In this fashion we progressed until we eventually reached the edge of the plateau where the land began to fall away sharply to the bed of the Anekal Vanka stream, which we could see between breaks in the tree-tops below us, the sun glinting on the silvery surface of the water as it meandered from side to side on its sandy bed. The stream itself was three-fourths dry at that time of the year.

A little later we came across the first concrete evidence that the panther had begun to feel the effects of his wounds. He had lain down in the grass at the foot of a *babul* tree and had even rolled with pain, as blood was to be seen in patches and smears where he had rested and tossed. Kush spent a long time at this spot and evinced another unusual characteristic by licking at the blood. Ordinarily a village cur is terrified of a panther, but Kush, as I have said already, was an unusual animal, and it was indeed very lucky that her owner had been willing to bring her along. Normally, villagers who will not hesitate to lop off the ears of a puppy at their base will vote that it is a cruel practice to employ a dog for tracking down a wounded panther or tiger and will flatly refuse to be parties to such a deed. As it was, without the invaluable aid rendered by this bitch, we would never have been able to follow the blood trail as we did that morning. It would not have been visible to normal human eyesight in the heavy underbrush.

As we descended the deep decline, vegetation became sparser and the ground became bare and rocky. Boulders were scattered everywhere, interspersed with tufts of the tough long-bladed lemon-grass.

Then we reached a stage where there were only boulders, big and small, and the descent had almost ended. This was the high-level mark reached by the waters of the stream when in spate during the monsoon.

Here, with the end of the vegetation, tracking became easy. Drops of tell-tale rusty brown, where blood had fallen from the wounded animal and splashed on the rocks, revealed its passage. Judging from the distance we had come and the quantity of blood that the panther had lost, it appeared to be more severely hurt than I had at first imagined. The wound must have been a deep one and the bullet had probably struck an artery. Had it been elsewhere, particularly in some fleshy part of the animal, there was a possibility that the bleeding might have lessened, if not ceased entirely, by the natural fat under the skin coming together and closing the hole made by the bullet.

We reached the narrow bed of the stream in which the water was still flowing. Here the panther had crouched down to drink, and there were two sets of blood marks, one nearer to the water's edge than the other. The marks further away indicated more bleeding than those closer. This was curious and it puzzled me greatly at the time, considering I had fired only one shot the night before. The solution was an even greater surprise.

At one spot the panther had stepped into his own gore and had left a clear pug-mark on a rock just before he had waded across the stream. The mark had been made by the animal's one of the forefeet and its size suggested a panther of only average proportions that was probably male. The blood had been washed off the foot by the time the animal had reached the opposite bank, but the dried drops on the stones and boulders continued.

After crossing the stream the panther had changed his course and had walked parallel with the edge of the water and alongside it for nearly two hundred yards, then he had turned to the left and begun to climb the opposite incline. The stones and rocks once more gave way rapidly to vegetation, and again we negotiated thickets of long grass, thorny clumps, small scattered bamboos and trees.

Up and up the panther had climbed, and now so did Kush on the trail, conducting herself as if she had been specially trained for the job. Eventually we came to the road which leads from Denkanikotta to Anchetty and which intersects the forest on its way downwards to the latter village. We had come out on this road exactly opposite the ninth milestone, which we now saw confronting us at the roadside. Incidentally this was the road on which I had parked my car near the fifth milestone when I had left it the evening before to walk to Sivanipalli.

Many carts had traversed the road during the night and in the earlier hours of that morning, and the scent was completely lost for a moment in the powdery brown dust. But Kush had no difficulty in picking it up on the other side, and we followed behind her.

The grass and bamboos gradually gave way to more thorns and more lantana, which tore at our clothing and every part of our anatomy they touched. In places, where the panther had crept beneath the lantana and thorn bushes, an almost impenetrable barrier confronted us. There was no way through and there was no way around, leaving no alternative but to follow by creeping on our bellies beneath the bushes.

My rifle was an encumbrance in such places and conditions, and I cursed and swore as the thorns tore at my hair and face and became embedded in my hands, body and legs. The plight of my three companions was infinitely worse, as they wore thinner and less clothing than I did. Perhaps their skins were thicker—I really don't know. But I am sure that the language that floated from all four of us would have won us prizes in any Billingsgate contest. Only Kush was unperturbed, and from her position ahead she kept looking back at us, clearly impatient at the slow, clumsy progress we were making.

But this time it was also evident that the wounded animal was heading for a large hill that lay about half a mile behind a hamlet named Kundukottai. This village was situated between the seventh and eighth milestones on the Denkanikotta-Anchetty road which we had just crossed. The top of the hill was known to hold many caves, both large and small, and what was worse, the arched roofs of some of the larger caves had been chosen by the big jungle rock-bees as safe and ideal places in which to construct their hives. I had often seen these hives as I had motored along the road to Anchetty on previous occasions.

I felt that my chances of bagging the black panther were becoming very dim indeed. Looking for him amongst those caves would be like searching for the proverbial needle in a haystack. In addition, the panther had the bees to guard him if his place of retreat happened to be one of the many caves they had chosen for their hives. I can assure you that these rock-bees, when disturbed, can be most formidable opponents.

We plodded along and broke cover below the line of caves where the thorn bushes thinned out and became less numerous owing to shelves of sloping rock, worn glass-smooth by centuries of rainwater as it ran down from above.

The scent led up and across the sloping shelf of rock to one of the larger openings that loomed above us. From where we stood we could see the black masses of at least half-a-dozen beehives hanging from the roof of the cave, each about a yard long by about two feet wide. The remains of old abandoned hives were scattered here and there amongst them, the wax sticking out from the rock in flatfish triangles of a dirty yellow-white colour, perhaps nine inches long.

My canvas-soled shoes enabled me to climb the slippery shelf without much difficulty, while the bare feet of my companions helped them even more. Kush's claws made a faint clicking sound as she scampered up the rock ahead of us.

We reached the entrance to the cave where a subdued rustling sound was all-pervading. It came from the movements of millions of bees as they crawled in and about the hanging hives above us. There was also a continuous faint droning, that arose from the wings of the busy insects as they flew in from the jungle with honey from the wild flowers, which they would store in the hives, and from those departing on a trip for more.

The little creatures were absorbed in their duties and paid no attention to us, but we realized that if we happened to disturb them, these same little creatures, so unoffending and peaceful now, would pour on to us in a venomous attack like a torrent of black lava and sting us to death in a matter of a few minutes.

We stood before the entrance of the cave, where the blood trail, very slight now, was still visible in the form of two tiny dried droplets. They showed that the wounded beast had gone inside.

Near its mouth the cave was comparatively large, some twenty feet across by about twenty feet high. Daylight filtered into the interior for some yards, beyond which all was darkness. I counted nine separate beehives, all of great size, suspended from the roof of the cave close to the entrance. The floor was of rock and appeared to be free of the usual dampness associated with such places. No doubt this accounted for the cave being inhabited by the panther—and the bees, too. For these animals and insects, particularly the former, dislike damp places.

I whispered to my three companions to remain outside and to climb up the sloping rock by the sides of the entrance to a point above the cave, and on no account to go downhill, as that was the direction in which the panther would charge if he passed me. They disappeared, and Kush and I entered the cave.

From that moment Kush seemed to know there was danger ahead. Gone was her erstwhile courage, and she slunk at my heels, gradually falling behind me.

I walked forward as far as I could see in the dim light that filtered in from outside. At most, this might have been for about thirty feet. Then we came to a halt. I could go no further as, not anticipating that my quarry would enter such a cave, I had not brought my torch with me from the village.

There were now two alternatives either to try to arouse the wounded animal, or to return to Sivanipalli for the torch, telling the men to keep watch from their position of comparative safety above to guard against the panther slinking out before I came back. I should, of course, have followed the second course. Not only was it safer, but more sure. I suppose, really, I felt too lazy to go all that way back and return again. So I thought I would give the first plan a trial and if possible save myself the trouble of a long walk.

I whistled and shouted loudly. Nothing happened. I shouted again. Kush, who had been simpering, then started to bark. Still nothing happened.

The cave had narrowed down to about half its dimensions at the entrance. Only silence rewarded our efforts. The deep, dark interior was as silent as a grave.

Had the wounded animal died inside? This seemed unlikely, as there was no evidence that the panther had lain down again after the first rest he had taken before crossing the Anekal Vanka stream. Had he left the cave before our arrival? This might easily have happened; but again there was no evidence to suggest that such was the case.

I looked around for something to throw. Just one large stone lay close to my feet. I picked it up in my left hand and found it heavy.

I am left-handed, for throwing purposes, although I shoot from the right shoulder. I had already cocked my rifle, and, balancing it in the crook of my right arm, threw the stone under-arm with as much force as I could muster. It disappeared into the blackness of the cave. I heard it strike the rock floor with a dull thud and then clatter on in a series of short bounces.

The next instant there came the all-too-familiar series of coughing roars as the panther catapulted itself at me out of the darkness. Being a black panther, I could not see it till it emerged from the gloom, two or three yards in front of my rifle. I fired—but the impetus of its charge made the panther seem to slide forward towards me. I fired again. The confines of the cave echoed and re-echoed with the two reports.

Then all hell was let loose. The sound of the bees, which had been registering all this while almost subconsciously on my hearing as a faint humming drone, rose suddenly to a crescendo. The daylight coming in at the entrance to the cave became spotted with a myriad of black, darting specks, which increased in number as the volume of sound rose in intensity. The black objects hurled themselves at me. The air was alive with them.

I had aroused the wrath of the bees. Gone was all thought of the panther as I whipped off my khaki jacket, threw it around my exposed back and face and doubled for the entrance.

The bees fell upon me as an avalanche. They stung my hands. They got through the folds of the jacket and stung my neck, my head, my face. One even got down under the collar of my shirt and stung my back.

The stings were horribly painful.

111

I slid down the sloping rock up which we had climbed just a short while before. As from far away, I could hear Kush yelping in anguish. As fast as I moved, my winged tormentors moved faster; the air was thick with them as they dive-bombed me mercilessly, I remembered comparing them to Japan's suicide pilots, who sacrificed their lives and their machines by literally throwing themselves upon the enemy. Similarly, each bee that stung me that day automatically sacrificed its life, for the end of every bee's sting is barbed, and in trying to extricate the point after it has stung an enemy the insect tears out its sting, with the venom-sac attached. These remain embedded in the skin of the victim. Thus, in stinging, the bee does irreparable damage to itself, from the effects of which it dies very soon.

I reached the foot of the sloping shelf with the bees still around me. In desperation I crawled under the thickest lantana bush that was available. Always had I cursed this shrub as a dreadful scourge to forest vegetation and a pest to man, encroaching as it always does on both jungles and fields, in addition to being an impediment to silent and comfortable movement along game trails; but at that moment I withdrew my curses and showered blessings on the lantana instead. It saved my life. For bees must attack and sting during flight, another resemblance they bear to the aforementioned dive-bombers. Clever as they are, they have not the sagacity to settle down and then creep forward on their feet to a further attack. The code with them is to dive, sting and die. The closeness of the network of lantana brambles prevented their direct *path* of flight on to my anatomy. And so I was delivered from what would have been certain death had the area just there been devoid of the pestiferous lantana I had so often cursed before.

For no matter how fast I had run, the bees would have flown faster and descended in their thousands upon me.

All the nine hives had been thoroughly disturbed by now, and the buzzing of angry bees droned and drummed in the air above me. I lay still and silent under the protecting lantana, smarting from the many stings the creatures had inflicted on me during my flight.

It took over two hours for the droning to subside and for the bees to settle down to work once more. I felt very sleepy and would have dozed were it not that the pain of the stings kept me awake. The hot burning sensation increased as my skin swelled around each wound.

It was three in the afternoon before I could crawl out of the lantana and wend my way downhill to the road; from there I walked to Kundukottai village. There I found my three followers. They had almost completely escaped the attention of the bees at their vantage point above the entrance to the cave. The bees had evidently concentrated their attack on the moving enemies immediately before them—myself and poor Kush, who was also with the three men now. She had been badly stung, and I had no doubt that the panther had also received their close attention.

All of us walked to the car where I had left it the day before. After we had piled in, I set out for Denkanikotta, where there was a Local Fund Hospital and Dispensary. It was quite late in the evening when we roused the doctor. He took us to his surgery in the hospital and with the aid of a pair of tweezers removed the stings embedded in Kush and myself. We had received, respectively, nineteen and forty-one barbs from those little demons in the cave. The doctor applied ammonia to our wounds.

We spent the night in the forest bungalow at Denkanikotta. The beds there are of iron with no mattresses. So I lay in an armchair. The three men slept on the verandah with Kush.

The stings brought on an attack of ague and fever. Kush suffered, too, and I could hear her whimpers. My neck, face and hands were still swollen. One bee had succeeded in registering a sting not far from the corner of my left eye, causing it partially to close.

Dawn made me look a sorry sight with my swollen eye and puffy face as I stood before the one blurred mirror the bungalow boasted.

We waited till past ten and then drove back to the ninth milestone. Retracing our steps—but this time along cattle and game trails where walking was comparatively easy—we came to the place below the rock-shelf where we had stood the day before.

The bees were once again busy at their hives. All was peaceful and serene.

Leaving the three villagers, I climbed the slope with Kush for the second time and cautiously approached the cave. I knew I was safe from the bees unless I disturbed them again. And I was almost sure my two shots the previous day had killed the panther. Even if they had not, the bees would have completed that work.

I was right. Lying a few paces inside, and curled into a ball, was the black panther, dead and quite stiff. Kush stayed a yard away from it, sniffing and growling. I put my hand over her mouth to quieten her for fear of disturbing those dreadful bees and bringing them down upon us once more.

Walking out of the cave, I beckoned to the men to come up to me. Together we hauled the panther down the slope. The herdsman, who carried a knife, then lopped off a branch to which we tied its feet with lengths of creepervine. All four of us then shouldered the load and carried it to the waiting car, where I slung the dead animal between bonnet and mudguard.

At the Denkanikotta forest bungalow I removed the skin. It was a male panther, of normal size, measuring six feet seven inches in length. The rosettes showed up distinctly under the black hairs that covered them. It was the first—and incidentally the only—black panther I have ever shot.

It was difficult to detect the bee-stings, embedded in the black hair, but I told the men to make a careful count of the barbs they extracted, which I personally checked. There were 273 stings in that animal, confirmed by the number of barbs extracted. There must have been many more that escaped our attention.

I rewarded the men for their services and returned to Bangalore well compensated for the punishment I had received from the bees—for I had a black panther skin, which is something very uncommon—and I had a wonderfully sagacious dog, Kush, whom I purchased from her owner for seven rupees.

There is one thing I nearly forgot to mention. You will remember that I had discovered two separate blood marks at the spot where the panther had stopped to drink in the Anekal Vanka stream. One of them had shown signs of greater bleeding than the other, and because I had fired only one shot I had wondered about it at the time. The reason was now quite clear. My one bullet, aimed between the eyes, had missed its mark, had furrowed past the temple and ear and embedded itself in the animal's groin. The second wound was the one that had bled severely. The first was only superficial. Evidently the body had been slightly twisted and crouched for the spring as I had fired that night, just in time.

Of the two shots fired in the cave, one (the first) had struck the panther in the chest, and the other, as the panther skidded towards me, had entered the open mouth and passed out at the back of the neck.

Five

Snakes and Other Jungle Creatures

MUCH HAS BEEN WRITTEN ABOUT THE ANIMALS OF THE INDIAN JUNGLE that is of great interest to people to whom any sort of animal and any forest form sources of secret attraction. Yeoman authors like Dunbar-Brander, Champion, Glasfurd, Best, Corbett and a host of others have blazed the trail and have recorded the habits of these animals as they personally experienced them. Some of them wrote a half-a-century ago, a time when, it must be remembered, the jungles of the Indian peninsula were literally alive with game, particularly carnivora. There writings were always appreciated, but it is only now that the real intrinsic value of their momentous works comes to the fore, and it will be safe to say that as the years roll by and the wild life of India becomes a thing of the past, the records of these great men will be of ever-increasing value, preserving for posterity knowledge that no riches could ever hope to buy.

It is a significant fact that the *shikaris* of India and even the great white hunters of Africa, who started their careers as trophy seekers or, in the latter case, as professionals, have during their lives invariably found an increasing love for the animals of the forests which they once hunted and killed. The great majority of them came to eschew the habit of killing in favour of the worthier but more difficult art of wild animal photography and the study of nature.

In the early years it was considered a rather hazardous undertaking to enter the jungle on a shooting trip. Apart from the dangers from the animals themselves which were deemed very great, there were the risks in the form of various poisonous snakes, scorpions, spiders and other creatures, and the threats to health in the jungle diseases such as malaria, black-water fever and so on.

For instance, in my father's day a journey to the forest at the foothills of the Nilgiri mountains, or to the jungles that clothed the districts of Shimoga and Kadur in Mysore state, or to the area around the Western Ghats, was considered a very risky undertaking. The mists that shroud these tracts in the early hours of the morning were regarded as a direct cause of bronchitis, pneumonia and particularly malaria. The jungle beasts were said to be most bold and terrifying.

The old writers have, on the contrary, shown us that the wild creatures were far from aggressive in their habits, and that almost without exception they were afraid of the human race. Science has since taught us that no poisonous spiders, lizards or frogs exist in India and only a few varieties of poisonous snake; also that bronchitis and pneumonia can be contracted anywhere, even in the hottest and driest cities of India. Sir Ronald Ross has shown that a particular species of mosquito carries the malaria parasite and not the damp mists and air of the forests. That parasite is found not only in jungles but throughout the length and breadth of the land. The malarial mosquito breeds in stagnant water and dirty drains, and such places abound even in the largest cities. Campaigns and measures by the authorities have done much to mitigate these evils, and medical science has produced rapid and almost certain cures for the complaints themselves, so that they no longer arouse the dread they once did.

As regards the dangers from wild animals and snakes, one's own experience has been and always will be the best teacher. But with a very few exceptions, and those in only particular places, it is safe and true to state that the dangers of a sojourn in the thickest of forests are far less than those run by a pedestrian when crossing any busy city street. The writers of the past have all shown this.

Of course a greenhorn to the game sometimes does something foolish that may involve him in trouble, but that trouble is entirely the outcome of his own inexperience and ignorance. Experience, particularly for him who is not only willing but anxious to learn, is easily acquired.

The tiger is acclaimed the king of the Indian jungles because the lion is not to be found anywhere except in the Gir Forest in the Gujarat peninsula, where it is very strictly protected. The tiger is a magnificent, beautiful and lordly animal, but it is the elephant who is in actual fact the real lord of the Indian forests by virtue of his great bulk, enormous strength and sometimes unpredictable temperament. As a rule he is certainly a far more dangerous animal than the tiger, and aborigines living in areas where both these animals abound treat the tiger, with the exception of course of a man-eater, with contempt, while they have the greatest respect for the wild elephant. Walk along a jungle trail with any of these aboriginal tribesmen. Even should you be so lucky as to spot a tiger or panther, he will point it out to you with good-natured indifference. But should the sound of the breaking of a branch come to his ears, he will immediately halt in his tracks and say the one word in his vernacular which means 'elephant', judge the direction from which the sound came and endeavour to find a way that avoids passing anywhere near the locality in which the elephant is feeding.

This inherent caution is the outcome of the accumulated jungle experience of his forebears and himself. They and he have come to know the uncertain nature of these mighty beasts, and so they avoid taking any unnecessary risk.

As a matter of fact the wild elephant is in general a harmless creature, subject to moods and subject to sudden excitement, fright and irritation. To this generalisation there are four exceptions.

By strange contrast, and unlike African elephants, the greater the number in an Indian elephant herd the less the danger from its individual members. The four exceptions are: the accredited 'rogue' elephant that has already killed a human being, a *'musth'* elephant in that periodical sexual state peculiar to the male of the species, occasionally a single male feeding apart from the herd, and a female accompanied by a young calf to protect which she will readily give her life. It is to be noticed that in each of these four cases the danger arises from a single animal and not from the herd. African elephants are reported to have the ability, when occasion demands, of acting collectively when they attempt to charge down upon a hunter *en masse*. The Indian elephant does not do this.

But in any of the four instances listed, the individual animal can be very dangerous and a creature of terrible destructiveness. It will pursue a human being inexorably, sometimes for as much as a mile, provided the man can keep going that far, till it can run him down. Then it will tear him literally limb from limb, or squash him to a pulp by stamping upon him and rubbing him into the ground with its feet, or beat him against the trunk of a tree or whatever happens to be handy, or toss him high into the air.

While sitting at a water hole deep in the forest I often amuse myself at the expense of the wild elephants that come there for their daily drink and wash-up, by calling like a tiger or imitating the sawing sound made by a panther. In the former instance, the elephants, if in a herd, usually trumpet shrilly and dash away to the accompaniment of much crashing of branches and underbrush. It is delightful to watch mothers with young babies practically carry their youngsters before them by supporting them under their bellies with their trunks, as they hurry away from the presence of that supposed tiger lurking somewhere in the bushes beside the water. Should an elephant have come alone, it invariably stands quite still when it hears the call, flaps his ears forwards to catch the sound and endeavours to scent the whereabouts of the enemy by 'feeling' the air with its trunk. Then it will turn around and slip silently into the jungle. An occasional elephant stamps its feet and tosses its head and trunk to and fro in anger, but within a minute, it too will disappear from the scene. I have not encountered a single elephant that stood its ground while I continued making the tiger-call. Obviously, despite their size and strength, they lack the nerve to remain in the presence of that dreaded feline. I have read somewhere that the elephant's eye has the property of magnifying the object it looks upon. Naturally this would make a tiger or a human being appear relatively larger to the elephant than they are in reality. Perhaps this is the real explanation of why elephants are afraid of tigers, panthers and human beings too.

Panther calls produce a somewhat different effect. If in a herd, the male elephants become aggressive and show signs of being prepared to defend the young. But a single elephant invariably makes off, although not nearly in such a hurry as when a 'tiger' calls. One or two have stamped the water or struck it with their trunks and then continued drinking. But it was clear they were decidedly nervous and uncomfortable.

These amusing little experiments of mine clearly indicate that elephants are far from courageous creatures, despite their great bulk and strength. On the contrary, they are decidedly nervous and timid. Perhaps I am safe in saying that, like all 'bullies', they will only take the fullest advantage of a situation in which their enemy shows signs of fearing them. But attack, apart from the four exceptions mentioned, particularly against anything that might retaliate, is not on the bill of behaviour of the average elephant.

Elephants appear to have an instinctive dislike for white objects. For this very reason milestones and furlong stones along roads in elephant-infested areas are painted black, for such objects, if white, would be immediately uprooted and flung away as soon as an elephant caught sight of them. For the same reason it would be unsafe to dress in white and roam in an elephant forest, for it would only invite attack. In years gone by white, solar topees were the vogue on the ground that, besides being sunproof, they kept the head of the wearer cool by reflecting the sun's rays. A gentleman of my acquaintance was once wandering in a jungle wearing such a white helmet. Why he wore it in the jungle I do not know, for apart from the aversion of elephants it would be very conspicuous and render hopeless any chance of successfully stalking living creatures. Anyhow, he wore it. He and his tracker, a Sholaga, were going along the ridge of a hill when they noticed an elephant about two hundred yards away, feeding on the other side of a clearing and a little higher up the hill. At the same moment the elephant saw them. Normally it would not have seen them at that distance, for elephants have extremely poor sight, and the breeze was blowing towards them, so that it could not have scented them. But that shining white helmet could not be missed against the green and brown background of the jungle. The elephant trumpeted and gave chase. The hunter and the Sholaga turned tail and fled. Fortunately the Sholaga was an experienced tracker, with years of recorded service and prestige in taking 'sahib log' into the jungle. He did not desert his protégé, but ran along behind him, telling him in which direction to run. The elephant gained on them rapidly. Then the Sholaga overtook the huntsman, snatched off his white hat and threw it to the ground, while urging the sahib to keep on running. The elephant reached the hat and lost interest in chasing them further. Needless to say, that nice piece of headgear also lost all semblance of shape by the time the elephant was through with it. He had not been interested in pursuing or harming them, but it had been too much to ask him to tolerate that dreadful white object. He just had to obliterate it.

Fights among male elephants have been known to go on, with but a few pauses for rest, for as long as three days. A fight may be occasioned by rival tuskers for the favours of a bulky lady, although such examples are few. More often it happens when driving a male elephant in musth out of the herd when his attentions to the ladies of the herd become too troublesome. Mostly it happens when a young bull, attaining the fitness that comes with the prime of his life, challenges the master bull of the herd for its leadership.

During such struggles, the bulls do great injury to each other by gouging with their tusks at any portion of the foe's anatomy that may offer itself. It goes without saying that during and after these fights the contestants are in the vilest of tempers and woe betide any living thing they may see.

There was an instance of a forester belonging to the Salem district Forestry department who came upon a pair of bulls engaged in such a struggle in the fastnesses of the Dodda Halla valley of the Salem district. In that case a strange thing happened. The erstwhile contestants forgot their enmity and thundered down upon him together. He was a sorry mess when eventually his departmental colleagues came upon his remains some days later.

I have written about 'rogue' elephants in some of my earlier stories, so I won't add much about them here, beyond saying that they are the nastiest customers one could encounter in a jungle. Once having heard their trumpet-like screams of rage and hate, and seen their huge bodies bearing down upon you through bush and undergrowth, with trunk curled inwards, ears extended and short tail erect, you will remember the experience till your dying day. The degree of punishment they will inflict on a human being if they catch him varies. One rogue in the foothills of the Nilgiris tossed a forest guard high into the air. In falling, he became impaled on the broken end of a bamboo stem and eventually died. The rogue elephant of Segur, shot by the Reverend Bull, was a comparatively small animal, but was noted nevertheless for his sagacity and ferocity. He would literally stalk a human being or ambush him from behind a rock or clump of bamboos. He caught a coolie woman on the Segur road, stamped her flat, rubbed her remains into the ground with his feet and then playfully tore off the silver anklet she was wearing, as well as the string of wooden beads around her neck, both of which he threw some yards away. There was the case of a convalescent forester in the Coimbatore district who was suffering from guinea-worm. After long periods on sick leave, he eventually became so lazy that he would not—or more probably could not—work. He was transferred to the Biligirirangan Mountain

Range, which is an area infested with elephants. It also harboured a rogue at that time, which had long been proclaimed as such but had never been shot. One day this man had the misfortune to meet the rogue. It chased him. In running he twisted an ankle while crossing a stream. The rogue caught up with him and tore him apart. It rampaged around his scattered remains for three days after that and would not permit any traffic to pass, before it had the grace to leave and allow his relatives to gather for cremation what remained. There was another rogue near Bailur in the same district which threw a bullock cart with its oxen off the road. It was killed by Mr Van Ingen, the famous taxidermist of Mysore.

It must be remembered that the incidents I have mentioned above were committed by rogue elephants and hence are unusual. The normal elephant, as I have tried to show, is a timid, retiring creature without any signs of boldness or bravery in its make-up.

For sheer, unsung grit, a wounded wild boar is the biggest-hearted animal in the Indian jungle. Within his comparatively small bulk, contrasted against the much larger animals, he packs more courage, more ferocity and determination, and above all more individual dash and stamina and thirst to kill than any animal I know. Wounded elephants, bison, and even tigers and panthers will invariably try to escape at first and only retaliate when cornered. But wound the old wild boar and just let him know where you are, and down he comes upon you. No lancer at Balaclava ever charged with more gallantry and determination than will 'porky' if you wound him and then reveal your position.

The tiger very closely follows the elephant as the most interesting animal in the jungles of India. I think he is fascinating. Except for the periodic man-eater which takes to killing and eating human-beings and becomes a terror within an area perhaps of some hundreds of square miles, the tiger otherwise well deserves the label of 'gentleman'.

Hunting him might very truly and justifiably be considered the king of all sports. Following him up when wounded is indeed a hazardous undertaking and calls for the best possible junglecraft on the part of the hunter. But to leave a wounded tiger in the jungle without attempting to finish him off is not only cruel, in that the wounded beast continues to suffer, but cowardly too, having regard to the poor folk who live in and near that area. For that very wound may be the point in his life that turns him into a man-eater. Moreover, he is a gallant opponent. He tries at first to avoid a conflict, but if followed and pressed too hard invariably turns and fights to the last.

A well-known military person of Bangalore, the Rev. Mr. Jervis, once followed a wounded tiger in Kumsi in the Shimoga district. It attacked him and practically chewed through his arm. His Indian car driver, who was also acting as his gun-bearer, but unfortunately knew nothing about using firearms, most pluckily drove the beast off his master while it was mauling him, by attacking it with the butt-end of the spare shotgun he was carrying. Very richly did he deserve the reward he was given by the congregation of the church for this heroic act. The unfortunate padre was carried to the Kumsi travellers' bungalow, where the local doctor, with the best means available to him at that time, amputated the minister's arm, which was torn to shreds. The arm was later buried in the compound of the bungalow beneath a tree. A special carriage was attached to the next train running to Bangalore and the Rev. Mr. Jervis was sent back, though he died in the Bowring Hospital in Bangalore the next day and was duly buried with full military honours.

The panther does not approach the tiger in size, strength or grandeur. He can also be a very mean foe. I have said before that even man-eating panthers, despite their proclivity for human flesh, generally share the fear of the human species that is distinctive of the rest of their kind. They will rarely attack from the front, but will almost without exception creep upon their prey unawares from behind, as a rule favouring the hours of darkness for such an attack.

The average panther has a propensity for dog flesh which he appears to regard as a delicacy. There were a couple of panthers living on a small hillock crowned by a temple, hardly a mile out of Kollegal town in Coimbatore district. They made themselves a perfect nuisance to the American missionaries who lived not far from the foot of that hill, by eating up their dogs just as fast as the worthy missionaries could replace them. Eventually the panthers became so obnoxious that the local Sub-Inspector of Police, accompanied by some youths of the town, volunteered to get rid of them by smoking them out of the cave in which they lived. As a preliminary step, the grass in the area was fired. When that failed to expel the miscreants, lighted torches were thrown into the cave. This had the effect of bringing them out at the double, and in the fracas that ensued one panther was killed and some boys were hurt. The other got away after mauling one of the older members of the party. A missionary by the name of Buchanan went after it but was mauled, while the panther escaped.

'Bruin', the sloth bear of the south Indian jungles, is a short-sighted, bad-tempered animal; not brave by any means, but extremely excitable. He is generally a coward. Very recently a family party of three sloth bears—father, mother and rather a big junior—walked into a cave near Closepet in which a panther had already taken up his abode. The panther attacked the three bears. Junior fled on the spot. The two older bears tried to resist, but their courage turned to water before the razor-sharp claws of the infuriated panther, and they also fled.

Not only that, but the he-bear was in such a hurry to get away that he did not look where he was going and rolled down a rock about a hundred feet high and broke both his forelegs. The villagers speared him to death the next morning.

Should he see or hear you coming the sloth bear will dash off at speed. If you meet him suddenly at a corner, he will attack without provocation—not impelled by bravery but by fright and a desire to get away from your presence. Possibly he thinks you may try to prevent him doing so, and to make sure that you do not he sets about mauling you. And he will do that very thoroughly, his objective being the eyes and face of the offending being, which he will invariably tear with his blunt four-inch talons. And he will make a better job of it by biting too. I have seen jungle-folk who had been attacked by bears: the wounds inflicted have been really ghastly, leaving the victims with disfigured faces for the rest of their lives.

Bruin often behaves like a clown when digging for roots or burrowing into the nests of white ants. The sounds he emits can resemble anything from a bagpipe being inflated to the droning of an aeroplane, from the buzzing of an angry wasp to the huffing of a blacksmith's bellows, the latter being a sort of background accompaniment to the buzzing and humming sounds. He will twist and contort his body into all shapes provided he can get at those tasty roots or at those most delectable and delicious termites. He is a heavy sleeper, often sleeping in the shallow holes he has dug in the ground, or between rocks, or in caves, or under shady trees and in grassy areas. He snores so audibly as to be clearly heard at a distance. When he is not snoring, an unsuspecting man may almost tread upon him before he awakens. That sudden awakening will almost certainly cause the startled bear to attack without a second thought.

The Sholagas of Coimbatore are very plucky in dealing with bears. They have been known to split open the skulls of many of these animals with their short, sharp axes. The bear rises upon its hind legs to reach for the face of its victim, thereby exposing its own head, face, throat and chest, and rendering it vulnerable to the sweeping stroke of an axe wielded by a powerful and determined man. The short, black woollen blanket, which a Sholaga generally carries wrapped around his left arm, serves as the only shield.

Although a vegetarian or insect-eater by nature, 'Bruin' is not averse to carrion. I have caught him several times robbing rotten meat from a tiger's or panther's kill.

One of the potential dangers of any jungle are the many varieties of reputedly poisonous snakes that are said to infest the forests. Actually the great majority of snake stories told to the visitor are grossly exaggerated. As a rule, snakes of all varieties are comparatively few in jungle districts and are not often encountered. They exist in much larger numbers in fields and near villages, the reason being that in such places grain is grown. Millions of field-rats live in holes in the ground to eat the grain. And the snakes eat the rats.

Furthermore, as far as humans are concerned, in the whole peninsula there are only five varieties of poisonous snakes capable of inflicting a lethal dose of venom. There are other species of poisonous snakes, too, but their bites would only cause a local swelling and some pain. The deadly varieties are the king cobra or hamadryad, the cobra, the Russell's viper, the saw-scaled viper or 'pursa', and the krait. The coral snake has a very poisonous bite, but its mouth is so tiny as to prevent it from getting a grip anywhere on a human being; apart from which, it has a very docile nature. The pit vipers are all poisonous, but a bite from them is never fatal except in very rare cases where the person bitten suffers from a weak heart and dies more from shock than the effects of poison. Most of the sea snakes are extremely deadly, some of them having venom as much as twelve times the strength of the cobra's; but of course they are only to be found in the sea.

Roughly speaking, the strengths of snake venoms and their consequent fatality, is as follows: a Russell's viper's poison is about twice as lethal as that of the saw-scaled viper; the cobra's poison three times as strong as that of the Russell's viper; and the krait almost twice as poisonous as the cobra. The king cobra's venom is not quite as strong as that of the ordinary cobra, bulk for bulk, but being a big snake, measuring sometimes fifteen feet and more in length, it makes up in quantity for this slight deficiency of strength, injecting about four times as much as is held in the glands of a cobra, so that a bite from this snake, which is incidentally about the largest poisonous snake in the world, causes death about three times as fast as an ordinary cobra's bite would do.

The hamadryad is found only in hilly regions in the midst of the evergreen forests where the rainfall is very heavy. It lives entirely in jungles and avòids human habitation as far as possible. Its food consists of other snakes, which makes it very difficult to keep in captivity. A specimen died in the Mysore Zoo recently after a full year of starvation, during which every effort was made to provide it with food in the form of various snakes of the nonpoisonous varieties, all of which it steadfastly refused to eat till eventually it died of starvation. Its death caused quite a controversy in the Press of Mysore, where some of the people of the city, on religious grounds, ventilated their strong disapproval of this cruel act on the part of the authorities at the zoo.

The hamadryad, as I have said, is a huge snake, generally of an olive-green colour, banded with white. In Burma and the Malayan region the male is said to be almost jet black, although the white bands still persist. The hood is not so well developed in proportion to the length of the snake as in the common cobra, and does not bear the well-known 'vee' mark. It is said to be very aggressive, attacking on sight, particularly the female of the species while guarding her eggs, which she lays in a nest prepared from fallen, mouldering leaves. However, this aggressiveness I have not experienced myself, although I twice met a hamadryad at very close quarters. The first time I was digging out tree ferns for my garden in Bangalore, while at the same time attempting to catch some rare fish with flaming-red tails that were swimming in a stream deep down in a valley of the Western Ghats, near a place called Agumbe. The fish, by the way, were for my aquarium at home. I saw what looked like the head of an iguana lizard peering at me from a thicket of ferns. I was wading in the bed of the stream at that moment and approached to have a closer look, when the hamadryad—and not an iguana as I had thought—reared up and towered quite six feet above me from its elevated position on the bank. The reptile was trembling with rage, and its black eyes glittered as it exhaled the air noisily from its body. I was not carrying even a stick, so I stood perfectly motionless. After some moments the trembling subsided, the inflated hood went down, the snake lowered itself and slithered across the stream not five feet away. Halfway across it halted, and regarded me again to see what I was going to do. I did nothing and I still did not move. Then it resumed its course and disappeared amongst the ferns on the other bank.

On the second occasion I was sitting behind a tree on a forest fire-line near Santaveri, on the Baba Budan hills, while a tiger-beat was in progress. Suddenly I heard a peculiar whistling sound from the jungle behind my back. It somewhat resembled the alarm signal made by a bull-bison, and accordingly I expected the bison to show up, when a hamadryad broke cover and crossed the fire-line quite close to me. In that case, however, I doubt if the snake even saw me as I did not move a muscle.

Most people to whom I have related these two incidents say that I saved my own life by not moving, and that had I done so the snakes would have attacked at once. Having never been attacked before by one of these big reptiles I cannot offer any opinion. However, there is no doubt that I was more lucky than the unfortunate German zoologist who came to Agumbe some years ago to catch a pair of hamadryads for a zoo. He caught the male first without trouble. A couple of days later he attempted to catch the female. She bit him. He died there in the jungle itself. In that instance the old proverb that 'the female of the species is more dangerous than the male' proved itself to be literally true. Against this I remember witnessing many years ago at Maymyo, in Burma, the performance put up by a wayside snake charmer. Incidentally she was a Burmese lady, and a very beautiful one at that, as I can still recollect. She took a hamadryad out of a basket and danced before it till it had extended itself some feet above the ground with hood inflated. Then she deliberately kissed it on the mouth. I examined the snake later. It had its poison glands and its fangs. But the hamadryad was a male I remember, and as I have said, she was a very lovely Burmese lady. Perhaps that was why she met with more chivalrous treatment than that unfortunate German scientist.

The ordinary Indian cobra is too well-known to require much description. Contrary to the stories told, it rarely exceeds six feet in length. There are two varieties in India, the first with the widely-publicised spectacle 'vee' mark, which is called the 'biocellate' variety, and the other with only a single white spot on its hood, ringed with black. This is known as the 'monocellate' variety. Here and there specimens are met with that have no mark at all, although their hoods are just as well developed.

Colouring is a very unreliable means of identifying cobras, as they are to be found in all varieties and shades from jet black to various kinds of brown and even reddish, whitish or greenish hues. Grey and brown are the most common colours. Even young cobras, when they are hatched and are just six inches long, are deadly venomous. They are also far more aggressive during the first two years of their lives. They mellow in temperament as they grow older, and very old specimens are not given to biting without extreme provocation. At this age they can be completely tamed while in full possession of their fangs and poison sacs.

Cobras lay quite soft-shelled eggs, about fifteen in number, each about the size of a pigeon's egg, in a shallow hole or among decaying leaves. To hatch these eggs successfully requires indirect heat from the sun together with considerable humidity. Without humidity they shrivel up.

The krait averages about three feet in length and is a slender black snake with white rings around its body. It is very swift in movement, but at the same time is very shy and nervous and generally dies in captivity within a day or two of being caught, for no apparent reason.

The king cobra, the cobra and the krait are known as 'colubrine' snakes, and their venom causes a collapse of the entire nerous system as a primary symptom. Each has two fixed fangs, the length of the normal cobra's being about a quarter of an inch, the hamadryad's about half an inch, and the krait's about one-eighth of an inch.

The 'viperine' snakes are the Russell's viper and the saw-scaled viper. They also have two fangs, one on each side. These lie flat against the back of the mouth when not in use, but can be erected and rotated about their base as an axis. The fangs of a big Russell's viper grow to a full inch and can pierce through a soft-leather boot, *putties,* pants or thick woollen stockings. A cobra's or krait's fangs, being 'fixed' and not rotatable, cannot do this. The Russell's viper itself is a stout snake growing to a little over five feet in length and possessing three rows of diamond-shaped markings running down its back (one to the centre and one on each side), joined together in chain-like fashion and of a rich dark brown. For this reason it is sometimes called the 'chain-viper'.

The saw-scaled viper hardly exceeds two feet in length and is a brown snake with white 'notch' markings across its back. Its distinctive feature is that it possesses rough keeled-back scales. When annoyed, it coils round and round against itself, the scales producing quite a loud rasping sound in the process. This gives it its Indian name of 'pursa', 'poorsa' or 'phoorsa', which is a phonetic rendering of the sound made by the rasping scales.

The 'colubrine' snakes have grooves down the backs of their fangs along which the venom trickles when ejected from the poison-sacs. The 'viperine' snakes have channels down the centre of the fang itself, like the needle of a hypodermic syringe, for the passage of the poison. Naturally, because of this, the wearing of thick socks, *putties*, long trousers and soft boots is practically no obstruction to the bite of a viperine snake, although they may do so to that of a colubrine, for, being exposed, most of the venom will be absorbed by the material itself or dispersed against the leather of a boot. The longer, rotatable, hypodermic-like fangs of the two deadly vipers ensure that the unfortunate victim receives a lethal dose more or less intact, just as it is expelled from the venom glands. This is particularly so in the case of a Russell's viper, the tremendously long fangs of which will penetrate any normal material.

The chief effect of viperine venom is to cause haemorrhage, which gives the victim a good deal of pain.

Of course, it is impossible to name more than average periods of time for a bite by any one of these reptiles to prove fatal to a human being. The other factors involved are the age, health, constitution and physique of the victim; the size of the snake itself and whether it has bitten any other creature recently; and the amount of venom that has actually entered the victim's blood stream. The average time in which death normally occurs might be as follows:

In the case of the hamadryad, about ninety minutes; the krait, two to three hours; the cobra, four to six hours; the Russell's viper, twelve to thirty-six hours; and the saw-scaled viper, anything from three to seven days.

The nonpoisonous snakes of India are very many in number. Perhaps the most interesting is the python or rock-snake, which may measure up to eighteen feet in length, while the Malayan variety grows to thirty-five feet. It kills its victim by coiling around it and crushing it to death, after which it swallows the whole animal. The victims, of course, range in size from rats and rabbits to pigs and small deer, according to the size and capacity of the snake itself. During the Burma campaign against the Japanese an account was given of the shooting of a 'reticulated python'—which is the name given to the Malayan species which is also to be found in Burma—over forty feet in length. In its death-throes it vomited the body of a Jap soldier it had swallowed, complete with helmet. I do not vouch for the truth of this story, although it appeared in the Press. The idea that a python covers its victim with slime before swallowing it is quite erroneous. Its jaws, like those of all snakes, are not hinged together, but are quite separate units. The outer skin being very elastic, it is easy to see that a snake can swallow creatures several times the size of its head and girth.

Other nonpoisonous snakes include many varieties of ground snakes; several species of very slender whip-like and fast-moving tree snakes; stout, lethargic worm-like sand snakes; and a large number of fresh-water snakes. One of the sand snakes possesses a blunt tail which looks like a second head, so much so that it is still widely believed that this reptile has two heads, one at either end.

I have always been fascinated by snakes, and for no other apparent reason I formed the habit of keeping them as pets at the age of eight years. As a result, I was considered quite frightful among the girls and something of a terror at school. I know I got quite a kick out of releasing reptiles in cinemas, in Sunday school and even in Church. The name of 'snake-charmer Anderson' still clings to me to this day, in my forty-eighth year.

Snake venom has many medicinal uses, and I am certain is a still unknown remedy for many ailments and conditions. The fact is that this field has not yet been thoroughly investigated and exploited owing to the danger consequent upon experimenting on a human being with these venoms. Viperine poison in small diluted doses and in accordance with the laws of homoeopathy, where the small dose of a particular poison is known to counteract a large dose of that same poison has been proved of sterling value for the very condition of haemorrhage which it produces when a large or lethal dose is administered. This venom is used by dentists and others to stop excessive bleeding after a tooth extraction or minor operation.

Similarly, colubrine venoms, which in large doses bring about a complete collapse of the nervous system, are efficacious in minute doses in cases of epilepsy and other nervous complaints.

The Haffkine Institute in Bombay prepares a series of anti-venom injections as an antidote for the bites of all five poisonous species, obtainable separately for any of the varieties, provided the offending snake has been identified; or in a combined form for all the species, if there is no certainty as to by which snake a person has been bitten. The serum is prepared by progressively injecting horses with increasing quantities of snake-venom, beginning with a minute dose, till they become immune and are able to tolerate three to four times a lethal dose without ill-effect. Then blood is drawn from a vein in the thigh of the horse so immunised, and from this blood the anti-venom serum is eventually prepared.

When I came to hear of how the serum was prepared I was greatly intrigued and determined to prepare my own stock. I procured two old ponies and a donkey from sources I still hesitate to reveal and started to immunise them with initial doses of cobra poison, injected with a small 3 cc hypodermic syringe I had bought for the purpose. Unfortunately my knowledge in those days of the initial dose to be given was rather sketchy, with the result that within a very few hours I had to arrange for the disposal of the corpses of the said two ponies and the donkey. I also recollect that my father was very annoyed.

Just before the last war I was doing quite a good business in exporting snake venom in crystallised form to interested institutions in the USA, particularly cobra venom. The average cobra produces roughly one cubic centimetre of venom every four to five days, which when crystallised weighs about one gramme, for which I was getting approximately one and a half dollars. I had twenty cobras, which therefore earned me thirty dollars worth of poison every five days, or a hundred and eighty dollars a month. Not a bad business considering the snakes cost me nothing whatever to feed beyond a frog or lizard each every ten days. These were caught for me by a fifteen-year-old Indian boy, such a servant being known as a 'chokra'. His salary for this work was seven rupees a month which, shall we say, is the equivalent of ten shillings in English money.

The venom is collected from a reptile by holding it by the neck with its mouth pressed against a glass cup covered by a thin piece of diaphragm rubber or bladder-skin. The snake bites the rubber, and in doing so ejects the poison from its glands, which trickles into the cup. The idea of the very thin rubber is to avoid loss of venom at the surface. Some care has to be taken not to injure the reptile by allowing it to break its teeth against the glass. Some layers of electrical insulating-tape around the edge of the cup serves this purpose.

Cobras are easily handled, as they expose their heads by raising themselves for about a third of their length off the ground while inflating their hoods. It is then comparatively simple to press a stick down firmly across the back of the hood, pin the snake to the ground and grip it by the back of its neck. Russell's vipers, saw-scaled vipers and kraits are far more dangerous, both because they hide their heads beneath the coiled folds of their own bodies and are, moreover, exceedingly quick in movement, far outclassing the cobra. In addition, the exceedingly long and rotatable fangs of a Russell's viper make him a nasty customer, requiring very careful handling.

Cobras in general are also easily tamed. The specimens in the itinerant snake charmer's basket have been rendered harmless by removing their fangs and poison-sacs. The fangs grow again, roughly in a month's time, but once the poison-sac is removed the reptile is harmless for life, as the venom cannot be secreted. A Russell's viper's poison-sacs cannot be removed because they are situated very near the brain and close to a big artery in the mouth. An operation to remove the sac causes this snake to die not only of blood, but it injures the brain, to which it succumbs in a short while. The snake-charmers therefore stitch the upper and lower lips together at both corners with needle and thread, and feed the unfortunate reptile once a week through a bone funnel inserted down the throat from the centre of the mouth. An egg-flip is the usual nourishment. The same artificial and forced feeding is practised on cobras that frequently refuse to swallow their natural food when in captivity.

Their habit of infrequent eating is what makes all snakes so easy to keep. Normally a meal of a rat, frog, lizard or small bird will be sufficient for a period of a week or ten days, according to the size of the snake. In this respect, strange to say, the smaller species are more voracious than the larger. Pythons eat less frequently, at intervals of fifteen days to a month, according to the size of the animal that formed the last meal.

In writing this rather long account of snakes my purpose was to depict the interesting features shown by each of them. One feature is common to all snakes, both poisonous and nonpoisonous, except, it is said, the hamadryad; that they are all afraid of and avoid man. They will not go out of their way to attack or bite a human, but will do their utmost to slither away out of sight when hearing one approach, and will only bite if actually trodden upon. This they do out of fear and in self-defence. Incidentally it is useful to know that snakes have no sense of hearing through an organ resembling an ear. Their 'hearing' lies in the ability to feel vibrations through their bodies. Thus the stories we hear of a snake-charmer's flute, and other musical instruments and sounds, 'charming' a cobra are a myth. It is not the snake-charmer's music that holds their attention, but the rhythmic swaying of his body, head and hands when playing the instrument the causes the cobra to move itself from side to side in keeping with his motions while watching them. By this token, shouting, singing or whistling when walking along some dark footpath in India will not serve to frighten away a lurking snake, whereas heavy boots or the tapping of a stick against the ground most definitely will.

Every snake casts its outer layer of skin two to three times a year. This comes off 'inside-out' in the manner of a removed sock or glove, and is accomplished by the snake rubbing and coiling itself against some rough surface or obstacle.

Both poisonous and nonpoisonous snakes are classified generally under two headings—oviparous or viviparous. The former lay eggs, which hatch out after some days, whereas the latter give birth to living youngsters. The possession or absence of venom has no bearing on this factor, as both poisonous and harmless species are to be found under each heading. For instance, the cobra lays eggs, whereas the Russell's viper and python give birth to their young alive.

Of all the five species of poisonous snakes, the ordinary cobra lives to a great extent close to human beings and will be found inhabiting ant hills and other holes in every field or near any dwelling-place. Strangely, he is rarely met with in a jungle. The hamadryad is just the opposite, as I have already said, and keeps entirely to the jungle. Russell's vipers are found more in forests and grassy places than near human habitations. Kraits are not very common anywhere, and the saw-scaled viper lives mostly in arid, sandy regions.

When in the jungle, short of carrying tubes of anti-venom injections, which in any case require to be kept in a refrigerator because they decompose rapidly, the only reliable remedy for a bite from a poisonous snake is immediate deep cutting into the wound with a sharp knife, followed by sucking out as much of the poisoned blood in the vicinity as possible, in order to minimise the quantity of venom absorbed. Incidentally, none of the venoms are poisonous if swallowed, so that there is no fear of secondary symptoms due to this sucking-out of poisoned blood. In fact, cobra venom is fed to trained cocks and partridges in order to make them more aggressive when participating in the staged fights often conducted by the Moslems in this part of India. High sums of money are placed as bets on the winner, and this is one of the standard methods of winning the jackpot.

The tying of an effective ligature above the bite requires time and some skill. Also the method is impracticable if the person happens to be bitten anywhere on the trunk. In any case, before the ligature can be effectively tightened, the venom has invariably entered the bloodstream. Pouring crystals of potassium permanganate into the bite helps to neutralize the venom to a slight extent through chemical action, but deep incisions have first to be made before the crystals can effectively penetrate the tissues and play their part. For this reason I always carry a small razor-sharp penknife in my pocket when in the jungle.

I know a man who was bitten in the foot by a cobra. He was a poacher and he had the presence of mind to pour a heap of the loose gunpowder he was carrying in a bag for his muzzle-loader on to and around the bitten part. Then he ignited the powder with a match, with the result that he burned a deep hole in his leg which still causes him to walk with a slight limp. But he lived. I know another man, a snake-charmer, who was bitten through his thumb by a cobra. He placed a knife over the second joint and brought a heavy stone sharply down on the back of the knife with his free hand, requiring more than one blow to complete the amputation. He must have suffered agony and almost bled to death; nevertheless, he pulled through and is alive today. In a third instance I was once camped at Muttur forest bungalow when

SNAKES AND OTHER JUNGLE CREATURES

a man awoke me at dawn to say he had been bitten in the foot by a cobra nearly an hour earlier. He said he was a cartman returning to Pennagram with a cartload of cut bamboos; the evening before he had encountered a herd of wild elephants by the roadside. Being afraid, he had turned his cart about and returned to the fellers' camp. About 4 a.m. that morning he had set forth again, walking behind his cart so as to be able to escape more easily if he ran into the elephants again. Probably the cartwheel had passed over the snake and injured it. He said he felt a sharp pain and looked down to see a snake fastened on to his foot. He kicked out, and the snake let go and made off, but not before he had had time to see by the inflated hood that it was a cobra. After being bitten he had walked the two miles to the bungalow, hoping someone could help him. I lost no time in lancing the wound deeply, and with the aid of a forest guard walked him up and down the verandah to keep him from falling into a coma. But it was not long before I could see that my efforts would be in vain. The unfortunate cartman began to drool at the mouth, his eyes rolled upwards, he staggered like a drunken man and his speech became inarticulate. I managed to get his name and that of his family, who lived in the village of Erigollanur, a mile beyond Pennagram. Then he suddenly became a dead weight in our arms. He had lost consciousness. By 8.30 a.m. he was dead. I sent the forest guard to inform his relatives and the Pennagram police. The relatives came in a bullock-cart by 2 p.m., and set up a loud wailing. Then came the police. They wanted to know why there were blood marks all over the floor of the forest bungalow where we had walked the man about; why I had cut him; why he had died. Finally the corpse was put into the bullock-cart and sent to the police station, and I was asked to go too. I refused point-blank. The chief constable pondered over my refusal awhile and then compromised with instructions that I should remain in the forest bungalow till the results of the post-mortem, which would be held on the dead man, had been reported. I readily agreed to do that. Then the party left for Pennagram, seven miles away, from where the body was sent by bus to the General Hospital at Salem town, forty-two miles distant, for a post-mortem. Back came the answer after three days. The cartman had died of cobra bite. On the fourth day the police informed me that I was no longer under suspicion.

In the whole thirty-nine years during which I have handled snakes, I have been bitten only once, and then by a cobra. It happened in 1939. I had just caught the snake when it slipped from my grasp and bit me on the second finger of my left hand. But I am still alive; nor did I have to blow up or cut off my finger. For fortunately the incident happened on some land I own nine miles out of Bangalore and I was able to drive in my car to hospital and receive antivenom treatment. As a result, the bite itself produced no unpleasant symptoms; but the injection certainly did, for on the third day I suffered a very severe reaction and temporary partial paralysis of both legs. However, calcium and other injections put that right within a day.

In conclusion, I would like to mention a strange belief that was widely held in southern India, that a stationmaster named Narasiah, working at Polreddipalyam Station on the Southern Railway and situated not very far from the city of Madras, could cure any person of poisonous snakebite provided he was informed by telegram. The belief became so widespread that the railway authorities gave preference on its own telegraph system to any such message addressed to this stationmaster. I had heard many accounts of his miraculous cures from authentic sources, and there are hundreds of people alive in southern India today whose lives were saved by him. The *modus operandi* was that, as soon as Mr Narasiah received a telegram informing him of someone being bitten, he would go to a certain tree growing in the station yard, tear off a shred of his *dhoti* or loin cloth, tie it to a branch of the tree, say a prayer, and then send a telegram in reply informing the patient that he would live provided he abstained from tobacco, alcohol and coffee. Invariably the victim survived.

Alas! Mr Narasiah had to answer the great call himself and has since passed away. But he will never be forgotten. I do not know if his secret died with him, but I fear so, as no reports of any successor to his healing work in the realm of snakebite have come to me since then.

Six
_____

The Killer From Hyderabad

NORTH OF MYSORE STATE, IN THE DAYS OF THE BRITISH RAJ, LAY THE districts of Bellary, Anantapur, Kurnool 'and Nandyal, all belonging to the former Madras Presidency. North of these again lay Hyderabad state, which was the dominion of the Nizam of Hyderabad, a staunch ally of the British regime and a descendant of a ruler who was an off-shoot of the once all-powerful Mohammedan Moghul Emperor at Delhi.

Hyderabad state now no longer exists and part of the Nizam's wide dominions have been amalgamated with Anantapur, Kurnool and Nandyal to form a portion of the linguistic Telugu state of Andhra Pradesh, which is about the second largest in the new Union of India, being exceeded in area only by Madhya Pradesh to the north.

However, this story dates from long ago when these areas, although predominantly Telugu-speaking, belonged to Madras.

In those days these districts were largely undeveloped because the rainfall was scarce, the climate viciously hot for ten months of the year (while the remaining two months are simply uncomfortably hot) and the population by no means dense. Except for the towns of Anantapur, Kurnool and Nandyal, which gave their names to the districts of which they formed the capitals, the rest of the land was peopled by small villages scattered widely over the area.

The railway line from Bombay to Madras was the principal arterial link which traversed the districts. It passed through a railway colony known as Guntakal Junction. This main arterial link was a broad-gauge section, with its lines 5 ft. 6 ins. apart. At Guntakal three separate metre-gauge sections branched off. One led westwards towards Bellary and Hubli; one led southwards towards Bangalore in Mysore state; the third led eastwards, passing through Dronachellam and Nandyal to Bezwada, and thence to the east coast of India. At Bezwada it linked up with another broad-gauge arterial section joining Madras and Calcutta, while at Dronachellam a metre-gauge line branched northeastwards to Secunderabad and Hyderabad. The metre-gauge engines and rolling stock were naturally smaller and much lighter than those of the broad-gauge lines.

After leaving Guntakal, Dronachellam and Nandyal, the eastern metre-gauge line passes through an area of forest for five stations, named in order Gazulapalli, Basavapuram, Chelama, Bogara and Diguvametta, before going on to Bezwada. This forested portion, which forms the setting of my story, is more or less in the midst of a jungle belt stretching northwards across the Krishna river into the former Hyderabad state, and southwards towards the town of Cuddapah.

The metre-gauge trains are slow, and it is still a common experience for the drivers of the up and down mails that pass

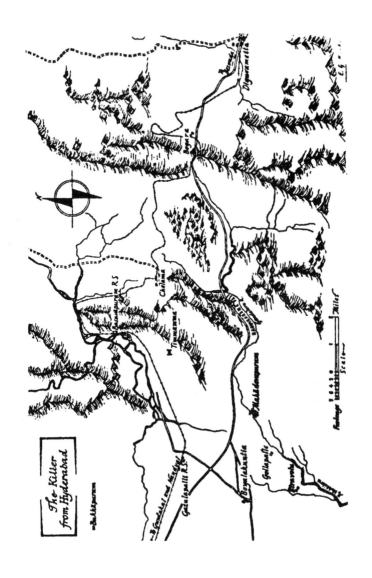

in the night to see wild animals running across the lines in the beam of the engine's headlight, or to run down a wild pig or a deer that attempts a last-minute crossing.

From the five stations which I have named only rough and stony cart-tracks and footpaths wend their way into the surrounding jungle. There were no motorable roads in those days. This was one of the main factors that helped to preserve the fauna of the locality from being badly shot-up, as has happened in jungle areas traversed by good roads. Enthusiastic but misguided and unsporting hunters use these good roads by spending their time from dusk to dawn shining spotlights from motorcars into the jungle and shooting at any animal whose eyes reflect the glare. More often than not these hunters are not even aware of the kind or nature of the animal at which they fire. This wanton and wicked practice has done and continues increasingly to do immense damage to wild animals, as the females and young of all species are being indiscriminately slaughtered, while a still larger number crawl away sorely wounded to die lingering and agonizing deaths in the jungle. The British government in its time tried to stop this poaching, and the Indian government is still trying. The first was, and the second is, altogether unsuccessful, and the terrible havoc still goes on. What is more, this will always be the case till either the public becomes conscious of the fact that wild life is a national asset and should not be wantonly destroyed; or alternatively, until wild life itself is completely wiped out.

However, as I have said, because of the fortunate absence of motorable roads, the Gazulapalli-Diguvametta area has so far been spared to some extent the curse of the night-prowling motorcar butcher, and there one may camp in the jungle reasonably sure of not hearing the hum of a car, followed by a dazzling beam of light, the sudden cessation of sound as the car is brought to a halt, the report of a gun or rifle and perhaps the agonized shriek of a wounded or dying animal.

The indigenous inhabitants of this area are a Telugu-speaking tribe known as Chenchus. Like all aborigines, they go about scantily clad, the main items of clothing in both men and women being torn and dirty loin cloths. The men carry bows and arrows, and most of them adorn themselves with beads or feathers around their necks. Peacock feathers are a favourite ornament for special occasions when stuck into their matted hair. They are fond of alcoholic liquor, which they make from the juice of the sticky *mhowa* flower, or from the bark of the *babul* tree. Indeed, because of the presence and abundance of the *mhowa* tree, these people were always a great problem to the excise officers in the days of British rule, and they are a still far greater problem to the Andhra government where the policy of 'Prohibition' prevails in certain parts of the state.

However, this tale did not set out to be a protest against night shooting from cars, nor as a discussion of the policy of 'prohibition'; nor is it even a sketch of life of the Chenchus. It concerns a man-eating tiger that terrorized the area, off and on, for some four years. This animal began his activities in the forests which belonged to Hyderabad state, where he fed on Chenchus and lonely travellers for half a year before he wandered southwards and dramatically announced his arrival at Chelama by carrying off and devouring a ganger who left the station early one morning on a routine patrol of the railway line in the direction of Basavapuram to the west.

In those days, particularly, the area was always well stocked with tigers, but these, due to the plentiful supply of natural game, seldom interfered with the local people except occasionally to carry off cattle. The disappearance of the ganger was therefore not attributed to a man-eating tiger at the time, as his remains were never found, and it was thought he had just decamped from the area for reasons of his own. Only in the months that followed, when Chenchus vanished here and there, were suspicions aroused that something untoward was happening, and people began to think that a tiger might be the cause of these disappearances. Even then there was no definite evidence of the presence of this man-eater, as tiger tracks along the jungle *paths* were common and there was nothing to connect the missing ganger and other Chenchus with earlier victims in the more distant northern parts of the jungle within Hyderabad state.

It was some three or four moths after the incident of the ganger that this tiger revealed his presence. Two charcoal burners were returning one evening to a tiny hamlet known as Wadapally, near the fringe of the forest. They were walking one behind the other when about half a mile before reaching their destination the leading man noticed the speckled form of a hen-koel fly from a nest rather high in a tree. Now you may wonder why I stress that this bird was a hen-koel of speckled plumage. It is because the male koel is jet black and therefore quite unidentifiable with the female, which is a deep grey speckled with white. The koel is perhaps the largest member of the cuckoo family, the Indian 'brain-fever bird' being another. Like all cuckoos, the koels do not build their own nests, but lay their eggs in the nests of other birds and leave the hatching to them.

Now the fact that the leading Chenchu had seen the speckled hen fly from a nest was irrefutable evidence that she had just laid an egg there. Chenchus not only find koel's eggs hard to come by, because they might be laid in any bird's nest, but they regard them as a great delicacy. He drew the attention of his companion to the lucky circumstance. The second man, who was younger, began to climb the tree with the intention of plundering the eggs. He had almost reached his objective when he heard a scream below him. Looking down, he was amazed to see a tiger walking away into the jungle with his companion dangling from the beast's mouth and screaming for help.

The man on the tree scrambled to its topmost branches while the tiger faded from sight with his still-wailing victim.

Night fell, but the Chenchu in the tree dared not risk coming down. He spent the next twelve hours there, shivering with fear and cold, and expecting the return of the tiger at any moment. Next morning, when the sun was well up, he started yelling at the top of his voice in the hope that someone on the outskirts of Wadapally might hear him. The wind happened to be blowing in that direction and his cries were eventually heard, when a party of villagers set forth to find out what it was all about.

Thus it was that the man-eater officially announced his presence in the Chelama area.

The Chenchus from Wadapally conveyed the news to the stationmaster at Chelama, who telegraphed up the line to Nandyal, from where in turn the news was conveyed to the Police, the forestry department, the railway authorities, and to the Collector of the district. Tongues began to wag, and the various mysterious disappearances of the other Chenchus and of the ganger, four months previously, were linked together and laid at the door of the man-eater.

Normally, when the presence of a man-eater in any particular area of jungle is confirmed, the Forestry department throws open the surrounding forests for 'free shooting' without licence, to encourage hunters to eliminate the killer. This step was automatically taken, but the announcement by the Forestry department met with no appreciable response, because few sportsmen cared to try their hand at bagging a man-eater in a district almost bereft of roads, where they would need to walk every inch of the ground without any transport.

One or two railway officials made half-hearted attempts by 'trolleying' up and down the line between Gazulapalli and Chelama with loaded rifles expecting, or at least hoping, to come across the tiger very obligingly seated beside the track, just waiting to be shot. But their expectations and their hopes did not work out, nor did the man-eater oblige. And not only did they see no tiger, but more Chenchus began to fall victims to the invisible devil week by week, till the death toll, inclusive of the ganger, rose to eleven. Of these only two victims were followed up by bands of villagers armed with staves, hatchets and bows and arrows, and their scattered remains recovered. No trace was found of the others, due both to the difficult terrain and the unwillingness of the people to risk their lives in attempting to save what they well knew to be carcasses already half-eaten.

Such behaviour may be regarded as indifferent and callous. But I would remind the reader that these poor folk were unarmed and not organized to deal with the man-eater. The jungle covered a vast expanse of heavy forest, with but few footpaths winding through the dense undergrowth, piled boulders and wooded ravines which lay in all directions. Everybody knew that should the man-eater be bold enough to charge a group of persons, at least one of them would fall a victim. Nobody wanted to be that victim. So who could reasonably blame them for not venturing out? In true eastern philosophy there seemed to be no sense in sacrificing another life to find the body of one who was already dead.

After these eleven killings, the man-eater appeared to have left the area for some time, as no further incidents were reported there for three or four months, though they began to appear again near the Krishna river. Then, and then only, did it become apparent that the former Hyderabad man-eater and the man-eater of Chelama were one and the same animal.

In Hyderabad state the call for hunters to kill the tiger met with greater response, and one or two of the Mahommedan Nawabs (or landowners) started active operations against the animal. Eventually the tiger overplayed his role by killing a traveller quite close to a hamlet named Madikonda. In this case he was driven off before he had time to eat even a portion of his victim, and news of the incident was carried to the Nawab of the area, who happened to be in camp a few miles away.

The Nawab answered the call and came posthaste to the spot, very fortunately before the body of the victim had been removed for cremation, and he was able to construct a *machan* on an adjacent tree in which to await the tiger's return to its undevoured prey. Being a nomad, the unfortunate victim had no relatives in the locality to claim his body, and this factor had provided the only chance this tiger had so far afforded of being shot.

But at this stage the Nawab's good luck was impaired by an unexpected thunderstorm which almost synchronized with the return of the tiger. Or that was what the Nawab claimed. Whatever the cause, he unluckily failed to kill it when he fired, and the morning light revealed a few traces of blood which had not been washed away by the rain. At least, he had the satisfaction of knowing that he had hit the tiger, although nobody was able to follow up and locate its carcass the next day. The Nawab hoped that it was dead, and so did everybody else.

Again an interval of some weeks elapsed. Then a Chenchu, who devoted his time to snaring partridges and jungle fowl near Gazulapalli, failed to return home for his midday meal. He had set out that morning on a visit to the traps that he had placed in various parts of the jungle the day before, saying he would be back by noon, as was his habit. But midday passed and the shades of evening fell and still he did not show up, and his wife and only son, a boy of twenty, grew anxious. Of course they had heard of the killings in the vicinity of Chelama, but those had taken place some months previously and everyone had since forgotten about the incidents. Now, with the absence of the trapper who was the breadwinner of the family, their misgivings and fears returned in full force.

In recording the exploits of man-eaters, it is rather noticeable that they follow a more or less regular pattern of happenings. The 'villain of the piece,' the aforesaid man-eater, makes his appearance suddenly, generally after being incapacitated from pursuing his natural prey through being wounded by some hunter. More rarely he, or quite as frequently she, has learned the habit from a parent who had a weakness for human flesh. The killings of human beings, few and far between at first, increase in number as the animal gains confidence in its own prowess and power over the helplessness of the human race as a whole. A strange feature in all man-eaters, whether tiger or panther, is the fact that, despite their growing contempt for humanity in general, a subtle sixth-sense of caution, which some hunters think is cowardice, pervades their whole nature. They will always attack the victim unawares, generally when he is alone or at least at the end, or at the head of, a moving file of persons. Instances are very very rare, indeed, when such a man-eater has charged a group of people. On the other hand, instances have been many in which the would-be victim has resisted and somehow fought for his life, and the man-eater has abandoned its attack and fled. This is more the case with panthers than with tigers, for the simple reason that the latter are such powerful animals that few live to tell the tale once a charge has been driven home. It is this inherent caution or cowardice, call it what you like, which is the common feature of all man-eaters and makes their early destruction a most difficult problem. As various attempts to circumvent them are made, and fail, the hunted animal naturally becomes more and more cautious and cunning as it appears to realize that a special price has been placed upon its head.

The man-eating tiger has a habit of following a particular 'beat' or route, which may extend over some hundreds of miles, halting in the vicinity of villages or hamlets for a week or two and then moving on again. In this way, not only does he escape when things are becoming too hot for him, but he arrives at fresh pastures and fields of opportunity where the inhabitants are unaware of his coming. By the same token, when he leaves a particular locality and the killings cease, the natural apathy and forgetfulness of the villagers makes them feel that the danger has passed and they become careless in their movements, ensuring another easy victim for the tiger when he eventually comes that way again. For he works around the territory in a huge and rough circle, and according to the extent of his beat will surely pass that way once more— maybe after a month or two, maybe much longer.

As I have mentioned earlier in this book, if one has the patience, and provided sufficient information is available, which is often most difficult to achieve, with the aid of a map of the area and by means of marking with a cross the locality of each human kill with the date on which it occurred, it is possible to assess not only the whole extent and area of the tiger's range of operations, but to anticipate its return to each locality within the margin of a fortnight. This is one of the main factors that helps the hunter who scientifically plans the killing of a man-eating tiger to accomplish his task.

In the case of a panther there is no evidence of a regular beat. He is here, there and everywhere. He kills mainly at night and very rarely during the hours of daylight. Being small, a man-eating panther can hide anywhere. As he grows bolder and bolder he often reaches a stage where he attacks and drags inmates out of their huts. I believe there are few authenticated cases of tigers doing this. On the other hand, a tiger will attack his human prey at any time of the day, lying in ambush beside forest *paths* or near the outskirts of a village.

I have related the story of the coming of the 'Chelama Man-eater', or, as he came to be better known, the 'Killer from Hyderabad', as I pieced together the facts at a much later date. To follow his exploits in detail after he killed and partially ate the Chenchu bird-trapper who used to live in Gazulapalli, and whose remains incidentally were recovered by his son, might bore you. Each incident was much the same in nature, the tiger repeatedly changing his location between the Gazulapalli-Chelama section in the south and the Krishna river in Hyderabad to the north. This area of operations was immense, as you will understand if you glance at the map. Moreover, after the wound inflicted on him by the Nawab at Madikonda, he doubled and redoubled his normal man-eater-like caution, till he gained the reputation of being a very devil incarnate—a sort of supernatural fiend. That unfortunate affairs caused him to adopt the practice of eating as much as possible of his human victim immediately after the killing, when he would abandon the body and very rarely return for a second meal. Not only did this habit immeasurably increase the difficulties of the few *shikaris* who went after him, but the killings themselves soon increased in number as the tiger was forced to prey on a fresh victim more often than would ordinarily be the case in order to appease his hunger, each time abandoning the remains of the last one. The area being large and remote, little publicity was given to the animal's depredations; and when it was given, all that appeared was a brief paragraph in one of the local newspapers, at infrequent and sporadic intervals, informing a disinterested public that the man-eater had claimed yet another victim. In this manner, in some three and a half years of activity, the tiger accounted for about eighty persons before serious notice began to be taken of the very real menace he had become.

The death of eighty persons in the jaws of a single tiger might appear colossal to the man living in a city. It certainly is so by all Western standards. But in a land as vast as India, where the average expectancy of life is at present well below thirty years, and in former days was very much lower— where famine, flood and sickness account yearly for thousands of lives; where snakebite causes the deaths of many thousands more; and where the birth rate is advancing to an alarming figure each year in spite of early mortality and all the causes of death—eighty people being eaten by a tiger was but a drop in the ocean, and nothing to worry about unduly. Indeed, relatively speaking, it reflected in the tiger's favour as a connoisseur in human flesh, considering the fact that he had only achieved this total in a period of some 1,300 days. It not only dubbed him as a very modest eater of human-beings, but what was very important to the hunter, indicated that he was obviously varying his human diet by killing animals for food, both domestic and wild. He would therefore not be averse to taking a bait should the hunter afford him the opportunity.

Apart from the man-eater of course, there were many other tigers, and panthers too, operating both in the Hyderabad jungles and to the south, so that the number of cattle and other domestic animals killed each year was always large. It was impossible under the circumstances even to guess how many of these 'natural' kills could be ascribed to the man-eater, and how many had been made by other carnivora; but it was certain that the man-eater had been responsible for a number of them for, as has already been indicated, he could not have subsisted on human kills alone for such a length of time. Here was another favourable feature. The man-eater could be baited with tethered cattle provided the hunter was able to estimate his line of 'beat' and could reasonably forecast his visit to a locality by allowing a plus or minus factor of a fortnight each way, before and after his due date of arrival. This plus or minus factor could be worked out on the map from his earlier record of kills.

I had read accounts in the Press from time to time about the depredations of this animal, and had received quite a few letters from officials in the Forestry department inviting me to try my luck at bagging it. To these I had turned a deaf ear, mainly because I found it difficult to spare the time from my work for a protracted visit, and also because the area in which it was operating was much too far from Bangalore to permit me to get there in time after receiving news of his arrival in any particular locality or of a human kill. At the same time, I have always been interested in news of the presence of a man-eater, be it panther or tiger, and the doings of a 'rogue' elephant. In this case I had already written to the Forestry department and Police authorities of both the Madras presidency and Hyderabad state to obtain all possible information about the animal, together with the most important data: the localities where human kills had occurred and the dates on which they had been perpetrated. This data I had jotted down on a map of the place and date of each incident. Thereafter, a study of the map indicated that this animal appeared to spend from two to three months operating between Gazulapalli and Chelama, before moving northwards into Hyderabad for the next four months or so. Then it returned again. The distance from Gazulapalli to Basavapuram is six miles, and from Basavapuram to Chelama five miles, and allowing for overlapping forest tracts the whole stretch of jungle between these areas covered a distance of about fifteen miles. Not only were these stations much closer to Bangalore than the more distant areas in Hyderabad, but they were much smaller in area, and were linked by part of the metre-gauge system of railway to Bangalore. The Hyderabad sections were not, and no motorable roads connected them. Lastly, the southern area was more populated, and I could therefore expect greater cooperation and earlier news of a 'kill' than would ordinarily be the case were I to start operations in the Hyderabad jungle.

You will see, then, that I had been toying with the idea of making an attempt for some time, when my indecision was brought to an end by the tiger himself. This happened when a permanent-way inspector (P.W.I.) on the railway was one morning carrying out a routine inspection of the line from Chelama towards Basavapuram by trolley. On the Indian railways these trolleys are simple wooden platforms on two pairs of wheels. The platform itself is scarcely more than six feet long, surmounted by a rough bench on which the railway officer sits. It is pushed by two coolies called 'trolley-men', who run along barefooted on the rails themselves. Practice makes them experts at placing their feet on the rails, necessitated in addition by the fact that were they to miss the rail and tread on the ballast they would find it very painful. They push the trolley uphill at a walking pace, run along the rails at some eight miles per hour where level ground prevails, and jump on at the back of the trolley when a downhill section is reached. The officer controls the speed of the trolley by a handbrake, and the whole assembly is lifted off the line at stations to make way for passing trains.

That day the trolley was negotiating a cutting through rising ground, when the P.W.I. applied his brakes and stopped it to get down and examine the ditches which draw off rain-water on either side of the track. The party had plenty of time at their disposal, as the next train was not due for another two hours. One of the trolley-men remained seated on the trolley, while the P.W.I. walked along the side of the ditch. The other man climbed up the bank of the cutting, which was about seven feet in height, seated himself on the top and took out a *beedi*. This is the name given to cheap Indian cigarettes made of uncured tobacco wrapped in its own leaf. He contentedly lit it and began to smoke.

The P.W.I. walked further away from the trolley, the man seated on it lay back and began to doze, while the smoker on top of the bank threw away the stump of his first beedi, took another and lit it, drew the smoke deeply into his lungs and regarded his superior officer with disinterested eyes while expelling the smoke from his nostrils.

The ditch had not unduly eroded and, after walking a hundred yards or so, the P.W.I. turned around to cross the line and retrace his steps along the other side and inspect the ditch there. As he did so, he glanced backwards and saw the trolley with the coolie sleeping on it, and then glanced upwards to the other coolie seated on top of the cutting smoking his second *beedi*. On either side the jungle bordered the line to within fifty yards, but some stray bushes had sprung up and grew much nearer. The P.W.I. noticed one such bush—a rather larger one—growing a little way beyond the smoker and what appeared to be a round 'something' sticking out from one side of it. This 'something' moved. The glare from the sun was reflected by the leaves of the bush in a myriad of scintillating points of light. In contrast the lower portion of the bush and the round 'something' lay in shadow. The mysterious object moved again, and the P.W.I. stared, wondering what it could be. Then it seemed to flatten itself and merge with the ground, and was completely lost to sight.

He crossed the track and started walking back to the trolley. Now his eyes scanned the opposite ditch. He had dismissed the object from his mind. But that was only for a few seconds. For he heard a piercing shriek. He looked up in time to see the coolie on the embankment being drawn backwards and then vanishing from sight, still screaming. Wondering what could be the matter with the man, the P.W.I. ran up the bank of the cutting to get a better view, when he saw a large tiger walking calmly away into the jungle with the coolie trailing from his mouth, his hands and legs kicking feebly. Then the tiger and the man were seen no more.

The P.W.I. was too shocked to move, but stood transfixed to the spot for a full minute or so. Then he was galvanised into action. He rushed down the bank to the railway track and pounded back along it towards the trolley as fast as he could. Meanwhile the sleeping coolie had been awakened by his companion's screams. In his confused state of mind he was not aware of what noise had actually awakened him, or of what was happening. He looked up to see his officer running towards him.

When the P.W.I. reached the trolley he shouted at the stupefied coolie, '*Bagh Reddi ku laikka gaiya*' (a tiger has taken Reddi) followed by the words, *Trolley ku dhakkalao, juldhi*' (push the trolley quickly). The coolie needed no further exhortation after that. Both of them commenced to push the trolley along the lines as hard as they could, till it reached the downward slope and began to roll on its own accord. Then they jumped on and allowed it to career madly downhill away from that dreadful place.

Much publicity was given in the Press to this latest killing, and the P.W.I. came in for severe criticism from all quarters, being dubbed a coward for deserting a fellow human being at a time of need, a moral murderer, and something which should have been born as an insect and not as a man. I wonder how many of his critics would have acted differently had they been in his place. You should remember it had all happened so suddenly. Further, he was completely unarmed.

I felt the time had come for me to try to meet this man-eater. So that night I was seated in the train that steamed out of Bangalore and the afternoon of the next day saw me detraining at Gazulapalli.

It seemed to me wisest to begin operations from one end of the area and work forwards towards Basavapuram and Chelama, rather than the other way round. To start haphazardly somewhere in the middle was unsystematic and depended too much on luck. Further, and most important of all, I needed local help and a guide, as I had little knowledge of the district, having visited it only casually once before. I had brought along with me the map on which I had marked the tiger's beat, and I hoped to be able to locate the son of the bird-trapper who had been one of the man-eater's earlier victims. I felt the youth would be a promising and useful ally.

As soon as the train drew out of the station I made friends with the stationmaster and the few members of the railway staff attached to the small station. When they became aware of my mission they clustered around and said that they were very glad that I had come, and that they would do everything they could to help me. I was a bit handicapped because the local dialect was Telugu, of which I could speak only a few words. This was partially compensated for by the fact that most people there seemed to understand a little Tamil and Hindustani, both of which languages I speak fairly well.

Somehow we got along and could understand each other. The stationmaster of course knew English, and he became my main interpreter.

To begin with, I explained that it was essential I should know some more about this tiger, especially any peculiarities regarding his appearance or habits, in order that I should distinguish him from any of the other tigers I might encounter. To this the station staff replied that all they knew was that he was a very large tiger. Of course, they had all seen tigers crossing the railway track from time to time, but they knew of no particular characteristic that would identify this tiger from any of the others. But, they suggested, one or other of the two forest guards who lived in the village might know better and be able to help me.

At this stage I asked if they could summon the son of the trapper who had been eaten by the tiger. They replied that they knew him by sight, but did not know exactly where he lived, beyond the fact that he lived somewhere in the jungle. They were sure the forest guards would be able to give me more information in this respect.

At my request a ganger was sent to call the forest guards, and in a matter of twenty minutes or so these individuals turned up. One of them was a Mahommedan named Ali Baig, with whom I could converse in Hindustani. The other was a Chenchu named Krishnappa, who spoke only Telugu. I waved them to the shade of a large mango tree growing behind the station, seated them on the ground, sat down myself and then got down to real business.

Using Ali Baig as an interpreter for the Chenchu forest guard, I played the opening gambit in the game of contacting the man-eater by offering a substantial reward to whoever first gave me the information that would lead me to it. At this both gentlemen pricked up their ears. Ali Baig said he would lead me to it even if it cost him his life. The Chenchu said—through Ali Baig—that he would do the same, except that he would not like to lose his life, and provided he knew exactly where the tiger was to be found, so as to be able to lead me there.

I appreciated that candid reply. Like all aborigines, I felt that the Chenchu was being truthful and practical too.

I began questioning them about the tiger. Both claimed to have seen him. Since the time the killings had begun they had never ventured into the jungle alone, but always together and armed with axes. Nor had they gone very far from the village. About ten days earlier they had seen a tiger crossing a fire-line about a mile away. The tiger had seen them too and had leapt into the jungle immediately. A month earlier they had encountered another, about nine o'clock in the morning, beside a water hole. That had also bounded away when they came into view. The occasion before that—it must have been about four months earlier—they had come upon a tiger hardly a quarter of a mile from the village; he had given them an anxious few moments, for he had not run away as other tigers had done. Rather, he had swung around, half-crouched, and growled loudly. They had been on the point of turning tail and running for their lives. But Krishnappa, the Chenchu guard, had whispered to Ali Baig that they should both shout in unison. They had done that. The tiger growled in return but did not charge. He had hesitated and then walked away, looking back at them over his shoulder now and again, still growling. When he was out of sight they had hurried back to the village.

Something clicked in my mind: four months! The interval corresponded with my calculations on the map, and the unusual behaviour of the animal confirmed the idea. They had seen the man-eater on his last visit to Gazulapalli, without a doubt.

They both thought so too.

More exciting was the fact that the four-month cycle had again appeared: the tiger had killed the trolley-coolie between Chelama and Basavapuram, and he had been the last victim. If my calculations were correct and fate was kind, the tiger should now be anywhere between Basavapuram and Gazulapalli at that moment. I became more excited. Luck seemed to be favouring me. But would it hold out?

I questioned them more closely about the tiger that had growled at them. Had they noticed anything peculiar about him? Ali Baig said that he was a huge tiger. Krishnàppa was sure that it was a male. He thought that it had a lighter, yellower coat than the average tiger. 'Remember, *sahib*,' he explained, 'we were very frightened at that time and had expected the tiger to charge us. Who would notice such things?'

I then asked them if they knew the boy I was looking for, the son of the Chenchu trapper I had read about as having been killed by the tiger much earlier. Of course they knew him. He lived in a hut in the jungle with his mother, wife and one child, over two miles away to the north. He was carrying on his father's profession as a bird-trapper, although how he was doing it with this 'shaitan' prowling about they could not imagine. It was against the forestry department's laws to trap birds in the Reserved Forest, and on several occasions during his lifetime they had prosecuted the father. But always he had carried on his profession after each case, and his son was doing the same thing now. Periodically, in the past, they had received a peafowl, or a brace of jungle fowl for their own stomachs, and this had often caused them to wink at the illegal practices of both father and son. Even these offerings had now ceased. But who could blame the poor boy? He must be finding it hard these days to trap birds for his own family, knowing this devil-tiger might be anywhere, behind or inside any bush.

I grew cheerful at the thought that I had found my first need—allies who would help me to locate my quarry. Scrambling to my feet, and slinging my .405 over my shoulder, I asked the two forest guards to lead me to this boy.

We crossed the railway lines and followed a footpath that wound into the forest. Light scrub gave way to heavier jungle, and soon we were walking in single file, Krishnappa leading with Ali Baig on his heels, while I brought up the rear. I had taken the precaution to load my rifle and carried it in the crook of my right arm, prepared for all eventualities. Not that we expected the tiger to attack just then, for we were three men together; but, should he make up his mind to do so, it was either Krishnappa in the lead, or myself at the end of the line, who were in any real danger. Ali Baig was quite safe as the middle man of the party.

After what appeared to me to be a distance of more like three miles than two, we crossed a stony channel through which a stream of water trickled, climbed a small hill and came upon the hut which was our objective. A pleasant-faced lad of about twenty years of age was seated at the open doorway, whittling bamboos with a sharp knife. Near at hand lay a half-completed contraption which I recognised as a bird-trap in the making.

At our approach he rose to his feet and *salaamed* respectfully. Krishnappa introduced me to him in the Telugu dialect, and the boy replied to him in a pleasant voice. Ali Baig then played his part as interpreter and told me that the boy's name was Bala. From the hut two female heads appeared, one of an old hag whom I took to be the boy's mother, and the other of a girl of about sixteen or seventeen. Supported by her arm, and contentedly sucking at her breast, was a naked infant about a year old. Without doubt, these were the lad's wife and son.

We squatted down on the grass a few feet from the hut and I began to ask questions, each of which Ali Baig translated to the boy in Telugu, translating also his reply. Krishnappa broke in frequently, clarifying some point that was vague to one or the other. Yes, he was certainly willing to help the white *dorai* to kill the tiger, for had it not devoured his own father? No, he would not accept money or reward in any form. His father's spirit would be very angry with him if he did so for, as his only son, the spirit expected him to claim vengeance on his slayer by direct means if possible, or at least to bring about the death of the tiger somehow. Oh yes, he had often seen the man-eater with his own eyes. Once he had gone down to the very rivulet we had just crossed to bring a pot of water to the hut. It had been about noon, just before the family had sat down to their midday meal. As he had dipped the pot into the stream, he had happened to look up and saw a tiger slinking down the opposite bank. Fortunately he had seen the beast in time, perhaps a hundred yards away, creeping directly towards him. He had left the pot of water and bolted for the shelter of the hut, where the family had closed and barricaded the door of thorns as best they could, expecting the man-eater to make an onslaught on the flimsy structure at any moment. Nothing had happened. He had very often heard the tiger calling at night, and he frequently came to drink at the rivulet. He was a large male tiger, with a rather pale yellow coat. Did the *sahib* want to know if he had seen anything peculiar about this tiger? Then Bala closed his eyes in thought; finally he looked up with a hopeful expression. All he could say was that the black stripes across the pale brownish-yellow skin were abnormally narrow. Would that help the *dorai*? He had seen very many tigers in his short life, but he could not remember ever having seen another with such narrow stripes.

When had he last seen the tiger? Again there was a slight pause for thought, and then Bala replied, 'About four months ago.' Had he seen any tiger after that? Certainly he had; twice. But they were ordinary tigers, not the slayer of his father. How did he know this? Well, for one thing, they were smaller and darker, and they had disappeared as soon as they had seen him.

Then Bala came out with the news I was hoping so much to hear. He thought the tiger was in the vicinity once again, for although he had not seen or heard him, he had discovered large pug-marks a short distance down the banks of the stream. Those large pug-marks had synchronised on previous occasions with the man-eater's visits. They had been present around the half-devoured remains of his father.

I got to my feet as I made known my wish to see these pug-marks for myself. Bala took the precaution of telling the womenfolk to keep inside the hut and barricade the door during his absence, and then led us back to the stream almost at the same point at which we had crossed it when coming. He turned, and began to lead us downstream. Some three furlongs away the stream broadened, though the water kept to the centre of the channel. Due to its broadening, however, there was a narrow stretch of sandbank on either side. This had been crossed by a tiger two nights previously, from east to west. The tiger's pug-marks were so large that they were clearly visible to me long before we reached them.

The spoor was that of a very large animal, undoubtedly male. As I stood looking down upon it, I decided that, even allowing for the exaggeration caused by the imprints spreading in the soft sand, the animal that had made them was exceptionally big.

We returned to the hut, where I suggested to Bala that he should take his family away to Gazulapalli village for the duration of my visit at least. This would leave him free to assist me with an easy mind. The thought of that old woman, the girl wife and her infant son, not to mention Bala himself, in that pitiful hut deep in the jungle, just awaiting the day when one of them would be taken by the man-eater, was something dreadful even to think of. In these modern days of strife and warfare, it is commonplace to read accounts of valour on the battlefield for which men have been awarded medals, for which their praises are loudly sung. We have read, too, of the lonely death of spies and agents who have gone voluntarily into the jaws of death and have sacrificed their lives for their country before a firing-squad, to fill an unmarked grave, their praises unsung. Thrilling tales of bravery, no doubt, that liven the blood in our veins. But my blood that day tingled in humble and respectful admiration for this little aboriginal family that had so bravely but simply faced the long months in their lonely home with the killer literally at their very door—the killer that had already taken the life of the breadwinner and head of their home.

The Chenchus hesitated for quite a while, but when I pressed them further, with the strong backing of both Krishnappa and Ali Baig, they eventually consented. The two forest guards and I sat under a nearby tree and waited while they packed up their few miserable goods into three ragged bundles. Then Bala closed the thorn door of the hut behind him, and with each of them carrying a bundle as a head-load, the mother still suckling her child, we set off in single file for the village.

That night the stationmaster invited me to his quarters for dinner. He was a vegetarian, but his wife had put up a noble effort and prepared one of the most tasty vegetarian curries that has ever been my good fortune to taste. A large bowl of delicious curd was an outstanding item, the whole being followed by big mugs of coffee. We had decided to hold a 'conference' after dinner to determine my next line of action, and Mr Balasubramaniam, the stationmaster, suggested that we hold it on the station premises, as his presence was required there during the night when the mail train to Guntakal would pass through, and two or three goods trains as well. So we repaired to the station, where we seated ourselves upon a bench on the open platform, with the two forest guards and Bala squatting on the ground before us.

To my way of thinking, the best plan appeared to be to tie out a couple of live baits the next day, one at the spot where the tiger had threatened the guards, and the other beside the stream midway between Bala's hut and the sand-bank where we had seen the pug-marks. Bala and Krishnappa would remain behind to watch them and report if they were killed, while I would take Ali Baig as interpreter and proceed up the line to make further enquiries at Basavapuram and Chelama. If either of the baits was killed, Mr Balasubramaniam was to receive the report and telegraph the news up the line to me at either Basavapuram or Chelama, wherever I might be camped.

Taking me to his office, the stationmaster called up his colleagues at both those stations and asked for *khubbar* or information. They reported no fresh news of the man-eater's presence, but added that everybody was on the alert and not a soul would venture out during the night. The stationmaster at Chelama also added that the trolley had been brought back to his station and was at present lying on the platform there. He suggested that Balasubramaniam should send a telegram down the line to the P.W.I., whose headquarters were at Nandyal, asking that I should be permitted to use the trolley if I should require urgent transport between the stations. No sooner said than done, my friend Balasubramaniam put his suggestion into practice at once, by transmitting a service telegram to the P.W.I. at Nandyal for urgent delivery, asking for the required permission. I was gratified by the enthusiastic co-operation shown by these railway officers. Throughout this adventure they did everything they could. Leaving the stationmaster to his work for a short time, I took my three henchmen down to the village. Although it was late at night, we did not want any delays the next day, so went to the house of a cattle-owner, awoke him from his sleep, and explained that our mission was to buy two half-grown bulls to use as baits.

The purchase of animals for this purpose in the jungles around Bangalore and particularly in Mysore state is always most difficult and has to be conducted with the utmost tact, as cattle-owners there consider it an evil practice to tie out live baits to be killed by a tiger or a panther, even with the object of eliminating an animal that has taken toll of human life. The people are not interested in selling for this purpose, and to obtain their co-operation sometimes takes hours of persuasion. To approach an owner for such a sale at dead of night would usually have been a hopeless undertaking. But the people in this particular area appeared to take a very realistic view. No sooner did the herdsman know of my purpose than he readily acquiesced. He even became enthusiastic and invited me to make my own selection.

The cattle-kraal stood behind his house, and with the aid of my torch I chose two half-grown brown bulls. The owner sold them to me for thirty-five rupees each—less than three pounds in English currency. I paid him the money, thanked him for his assistance and asked him to allow the animals to be kept with his herd till morning, when my followers would call for them. To this he agreed at once.

We returned to the station to find a goods train had since drawn in and stood on the line. The Anglo-Indian driver was chatting to Balasubramaniam in the latter's office, a thermos flask of coffee in one hand, while he sipped from a mug in the other. Evidently the stationmaster had been talking to him about me, for at my approach he introduced himself as William Rodgers, offered me his mug of coffee and volunteered the information that only four nights ago he had seen a tiger jump across the track about a mile down the line in the direction of Nandyal. I asked him if he had noticed anything remarkable about the tiger or its colouration. He reminded me that the headlight of his engine would not reveal such details at that distance, but that the tiger appeared to have been quite a large animal. He also told me that if I cared to shoot a good chital or sambar stag, or even wild pig, they were more plentiful in the vicinity of Diguvametta than around this station.

I thanked Mr. Rodgers for his information and told him I would consider shooting deer after disposing of the tiger. He shook hands with me, took the 'line-clear' token from the stationmaster, waved us goodbye and sauntered back to his engine. A minute later its shrill whistle broke the stillness, and with a loud puffing and clanking the goods train rumbled on, the red light at the rear being lost to sight as it passed around a curve. Once again the station was shrouded in stillness.

Just then the telegraphic reply from Nandyal arrived, conveying the P.W.I.'s agreement to the use of the trolley lying at Chelama station.

The stationmaster opened the waiting-room. I struck a match and lit the solitary oil-light that hung from the ceiling. Bala brought in my rifle, bedroll, water-bottles and tiffin-basket. There was no water in the bathroom, and it was far too late to ask Balasubramaniam to arrange for any to be brought to me. Nor was there any bed in the room, but only a table, two armless chairs, and an armchair with a large hole in its centre. Grateful that at least I had a roof over my head, I blew out the light and found my way to the armchair. Half my rear end sank through the hole in the cane bottom, but the other half managed to keep above. I removed my boots, lay back in the chair, cautiously raised my feet to place them upon the extended leg supports, and was asleep before I even knew it.

Another goods train rumbled through at about 4.30 a.m. After that I fell asleep again, but it seemed only a few minutes later that Bala came into the room and called to me softly. I awoke to see that it was daylight. I found out that Balasubramaniam had gone to his quarters to snatch a few hours of well-earned rest; so, while Bala got busy on my instructions to gather three stones at the end of the platform, find some sticks and light a fire to brew tea in my travelling-kettle, I got out my small folding Primus stove, lit it and fried some bacon. The tea-water had not yet come to the boil when I finished the bacon, so I sauntered down to the 'water-column' at the opposite end of the platform, which supplied water to such thirsty locomotives as required it. I carried my towel, toothbrush, toothpaste and soap and a change of clothes with me. Stacking these articles some distance from the water-column, I removed all my clothes and knotted the towel around my waist. Then I got beneath the leather hose and with one hand turned the wheel that opened the valve and let the water into the column from the ten thousand gallon storage tank standing high on its four stone pillars nearby. The quantity of water that suddenly descended upon me was tremendous and almost knocked me off my feet. However, I enjoyed my bath, combining it with my morning toothbrushing routine. Although I generally do not bother to shave in the jungles, to keep clean and feel fresh is very necessary. I had no second towel to dry myself with, as the one around my waist was wet, but it was of no account, for the morning was far from cold. In a few minutes I was able to don dry clothes and go back to Bala, to find the kettle boiling merrily. The tea, bacon and remains of the *chappatis* I had brought from Bangalore, which had become bone dry by then, served as 'chotahazri', which is the white man's exalted name for breakfast in India. The Hindustani adjective 'chota' signifies 'small', while 'hazri' indicates 'a meal'.

By the time I had finished all this, the two forest guards had come back from the village where they had gone to spend the latter part of the night. The four of us then set out, after collecting the two young bulls I had purchased the night before, to tie them at the places we had already selected. If you remember, the first of these was to be where the two guards had seen the tiger that had adopted such a threatening attitude. This was a spot on a narrow fire-line within a mile of the village. Krishnappa lopped off a branch with his axe, cut off about three feet and sharpened one end of this. We selected a tree on which a *machan* could be conveniently tied, provided the tiger obliged us by killing this bait, drove the stake that Krishnappa had just made into the ground at a suitable spot some fifteen yards away, and tethered one of the brown bulls to it by its hind leg, using a coil of the stout cotton rope I had brought with me in my bedroll. Then we walked back to the station, crossed the lines and traversed the three miles to the stream near Bala's hut. No fresh tracks were evident, so we tied the second calf beneath another tree on the slope of the stream about fifty yards short of the sandbank on which the tiger had left his pug-marks.

We got back to the station shortly before noon, when the stationmaster started insisting I should have lunch with him again. So as not to wound his feelings I very politely declined, as I knew my presence in his house was irksome to him as a high-caste individual, although he tried very gallantly not to show it. Instead, I went to the village with the guards and managed to obtain a meal of sorts from the village 'hotel'— a one-roomed zincsheet-cum-grass-roofed affair. That done, we all returned to the station, where I gave instructions to the two Chenchus who were to feed and water the baits: they were to tell the stationmaster if either was killed. Mr Balasubramaniam needed no reminding of the part he was to play in the affair by sending a message to me should such a kill occur.

Let me here record my appreciation of this gentleman's co-operation. I knew it was violently against his religious principles to aid and abet me, or to assist me in any way by bringing about the death of a bull or cow, which to his caste are sacred animals. But in the larger interests that were at stake, he suborned his principles and went all-out in his efforts to help me.

The train that was to carry me to the next station, Basavapuram, six miles away, steamed in at 2.30 p.m. I asked the driver for permission to travel with him on the engine, which he very readily gave. I wanted to do this so as to view the jungle on both sides of the track. Ali Baig got into the first third-class compartment behind, and away we went.

The train took twenty-five minutes to cover those six miles. As I viewed the thick jungle through which we passed, my hopes of success sank very very low indeed. It was an immense area, heavily forested, and the tiger might be anywhere.

The railway station at Basavapuram closely resembled Gazulapalli. As I got off and thanked the driver, I began to think I had indeed been a super-optimist in tying those two baits at Gazulapalli while the tiger might be here at

Basavapuram, or even at the next station, Chelama, five miles further on.

The stationmaster here turned out to be as obliging as had been his counterpart. He was a non-caste Tamil named Masilamony, and after his first words of greeting, in which he made me feel quite at home, he urged me to make my headquarters in his waiting room, stating that the tiger would surely be found there in Basavapuram, being the centre of the affected district.

Once again I went through my routine of closely questioning the station staff, and the one forest guard who came from the village. He was a Telugu and told me, through Masilamony, that the other forest guard who shared with him the responsibility of looking after the area was suffering severely from malaria and had gone on sick leave to Nandyal. They had all seen tigers at various times, and each claimed that he had seen the man-eater. But nobody appeared to have noticed anything special about it, either in size or markings. This forest guard, whose name was Kittu, told me there was a water hole north of the railway line and a little over a mile away, where he had often seen tiger pug-marks when these animals came to drink water.

We walked to the water hole that evening, where I noticed some old pug-marks of a tiger, together with a recent spoor made by a large panther. I was annoyed to see the latter, as I was almost certain he would devour any bait I tied there long before the tiger showed up. It is a nuisance to bait for a tiger at a spot frequented by a panther, as one is almost sure to sacrifice the bait to the latter.

I spent the night in the waiting-room and bought a half-grown buffalo calf in the village next morning. This we tied in a clearing in the jungle half a mile short of the water hole, and I instructed Kittu to visit it each morning in company with his friends, to feed and water it, and to tell the stationmaster if it was killed. Masilamony readily agreed to follow Balasubramaniam's example and send me a message as soon as word was brought to him.

Once again I caught the afternoon train, which came a little late at 3.15 p.m., and travelled on the engine up the line for five miles to Chelama. The engine-driver, who was an Indian, as we passed through it, pointed out the cutting where the trolley-man had been taken. He said it was almost midway between the two stations.

We alighted at Chelama to follow much the same procedure. The stationmaster came up and greeted me, saying he had been told to expect my arrival by his colleagues in the stations I had recently left. He had also arranged with the two local forest guards to await me; they were, in fact, on the platform.

As a result of the conference that followed, I was told that word had been brought by the guard of a goods train which had passed through Basavapuram while I had been sleeping in the waiting room there that morning, that a woman had been killed at Diguvametta, sixteen miles further up, at the extreme eastern limit of the jungle belt. The guard had been unable to mention the matter to any of us at Basavapuram, as his train passed the station without stopping.

This latest news upset all my calculations, just as it dashed my hopes to zero. Not only did it increase enormously the area of search for the man-eater, but all my carefully cherished tiger-beat timetable was entirely upset. I had been almost sure that the man-eater would be somewhere in the vicinity of Gazulapalli. Instead, he had killed at Diguvametta, which was twenty-seven miles away.

Then I remembered that twenty-seven miles was, after all, no long walk for a tiger.

I asked the stationmaster to verify the news if possible on the morse-line to Diguvametta. After about fifteen minutes of tapping on the telegraph key, he said that the stationmaster at Diguvametta had confirmed it with the local policeman at his village, to whom a report had been made that a Chenchu woman, gathering *mhowa* flowers at the edge of the jungle, had disappeared the morning of the day before. People from her village had found her half-filled basket, but no traces of her. The Diguvametta stationmaster also sent his advice that, as he had heard I was tying up live baits at the different stations, I should on no account fail to do so at Diguvametta, and also at the small station of Bogada which lay between Chelama and Diguvametta.

Here indeed was a pretty kettle of fish. It seemed as if I would have to tie up baits at each station along this whole line to catch up with the elusive tiger.

It would not be very interesting to give you the details of how I tied up a bait at Chelama next morning. Perhaps you may wonder why I did not leave for Diguvametta by the next train, but you must not forget that two days had passed since the woman had been killed, and the tiger would have picked her bones clean by the time I arrived—assuming, of course, that I was able to find them. So I thought it better to finish tying the bait intended for Chelama before moving on.

But that same afternoon I caught the train to Bogada, where I tied another bait in the evening, catching a goods train for Diguvametta in the early hours of the morning. There I tied two animals, one near the place where the woman had been taken, and the other at a point where a forest-line, a large stream and a cattle-track leading into the jungle intersected. Diguvametta boasted of a forester, an intelligent and very helpful Indian Christian. This man assured me that many tigers had been shot in years gone by from *machan*s in the branches of the 'hongee' tree which grew at the spot where the latter bait was tied.

I had now spent some five days in this area, had seven baits tied out, had used up far more money than I wanted or expected to use, and was quite tired of only hearing stories about this elusive tiger without even hearing him roar—or any tiger, for that matter. The jungles had been exceptionally silent since my arrival.

During the evening of the day on which I tied the two baits at Diguvametta, I went for an extensive ramble into the forest, accompanied by Joseph, the Indian Christian forester. As he was a non-vegetarian like myself, and a bachelor withal, at his invitation and assurance that my presence would cause him no discomfort or inconvenience, I decided to remain at least a few days at Diguvametta and sleep on the verandah of his quarters. The stationmaster had previously offered the use of the station waiting room, but the passing trains at night disturbed me. Joseph's Malayali servant whom he had brought along with him from Calicut, who cooked his food and attended to his few requirements, would relieve me of the burden and waste of time each day that I had hitherto been compelled to spend in preparing some of my own meals, snatched and scanty as they had had to be.

Another reason for choosing Diguvametta as my camping-place, at least for the present, was of course the fact that it was here that the tiger had last killed, just over three days previously. You may wonder again why we had made no very serious attempt to locate the remains of the poor woman who had been taken. Firstly, it would have served no purpose. As I have already indicated, the tiger had had more than sufficient time to devour her completely, and at most we might have found but a few gnawed bones. Secondly, the jungle was intensely dry, and although I had cast about at the time of tying up my live-bait (a bull-calf), there had been no clue as to the direction in which the tiger had carried her. We had combed the area in a radius of well over two hundred yards and found nothing, not even a remnant of torn cloth from her garment. Lastly, there being no purpose as I have just said in finding her remains at such a late state, I did not want to disturb the area further, for it had already been disturbed by the party of men who had come searching for the girl and found her basket.

The jungle in the locality was beautiful and indeed a sportsman's paradise as regards feathered game and deer. We came upon several herds of graceful cheetal in the forest glades. The long spear-grass was bone-dry, and the ends of the stems bent down to earth with the weight of the barb-like dry seeds with which they were tufted. This factor greatly increased the range of visibility and enabled us to see between the stems of the trees and into the glades. We even came upon a lordly sambar stag with a beautiful pair of antlers, which crashed away at our approach. It had been a bit early in the evening for a sambar to be about. Nevertheless the presence of the stag advertised the fact that the jungle was undisturbed, but that natural game was so abundant suggested little hope or reason for the tiger to take either of my baits. By the very same token, with such abundance of food available just for the taking, there seemed no cause for the tiger ever to have turned man-eater at all.

I purchased Ali Baig's ticket, instructing him to return by the night mail to Gazulapalli, as his presence was no longer necessary, and made an early night of it myself. At least in Joseph's verandah I was not disturbed by the clanking of trains, so that I slept soundly for ten hours and awoke the next morning in a considerably more hopeful frame of mind. The Malayali servant had performed wonders while we had been sleeping. There was a jug of strong tea and plateful of 'hoppers' and 'puttoo-rice'. The former is made from finely-ground rice-flour, and the latter from the whole grains of a special variety of rice. They are specialities of Madras, and their presence before me that morning indicated that my new-found friend and host Joseph, undoubtedly came from that city. It proved a delicious and most welcome repast.

Then I had a cold bath inside the enclosure constructed for the purpose, built up against the wall of the house, its three sides consisting of bamboo mats, each about five feet wide. There was no roof.

Joseph was ready and waiting while I dressed. We then visited the two baits we had tied out the day before, in company with both the forest guards who worked under Joseph, and to whom he had delegated the responsibility of feeding and watering these animals. Both the baits were alive and untouched.

There was nothing more I could do but await developments. The area was far too extensive to warrant long walks in the jungle in the hope of stumbling upon the tiger by accident. It might be anywhere between Diguvametta and Gazulapalli, twenty-seven miles away, and searching for it would have been a waste of time and energy. Up to this stage, as I have already said I had not contacted any tiger whatever, but I had done some yeoman spadework, and I might expect to reap the rewards in a little while.

And once started, things really did begin to happen. The telegraph wires hummed at about nine the next morning when Masilamony, the stationmaster at Basavapuram, relayed the news that my bait had been killed the night before. I was not over-exuberant at receiving this information, for you may remember that this was the place where I had come across fresh panther-tracks near the water hole, and had deliberately tied my bait some distance away to keep it from that panther, if possible.

I asked the stationmaster at Diguvametta to speak to Masilamony and ask him to question the forest guard, Kittu, closely to find out whether it was a tiger that had taken my bait or the panther. There was only a short delay before the reply came back; Masilamony explained that Kittu was beside him at the telegraph instrument while he was signalling. Kittu stated the bait had been killed by a panther and advised that I should come and shoot it, as otherwise any other baits I might tie up would undoubtedly suffer the same fate at the hands of this animal.

This was sound logic. At the same time, I did not possess a regular game licence for the area, but had come on a special request to shoot the man-eater only, and nothing else, made directly by the Chief Conservator of Forests at Madras, who had issued a permit to cover my visit. I decided I would write to the Chief Conservator later and explain the reason why I had to eliminate the panther, while offering to pay the game licence fee should any objection arise. I therefore made up my mind to answer Masilamony's summons.

There was no passenger train in the direction of Basavapuram during the day, but fortunately a goods train was scheduled to pass through at about eleven that very morning. The stationmaster stopped the train for me, and I travelled in the guard's van to Basavapuram. Joseph insisted on going with me.

Kittu took me to the kill, which bore every trace of a panther's handiwork, from the fang-marks in its throat to the large hole that had been eaten in the animal's stomach, where entrails and flesh had all become mixed up together to form a repast. The panther had eaten heavily the night before, and because of that I feared it might make a late return. Kittu offered me the loan of his own *charpoy* or rope-cot, so, rather than build a *machan*, we went back for it. To return and tie it up took scarcely two hours, and everything was set by four o'clock.

It was far too early to sit up, so we returned to the station, hardly more than a mile away, and had a quick meal, consisting of biscuits, *chappatties,* bananas and several mugs of tea. Joseph expressed a keen desire to sit up with me, so we both returned and were in position in the *machan* by 5.30 p.m.

I have said that I expected the panther to come late. I was wrong. We had been in the *machan* for scarcely twenty minutes, and I was leaning back and taking it easy, when I heard a faint sound below me. I looked down. There was the panther sitting on his haunches beside his kill and contemplating it. A truly nice specimen, I was tempted to spare his life. This temptation I overcame only because his presence there would be a constant source of interference with my baits. I shot him behind the left shoulder.

Our early return to the station surprised both Kittu and Masilamony. Hearing the news, the latter asked me to give him the skin if I was not in need of it, to which I agreed, and we went back with a petromax light and four coolies to retrieve the dead panther. I supervised while Masilamony excitedly watched the skinning operation. I showed him how to preserve the pelt temporarily with a solution of copper-sulphate and salt till such time as he could send it to a taxidermist at Bangalore.

Next morning I bought another bait to replace the one that had been killed. We took this to the water hole where I had seen the old tiger pug-marks and there we tied it up.

It had been my intention after shooting the panther to return with Joseph to Diguvametta by the afternoon train, but when we got back to Basavapuram station after tying out the new 'bait, Masilamony informed me that he had just received a morse message from the stationmaster at Chelama, stating my bait there had been taken the previous night by a tiger.

This information came before ten o'clock. The train to Chelama would not arrive for at least another four hours. So I decided to walk the five miles to Chelama, to which Joseph at once agreed. We were there shortly after 11.30 p.m.

The stationmaster who had relayed the message, and the two forest guards who had brought it, were awaiting our arrival. They were all in a state of excitement, and the guards reported that when they had gone to inspect and water the bait that morning they had come upon its partially-devoured remains and the pug-marks of a large tiger in the surrounding earth. Delaying only long enough to cut some branches and place them across the carcass of the dead animal to hide it from vultures, they had hurried back to the station to send their message.

Now in all seven cases, when tying up these baits, I had chosen each spot very carefully and had taken care to place each animal close to a tree on which it would be convenient to tie a *machan*. This precaution had already made my task easy when shooting the panther.

The forest guards volunteered to get a *charpoy* for me, while Joseph and I, together with the stationmaster, went down to the only eating-house in the village for our midday meal. During this meal Joseph said he would like to sit up with me again, and it was with the greatest difficulty that I could dissuade him without wounding his feelings. His company was one thing where the panther was concerned, but quite another when it came to a tiger, especially so if the animal happened to be the man-eater for which we were all searching. The slightest sound or incautious movement by a person in a *machan* would betray our presence and drive the animal away. I had previously had experience of companions who had sat in *machan*s with me and made involuntary sounds which had rendered our vigil abortive. This is especially likely to happen if the sitting-up becomes a nightlong affair and the person gets fidgety and restless. I did not want to run this risk after all the trouble I had taken in tying up my baits over such a wide area.

The kill was about an hour's walk from the station and perhaps three miles inside the jungle, and was reached by traversing a tortuous footpath and then making a short cut downhill. I had the *charpoy* in position long before 3.30 p.m., but as the leaves to screen it had to be brought from some distance away, so as not to disturb the neighbourhood, and moreover had to be of the same species as the tree in which the *charpoy* had been fixed (in this instance a tamarind), it was nearly an hour more before I was in position.

While the two guards had been busy fixing the *machan*, assisted by Joseph, who passed the branches up to them from the ground, I studied the kill and the half-dozen or so pugmarks that the tiger had left. The earth was fairly hard, so that the marks were only partially visible, and in every instance the ball of the pad was not clearly outlined. I could see the tiger was a large one and a male, but it was quite impossible to say with any degree of certainty that he was the same animal whose footprints I had seen beside the stream near Bala's hut in Gazulapalli. There the marks had been made in the soft, damp sand which had served to spread and to some extent exaggerate their size. But here the ground was dry and fairly hard.

Just before 4.30 p.m. I was comfortably settled on the *charpoy*. I spent a few minutes arranging my tea-filled water-bottle beside the smaller one that contained water. The village 'hotel' had supplied three large *chappattis*, folded inside a portion of banana-leaf, for dinner. These I placed next to the bottles holding the liquid refreshments; then came my spare torch and cartridges. The nights at this time of the year were warm, so I had brought no blanket or overcoat; only my balaclava cap, which I donned. Finally I fixed my torch into its clamps along the rifle, and then all was ready.

I told Joseph and the guards that I could find my way back to the station on my own. They walked away, leaving me to start my vigil.

It was just getting dark when I became aware of a muffled tread on the grass directly beneath me. The leaves of the tamarind tree are tiny and soft, so that when they become dry and fall to earth they form a malleable carpet and emit no sound when trodden upon, beyond the vaguest rustling noises, hard to recognize or define. In this respect the dried leaves of teak trees provide the ideal medium to warn the watcher of the approach of any living thing, even a rat, for they rustle and crackle long before the intruder appears in sight. But I knew that those muffled sounds heralded the coming of the tiger, and so it was that I was not surprised when, leaning forward and looking down, I saw him almost immediately beneath me. The weight of his body on the grass and tiny fallen tamarind leaves had caused the slight sound that had betrayed his approach.

He then passed out of view for a few seconds, but reappeared soon and strode boldly towards the bull he had killed. This was in a direction away from me, so that I could not make out much of his head, but saw his left flank, hindquarters and tail instead. As I have said, it was just about getting dark. In the forests, at such a time, colours tend to lose their clarity and objects look much bigger than they really are. Anyone who has been in a jungle or even in the English woods at dusk, will tell you the same thing. The animal below me appeared abnormally large, but I could not make out whether his colour was pale or otherwise. The stripes were blurred and hardly visible.

It was too dark to take the shot without the aid of the torch, especially as I would not be able to see the foresight of my rifle clearly. So I pressed the switch with my left thumb. The beam shone forth, lighting up the left side of the tiger, and fell ahead of him on to the kill. As I aimed quickly, I remember noticing that the tiger was not aware of the fact that the light was coming from behind him. Rather, he seemed to think it was coming from the kill itself. He just stood still and looked.

I fired behind the left shoulder. He fell forward against the dead bull and then squirmed around on his right side. The white of his belly and chest came into view. I fired again. The tiger died as I continued to shine my torch on him.

I waited for perhaps twenty minutes, during which time I flashed my light now and again to make sure I had indeed killed him. Then I climbed down and made a close examination of my prize. .

He was a large male in his prime, but he was certainly not the same animal that Bala had described to me. This one had a rich dark coat, and his stripes were very far from being abnormally narrow. Had I shot the wrong tiger, or was this the real man-eater? Was the animal that Bala had seen some other ordinary, oldish, tiger? These questions sprang to mind, but I knew that the answer would only be known if another human was killed—or if there were no more human victims.

By the aid of my flashlight I was able to find the winding track that eventually brought me to the railway station a little before 9 p.m. Joseph was asleep in the waiting room, while the two guards lay on a mat on the platform. I awoke them and announced what had taken place. Their surprise at my early return gave place to great jubilation at news of my success, and Joseph shook hands with me in warm congratulation.

I thanked him, but said I was far from certain that I had killed the man-eater. He asked why, and I told him. But he and the guards were optimistic and said they were sure I had slain the right tiger.

The stationmaster then arrived to supervise the passing of the night trains, and he too was very pleased to hear the news. The two guards hurried off to summon a carrying party, returning in another hour or so with some ten men, a couple of stout bamboos, ropes and two lanterns.

We returned to the kill and were back with the tiger by 1 a.m. I had the carcass placed at the end of the platform, just outside the iron railings that marked the precincts of the station yard, and started to skin the animal with the aid of the two lanterns and my spare torch, held by Joseph. I did the job myself as the guards appeared not to know much about the art, and I was closely engrossed and halfway through the operation when the night mail train, going down the line to Guntakal, came to a halt at the station.

Everybody in that train got down, from driver to guard and including all the passengers, and stood around me in an enormous circle to get a clear view. I got much publicity that night and the train left more than fifteen minutes behind schedule. The running staff regarded the delay as of little consequence. Besides, the skin being taken off a large tiger at dead of night on a railway station platform is not exactly a common sight, even in India.

The standard application of a solution of copper sulphate and salt would temporarily preserve it for the duration of my trip.

The next day I rested, while the stationmaster relayed the news to the stations on both sides of Chelama, and everybody was happy. I was not so pleased myself, and decided to remain for a further week if possible. As I had tied out my baits and come prepared to stay up to a month if needed, I felt it would be better to remain where I was rather than return to Bangalore and then have to come out again and tie out my baits once more. For a strange premonition kept insisting to me that the man-eater was not dead and would kill someone very soon.

Four days passed. Then came the news from Gazulapalli that the tiger had killed Bala's young wife. Unknown to me he had taken his family back to his hut in the forest, thinking that the coast was clear.

The man-eater had kept to his expected schedule after all.

Joseph had meanwhile returned to Diguvametta, so I waited only long enough to send a message to Balasubramaniam to keep Bala in attendance and, borrowing the trolley at Chelama, as no goods train was due to pass for the next four hours, set out for Gazulapalli, propelled by two trolleymen.

We took a little over an hour and a half to get there and found Bala awaiting me, seated on the ground at a corner of the platform, weeping. Balasubramaniam was there, too, and the two forest guards, Ali Baig and Krishnappa.

The young Chenchu's tale was as brief as it was tragic. Hearing I had shot the man-eater at Chelama, and as neither of my live baits had been touched all this time, he had decided that the danger to their lives had passed and had taken his family back to their hut only two days earlier. At dawn that very morning his wife had wakened, laid their baby next to him, and had gone outside to relieve herself. A moment later he heard her cry out faintly. Realising that something terrible had happened, he had seized his axe and rushed outside. There was nothing to be seen.

It was not yet daylight, and Bala said that he could find no trace of anything having happened, except that his young wife was not there. He had called to her but received no answer. Frantically searching, he went to the other side of the hut where he knew she would have gone for the purpose she had had in mind. Still he found nothing.

The grass was wet after a heavy night's dew-fall, and as the light grew stronger he was able to pick out the course made by something that had walked away through it into the jungle.

He had found no blood trail, but he knew he was gazing at the *path* made in the wet grass as the man-eater had walked through it, carrying his wife. For the trail through the damp grass was clear, where it had been trodden upon or brushed aside by the passage of the two heavy bodies—the tiger and his victim.

Then Bala had done a very brave and a very foolish thing. Alone, and armed only with his puny axe, he had followed the trail.

With more daylight, after a couple of furlongs, he had come upon the first trace of a blood trail from the point where the tiger had laid his burden down among the dew-dripping bushes in order to change his grip on his victim. Thereafter, following the grim trail had been easy, and he had caught up with the tiger in the act of settling down to its meal at the foot of an old dead tree.

The man-eater had seen him. He laid back his ears and growled. In another second he would have charged. But the sight of his wife being devoured before his very eyes had proved too much for the young Chenchu. Some demon of recklessness and bravery had possessed him, and, burning with hate and screaming, he rushed upon the tiger brandishing his little axe.

I have often told you that all man-eaters appear to be possessed by a strange streak of cowardice. They will attack a victim unawares but will rarely face up to a direct counterattack. That early morning the man-eater of Chelama proved himself no exception to the rule. He hesitated till the little Chenchu was almost upon him. Then he turned tail and fled.

Fortunately, wisdom at last came to Bala. Had he attempted to follow the tiger, the latter might well have recovered his morale and wiped him out. Instead, he snatched up the corpse of his wife and ran back with it to the hut.

Hearing this simple tale, simply told by the little aborigine, my heart was filled with admiration and pride that India possessed such heroes, even among her most humble out-caste tribes.

At the hut Bala had wasted no time on tears. Leaving the body inside, and bidding his old mother carry the child, he had secured the door as best he could and set off for the railway station to get word to me. It was lucky that he had acted so quickly, for he and his mother were well on their way to the station before the tiger had time to recover from his fright and return to the body or the hut.

The little man was crying silently as he told me this story, and I made no effort to console him. His tears would be good for him. They were Mother Nature's own salve to the great nervous strain he had been through and an outlet for his pent-up emotions after the shock of bereavement. My lip-sympathy, on the other hand, would be quite useless. I could never even hope to look for an excuse to bridge the tragic gap that had been created in his young life, so early that very morning.

But the tears did not last for long. The aboriginal is inherently a fatalist. I did not want to interrupt or hurry him, but ten minutes later Bala stood up and announced himself ready for action.

I had been thinking quickly and deeply, and a plan was forming in my mind. To put it into effect would require the utmost sacrifice from Bala, and I hesitated to ask him to make it. Perhaps some affinity of thought between us, born of years of life in the jungle, he by birth and me by choice, bound us together. He looked up into my face, and once again tears welled from his eyes as he gently nodded his head. Then Ali Baig interpreted. 'She was my wife and I love her, *dorai*. But you shall have her dead body to serve as bait to avenge the death of this dear one, and of my father.'

Enough words had been spoken, and enough time wasted. I was determined to play my part in the role with which this humble but great little man had entrusted me. I waited only to eat a hurried meal of vegetable curry and rice which the ever-solicitous Balasubramaniam had got his wife to prepare for me, filled my two water-bottles with tea and water respectively, and set off for the hut with the two forest guards and Bala, carrying a *charpoy*.

The dead girl was a pitiful sight. The few rags she had been wearing had been torn away by the tiger, but Bala had covered her loins with the one saree she had possessed. The young face wore a strange expression of calm. Blood had seeped into the mud floor of the hut from her lacerated back, and its dark stream had trickled from her torn throat and breasts and dried on her dusky skin. We stood, all four of us, in respectful silence for a minute, regarding those mangled remains on the floor before us that had, only that morning, been a living and happy mother. Then I closed the door of the hut behind us as I motioned Bala to lead us to the spot where he had found the tiger about to begin his meal.

The sun had long since absorbed the dew, and the heads of spear grass that had bent with the passage of the man-eater and his victim were standing upright again, gently nodding in the light breeze. Bala walked ahead to the spot where the tiger had laid the girl down for the first time and changed his hold. From there the blood-spoor began and it led us in a short time to an old dead tree, at the foot of which the killer had set her down to begin his meal in real earnest, when Bala had driven him off.

We walked silently and did not speak, although all four of us were on the alert. But there was little actual danger, because of our numbers. At the foot of the tree we halted and looked at the ground. It was hard and covered with short dried grass. No pug-marks were visible, nor was there any need to look for them

I remembered that this tiger was accredited with never returning to his meal of a human victim after his earlier experience in Hyderabad when he was wounded by the Nawab. Would he return now? Would there be any use in my sitting up for him? These thoughts passed dismally through my mind. The only ray of hope in this case was the fact that he had not eaten even a mouthful of the girl. But against that was the fact that Bala had frightened him away. All said and done, the proposition appeared to hold out but little chance of success. But I knew I would have to try, for there was no alternative.

I looked around for a tree on which to put the *charpoy*.

The tiger had selected a densely-wooded spot for his repast, covered with bushes and undergrowth. The nearest tree, other than the bare dead one, was thirty yards away. When I squatted on my haunches at the approximate height of a tiger, I could see I would have to sit right at the top to see over the undergrowth and have a fair chance to shoot. Most probably the tiger would only return after dark, if he returned at all, and a flashlight could not penetrate the brambles should I sit any lower down.

I walked the thirty yards to the tree and looked up. Its higher branches were no thicker than my two fingers and could not possibly support my weight in the *charpoy*.

The next sizeable tree was some ten yards further away. I got to it and scrambled up. But I could only see the upper portion of the trunk of the dead tree where the tiger had been. The brambles hid its base and everything else below.

Here was a knotty problem. Where could I sit?

I walked back to the three men and sauntered around the dead tree. It had been a big tree in its day and the bole at its base was twelve to fifteen feet in circumference. There was no apparent reason why it had died: perhaps from some disease or an insect pest. Perhaps its roots had been eaten away underground. Whatever the cause, it had perished some years earlier; only the dead branches forked into the cloudless sky above my head.

White ants had already begun their work of demolition from below, and in a short while the weakened base would no longer be able to sustain the weight of the dead superstructure, and the whole would crash to earth and disintegrate as food for the termites and the myriad wood-beetles and insects of all kinds that would then attack it from the ground.

I walked closer to the trunk. At a spot just level with the top of my head three branches had spread out from the main stem. A crust of dried earth covered the busy white ants below. Raising Myself on tiptoe, I peered into the cavity that led down the stem. The inside of the tree was hollow.

This had not been noticeable from outside, particularly from the spot where the victim's body had been laid.

I motioned to the three men and whispered to Ali Baig to ask Bala to get inside the hollow trunk to see whether a place could be made for me there. Before sending him, however, I took the precaution to shine my spare flashlight into the hole, to make sure it did not shelter a snake or scorpion, or even a centipede. Having made certain it was tenantless except for the white ants, Bala nimbly let himself down. Being at least a foot shorter than me, he disappeared from view, but popped out again and stated that it was a close fit for him and could not possibly accommodate my greater bulk. Some extension of the interior was absolutely necessary.

I then noticed that the white ants had eaten much further into the wood on the opposite side.

With Bala pushing from within, and we three pulling from outside with our hands, aided now and again by a couple of gentle blows from Krishnappa's axe, we started tearing away the rotting wood from the hole by which Bala had entered. The termites had already done most of the work for us, and little by little we enlarged the hole, working downwards towards ground level. We increased the size of the entrance not only at the top, but by dint of removing the wood from the other side of the bole we completely exposed that side down to about knee-level. As the wood came away, to lay open the interior, we were able to get our hands inside and use Bala's short-handled axe as well.

It was hard work and took nearly two hours, but at last I was able to step into a hole that was sufficiently big to accommodate my feet up to my knees. Thereafter, I was free enough to move my hands and my rifle through the opening we had made in the off-side of the trunk.

There were several serious snags in my position. The main one was that I had my back to the point where the tiger had set the woman down, and to which he would most probably return—that is, if he did return. I could not turn and look in that direction because the tree trunk was behind me. Further, we had not been able to remove the wood from this part of the trunk, as the white ants had eaten more on the opposite side, as I have said. To do so we would have had to hack through the wood, for which we did not have the time, apart from the noise we would make.

All these drawbacks combined to suggest that, when we finally put the corpse of the girl-wife into place, it could not be at the spot where the tiger had left it. We would be compelled to change its position a little. If I did not do that and the tiger did come, he would either remove the carcass before I became aware of his presence, or he would sit and eat it within a distance of five yards from me without my being able to do anything about it. Of course, I could step out of cover and creep around the bole of the tree. But I was far too afraid to do that. Further, I would probably make some noise in stepping out of the trunk in the dark. The tiger would hear me and perhaps disappear; or, what was more frightening, he might meet me halfway around the trunk. That thought was difficult to relish.

A second major disadvantage lay in the fact that I would have to stand upright throughout the night. I could not even squat, because the hole below knee-level was just large enough for my legs.

Thirdly, if the tiger reconnoitered the place before approaching the body, as every sensible tiger would do, he would look straight at me as soon as he came opposite the gap we had cut. Of course, I would have the men put up some sort of camouflage to hide in, in the way of leaves and trailing creepers, but would I be able to deceive his jungle-bred eyes if he looked straight in my direction? At least, would he not become suspicious of these leaves and other things, suddenly appearing on the bole of a tree that had been quite bare only that very morning?

Again, if a cobra, scorpion or some other nasty creeping or crawling thing chose to select the hollow in the dead tree to keep itself warm on a chilly night, I would indeed be in a sorry predicament. There were so many possibilities of trouble that I shrugged them away. I would have to take the chance, although the odds seemed to be ten to one against success.

I laid my coat upon the ground, and on it we piled every bit of the dried wood we had removed, even to the last scrap. We then held the coat at the four corners and carried it away to throw the debris at a distance.

Then we returned to the hut, where Bala bravely lifted his wife's body on his shoulder. In single file and silence we walked back to the tree. I asked him to set the body down a little to the left of the opening we had made, so that the tiger in looking at it would not be in a direct line with the opening and myself. There was no room for anything inside the hollow but myself and the rifle with torch attached, so I swallowed a chappatti and some tea from my water-bottle before giving it to Ali Baig to take back.

I stepped into the hollow. Bala and Krishnappa then placed some sticks across the opening, between which they draped leaves and trails of ereepers to screen me as much as possible. This job Bala took very seriously, going back some paces to different angles of vision every now and again, to check whether I could still be seen inside. He wedged a larger bit of stick across the two sides of the opening at the level of my chest, so that I might rest my rifle upon it as I fired. I found I could slide my rifle before me, slowly up my body and then over this stick without making any noise. The two Chenchus draped the stick and the trunk on both sides of my face with creepers, hanging them downwards against the wood from the two higher branches of the tree. Finally, they wedged a great mass of leaves and wood down on the base of the three branches that bifurcated above me. I was truly bottled up inside that hollow.

Before leaving, Bala bade farewell to his dead wife. He kissed the cold forehead and he kissed her feet. Then he got down on his knees beside the body and prostrated himself on the ground, with his palms extended to earth, to seek her pardon for the indignities to which he was exposing her poor body.

When he got up again, there were no tears in his eyes. His face was resolute. He looked at me wordlessly. Once more the telepathy of jungle-loving people passed between us. His look said, far more clearly than any spoken word: 'I have done all I could and have even sacrificed the body of my dear one. The rest is up to you.' I resolved I would not fail him.

A moment later my three followers had gone on their way to the hut and I was alone.

I glanced at my wristwatch. The time was 4.45 p.m. Patches of bright sunlight filtered through the undergrowth and dappled the red and black of the dead woman's saree which Bala had wrapped around her waist. Her hair had fallen loosely and lay outspread on the ground, framing the head and face, now turned towards me, with its peaceful expression. Rigor mortis had set in and one hand lay folded stiffly across her breast, where perhaps her husband had laid it in the morning when he had carried her body back to their hut. The other had set by her side. The gentle evening breeze, swaying the grass, idly flapped a corner of the saree or lifted a wisp of her jet-black hair.

Except for the breeze stirring the leaves and grass, nothing else moved. Except for the faint tick of my wristwatch, and a dull thudding sound which took me quite some time to identify as the pounding of my own heart, I could hear no other sound.

I spread my feet gently, inch by inch, and eased them as far forward as possible while leaning back. They would have to bear my weight that whole night, and my least duty to them was to try to distribute that load as evenly as possible.

The jungle came to life forty-five minutes later, with the usual cries of roosting peafowl and jungle fowl. One grey cock strutted out into the clearing before me, and crowed his challenge to the dying day. 'Kuck ky'a ky'a khuk'm', he called, and in a few seconds the cry was answered by another junglecock in the distance. 'Wheew, kuck khuke'm', he replied. The first rooster ruffled his feathers and looked in the direction from which the reply had come. Then a gust of wind blew and the corner of the saree stirred. With a heavy flapping of wings, the rooster was gone.

'Mi-iao mi-iao' called a peacock, to be answered by similar cries from his own kind, as the heavy birds flapped one by one to rest in groups in some distant tree. Spurfowl cackled their fighting notes in the undergrowth, while the last of the *butterflies* and beetles sailed or buzzed their homeward way to the particular leaf or other shelter they had chosen for that night.

The daylight faded fast in the manner of all tropical countries. My feathered friends of the sunny hours were no doubt tucking their heads beneath their wings, or at least would do so very soon. With the fading light, something soft descended from the skies and came to rest on the ground a yard away. It was a nightjar, the harbinger of the Indian jungle night. 'Chuck-chuck-chuckoooo', it trilled, while its brown outline on the dried grass resembled just a stone. And then, with a graceful outstretching of its wings, it floated away. 'Cheep-cheep-cheep' came a sound from directly above me. Two bats circled their rapid flight around the tree, to snap up the belated day-insects that were just going to rest, in addition to some early arrivals from among the insects of the night.

I had seen and heard it all so very many times before; the diminuendo of the creatures of the day giving place to the crescendo of the creatures of the night. But never in quite the same position and circumstances as I was now in, I had to admit.

Then came darkness for a short while—but not for long, as singly and in groups the stars began to twinkle overhead, shedding a very diffused light on the jungle around me. That would be my only illumination till daylight came again, for this had happened during the moonless nights.

The mosquitoes took some time to find me out, but when their scouts finally made the discovery, they lost but few moments in reporting to headquarters. Then whole squadrons of dive-bombers made full capital out of it. With protruding under-lip, I blew them off my face and I stuffed my hands into my trouser pockets to outwit such of the more enterprising individuals as had flown inside my tree-trunk, bent upon sucking my blood.

Eight o'clock came. I lifted one foot after the other and wriggled my toes inside my canvas shoes in order to restore circulation to the soles of my feet. This tiger had the reputation of never returning to a human kill. And I had placed myself in this awkward and uncomfortable position for the night. Then a picture of Bala's tear-stained face and of that dead countenance, now lying out in the darkness so close to me but hidden from sight, appeared before my mind, and my reason assured me that what I was doing at that moment was the only thing possible for me to do.

My thoughts had been wandering when all of a sudden I became fully alert, every nerve at high tension. I had seen nothing; I had heard not a sound. But just as certain as I was of my own name, I knew the man-eater was near. The hair on my neck was on end and a faint nervous quiver ran through my whole being. Some undefined and indefinable sense had screamed the warning to me. Yes, without doubt, the tiger was there.

I strained my ears to the utmost to hear any sound. There was absolute silence. No warning cry from deer or other jungle creatures had betrayed the feline's movements.

Such complete silence and such delay in approaching the dead body meant only one thing. The tiger was suspicious. Was that the aftermath of the fright Bala had given him that morning, or had he seen or sensed something in his surroundings. Above all, had he seen or sensed me?

I would have given a great deal to know the answer to the last question.

After what appeared to be an eternity, I heard a faint snuffling noise; then that of something being dragged.

There was only one explanation. The tiger was dragging the body of the dead woman away. In another moment he would be gone.

I was on the point of casting caution to the winds and revealing my presence by bringing my weapon out of cover and flashing the torch to risk a shot, when the dragging ceased abruptly. Had the tiger disappeared with the body?

And then the sounds of eating began, and the crunch of bones. They came from the other side of the tree and from behind me.

The explanation was easy. For some unaccountable reason the man-eater had dragged the body back to the very position where he had left it early that morning. Instinct perhaps. At least it indicated one thing: the tiger was not suspicious or alarmed, as I had at first thought. If that had been the case, he would either have slunk away or bounded off with the body. Had he become aware of my presence, he might even have made an attack.

The fact that he had done none of these things clearly indicated that he was not alarmed, but only that he wanted to have his meal exactly where he had left it. Perhaps he had reasoned to himself that some earlier visitor, in the form of a jackal or hyaena, had shifted it.

I breathed a sigh of relief—until I recollected that I would now have to step out of my shelter into the open and around the trunk of the tree if I wanted to take a shot. Then all feeling of relief left me.

You will remember that Bala and Krishnappa had more or less 'fenced me in' with the aid of sticks, leaves, creepers and so forth. To step out, I would first have to remove these obstructions. In doing so some slight noise would undoubtedly result. The tiger would hear. He might run away, or, far worse than that, he might come around the tree to investigate the cause and find me before I was ready.

There was just one thing to do, and I did that thing. I let the tiger tuck into his meal right heartily.

Each time he tore the flesh or crunched a bone and chewed noisily, I gently untangled a leaf or piece of creeper or removed one of the sticks and slid it down the inside of the hollow tree towards my feet. Thus I cleared the way to step out while the tiger was eating.

Then I raised my right foot into the air and poised it for a minute to restore circulation, before lifting it ever so carefully outside the tree-trunk. I waited; but the tiger was still crunching bones. I steadied myself with my left hand against the hole and very cautiously brought my left foot beside my right one.

For a few moments I was unbalanced to take a shot, and it would have indeed been very unfortunate for me had the man-eater discovered me then. But mercifully he was far too engrossed in his meal.

An inch at a time, I shuffled myself forward around the bole of that tree. Then came the moment when another inch would reveal me. If the tiger happened to be facing the tree he would surely see me. If not, there was a chance that I would not be detected immediately.

The moment for action had arrived and I had to risk it. I raised the rifle, pointing skyward, and placed the stock to my shoulder. I edged an inch forward with each foot. Then I slightly craned my neck to look around the trunk.

My eyes had become accustomed to the diffused light and I saw the tiger lying full-length on the ground over a dark mass that was all that was left of the woman. He was half-inclined away from me, facing the direction whence we had come that evening. The foresight of the rifle would not be visible in that light, and I would have to use my flashlight for the shot.

I raised my left arm gently to support my rifle as I brought it to firing position at my right shoulder. My left thumb frantically groped for the torch switch. Something warned the tiger that all was not well. He looked back over his shoulder as the beam shone forth to frame his head and glowing eyes, while flesh and blood drooled from his lips.

My first bullet took him in the neck, and as he catapulted head over heels I worked the under-lever of my Winchester as I had never worked it before in my life. He was writhing furiously as I pumped into him a second shot, followed by a third. I really could not tell you what happened then. But he just disappeared.

He had been roaring with pain and rage after my first shot. He had roared during the fusillade. He was still roaring and tearing up the undergrowth in rage and agony, but I could see him no longer. He had leaped into the shelter of the jungle.

I dived back into the hollow of the dead tree as fast as I could scramble and awaited events. I wanted to replace the three rounds I had just fired, so as to have a full magazine ready. But a .405 Winchester does not lend itself to that kind of thing. A 'jam' is likely to occur when putting more rounds into a half-empty magazine. If that should happen, I would be helpless. I decided to leave well alone. There was still one round with which I could hold off the tiger. Although my rifle magazine held five rounds, I usually load only four, keeping one in the breach and three in the magazine when sitting up for carnivora. This is by way of an added precaution against a 'jam'.

I began to wonder if I had acted wisely in getting back inside the tree. Perhaps it would have been better if I had remained outside. I could at least see the tiger if he charged. Now I could not do so till he came out of the bushes and in front of me.

However, it was too late for regrets. I stood still. Perspiration saturated my body and my hands were slippery from holding the rifle. I felt terribly sick and my head ached.

The tiger was still roaring and tearing at the bushes, but in time the sounds subsided and then faded in the distance. The creature was not dead, but at least it had gone away and I was safe. And I was thankful. Then I retched—and felt all the better for it.

Unfortunately, the direction of the tiger's departing roars had not registered on my confused senses and I was uncertain which way he had gone. Under such conditions it would be suicidal to attempt at once to walk to Bala's hut in the darkness. I would have to use my flashlight to find my way there, and that would betray me if the man-eater was lying up in the undergrowth.

So I spent the rest of the night in that damned hollow, drooping on my tired feet. Dawn found me dejected, till I remembered I was lucky to be alive. For that I was glad.

As soon as it was light enough to see, I stepped out of the hollow tree and sat on the ground outside. Have you ever attempted to remain on your feet all night for a stretch of something like thirteen hours? Try it yourself sometime.

For fifteen minutes or so, while the light grew stronger, I rested. Then I got up to see what could be seen. The time I had taken to free myself from the sticks and leaves, and to step out from the tree, while the tiger had been eating, could not have been much more than ten minutes—perhaps fifteen minutes at the most—but the tiger had eaten more than half of the dead woman. Her head and arms had been parted from the body and lay scattered on the grass. One thigh and leg were there too, and part of the other foot. The rest of her was gone, except for the gnawed vertebrae with a few of the rib bones still attached.

The earth was torn up where the man-eater had ravaged the ground in his agony. Then he had made a jump into the undergrowth a couple of yards away. Here the stems of the bushes had been bitten through and the leaves were smeared with his blood. This had been the place from which I had heard him roaring and rampaging while I had been cowering in the hollow tree. From there the blood trail moved away into the jungle. I followed it for a few yards and found it was leading approximately northwards. I could return to the hut in comparative safety.

I did so. Bala and the guards had heard the sound of shooting from the hut, where they had been lying awake. With the coming of daylight they had advanced for about a furlong and were waiting for me. Indeed, the Chenchus would have come all the way to the dead tree, but Ali Baig cautioned them that I might have only wounded the tiger and there was no knowing where it would be hiding.

I told them all that had happened during that terrible night.

My watch showed that time was 6.25 a.m. I must have fired at the tiger about 8.30 the night before—ten hours previously. He must be dead by now, I thought. Or, if not dead, he must have lost so much blood and become so stiff from his wounds that he would be lying up somewhere in a bad plight. I could no longer restrain myself from following the blood trail.

As Ali Baig was unarmed, I asked him to go back to the hut and await us there. He replied that he was afraid to stay there alone and that he would rather accompany us and take his chance. So we returned to the dead tree.

I had told Bala that, as much as I had not wanted to do so, I had been compelled to let the tiger eat the body of his wife in order to preoccupy and distract his attention while I was freeing myself from the camouflaging sticks and creepers. He had accepted my explanation then. But when we reached the tree and he saw the torn remains of the poor woman, the shock had been too great for him. The little man broke down completely and wept loudly and bitterly.

He said he would not go on till he had cremated the remains. It took all that the two forest guards and I could do to stop him from setting about this business there and then. In fact, it is doubtful if we would have succeeded had not Ali Baig bluntly told him that all of us, and more particularly he, would be in trouble with the local police, who would expect a report about the incident, after which they would conduct some sort of inquiry and hold an inspection of the remains. They would not look kindly upon him if he should cremate the evidence before they had seen it. So we broke branches and covered the scene of carnage to keep off the vultures that would otherwise soon arrive.

We all hoped we would find the tiger, dead or dying, within a very short distance, and that we would be able to return soon to make the necessary report to the police.

That was where we were greatly mistaken.

The blood trail led through the bushes. As far as I could see, the tiger had been wounded in two places, one of them high up—no doubt by my first shot at his neck. The second wound had left a constantly dripping blood trail, and as we followed it we found a tiny piece of membrane mixed with the clotted blood. To me this indicated a stomach wound.

The animal had first rested beneath a tree within two furlongs of the dead tree. Here mounds of regurgitated, blood-soaked flesh—the flesh of that poor woman—showed that the tiger had suffered a severe fit of vomiting and confirmed that one of my bullets had entered his stomach.

He had carried on from there for another half-mile or so, where he had lain down upon the grass. Two small pools of blood established the fact that he had been hit twice. The stomach wound appeared to be the more severe one, as the bleeding there had been much more copious.

Nevertheless, the animal had still kept going. The blood trail, which had been very prolific at the start, was now less. Outer skin, membrane or fat had perhaps covered the exterior hole made by the bullet where it had entered his stomach, and so had stopped the bleeding. Probably it was only the neck wound that had continued to bleed thereafter and that no doubt accounted for the scantier trail.

We came to a stream between two hills where the tiger had lain in the water, which still held a faint pinkish tinge. A little blood streaked the mud on the further bank. Here the pug-marks were clearly visible for the first time along the whole trail. They were the large quarter-plate-sized pugs of a big male.

Still the trail carried on, but the bleeding had become markedly less. Soon there was only a drop to be seen here and there. I was amazed to say the least of it.

My first shot had been at the tiger's neck. I knew I had not missed, for he had made a complete somersault, which indicated he had been hit. I had fired twice after that and one of those shots had perforated his stomach. The quantities of vomited human flesh had established that also. We had been following a copious blood trail at the start, commencing from the place where the man-eater had torn up the undergrowth in pain and fury. He had rested more than twice after that. All these factors together, and all my experience over the past many years, cried out that by all the rules of the game the tiger should have died, or have almost bled to death, by now. We should have come across him lying up in a very enfeebled condition in some cover. In fact, we had expected the trail to be a short and easy one.

Instead of any of these expected happenings, however, the man-eater was still pressing on, heading ever northwards. Splashes of blood on the earth and leaves, as it dripped from his wounds or was smeared on the bushes as he passed, were few and far between now and the trail was becoming increasingly difficult to follow. We had travelled far from any footpaths and were many miles into the interior of the jungle, with only a game-*path* here and there. The terrain had become very hilly, crisscrossed by deep boulder-strewn valleys, each of which was the bed of a tiny, trickling stream. Water was far from scarce, and we could see the tiger had stopped to drink from many of these rivulets. The larger trees of the jungle had given way to dense undergrowth, mostly of lantana and other thorny varieties.

At ten minutes to one o'clock we could find no more blood drops, although the four of us fanned out and cast around in a wide circle. We had reached the journey's end and the trail was dead. The sun beat down mercilessly.

We were a silent party as we made our way back to Gazulapalli, and I was dog-tired when I threw myself into the old armchair that had almost no bottom in the station waiting-room. Sleep came before I could take off my boots.

Mr Balasubramaniam made a telegraphic report to the police that night, and next day the officials arrived by the afternoon train from Nandyal. We went with them to the old dead tree.

What had been left of the unfortunate woman was stinking by now. We could smell it a furlong away. Hordes of blue bottles nestled in swarms on the leaves we had thrown over the bits and pieces. But at least they had been protected from the vultures. I showed the sub-inspector of police the hollow in the tree-trunk where I had hidden the night before, while I related my story.

The notes he made covered some thirteen pages of paper. My statement alone took six.

Bala begged for permission to cremate the remains. The police officer was of the opinion that they should be taken to Nandyal for a post-mortem examination. I vouchsafed no advice, because I could see that the sub-inspector did not regard my action in having set the dead woman out for bait as quite the proper thing to have done. I felt that whatever I advised now might cause him to take exactly the opposite course of action. So I minded my own business. The presence and testimony of the two forest guards, however, eventually turned the tables in Bala's favour, and permission was given to him to cremate the remains. We were silent witnesses as he and the two guards gathered a pile of dried wood, set the decomposed remains thereon, topped up the pile with more wood and then set fire to the lot. It was a simple and sad ceremony, marred only by the awful stench of burning decomposed flesh. Out of respect for Bala's feelings, I remained there. The police officer went some distance away, leaned against a tree and was terribly sick.

I found it difficult to look Bala in the eye next day. I felt I had let him down. But the little man's intuition sensed this. He came with Balasubramaniam to the waiting room while I sat there and asked the stationmaster to interpret what he was about to say. It was just this. 'Tell the "dorai" not to feel worried because he failed to shoot the tiger. I know he did his very best. No other man—no, not even I—could have done more.'

And no man could have said more than that to relieve my feelings. I felt better and told Balasubramaniam to thank him for what he had said, and for all the cooperation he had extended to me. His simple tribute was one of the best I have ever received.

I remained in Gazulapalli for another week, but no more news came to me of the man-eater. A panther killed one of my baits at Diguvametta. I went there to verify this and proved it to be a fact. Joseph was not very pleased when I left the remains for the panther to have another feed that night.

At the end of that week I paid farewell to all my newly-found friends who had helped me so unstintingly and made my visit such a pleasure. The baits I gave away to the various forest guards at the different stations, with something more for Bala.

Three months passed after my return to Bangalore. Then a tiger killed a man near the Krishna river in Hyderabad state. Three months later a Chenchu was killed several miles north of Bogara railway station. News of human kills since then have been very few and far between. But they still come in.

Did the man-eater I wounded recover after all? Has he started operations again? Were there two separate man-eaters operating at the time of my visit, the one that had taken the woman gathering *mhowa* flowers at Diguvametta being quite different from the one that had killed Bala's wife?

Were the latest kills the work of one or other of these two tigers—if indeed there ever had been two? Or had they been made by quite another tiger, one that had newly appeared on the scene?

These questions worry me sometimes, for I cannot find an answer. But I would give a lot to know.

Seven

The Big Bull Bison of Gedesal

THIS IS NOT THE STORY OF A REGULAR HUNT, CONCLUDING WITH THE shooting or wounding of the Big Bull Bison I am going to tell you about. If you think that, you are in for a disappointment, for I never even fired a shot at this animal at any time, nor would I ever have done so. For I admire him too much.

He was a brave old warrior, and if he is still alive today he well deserves his title as lord and leader of the herd he cared for so faithfully. If he could understand me, I would be proud to call him my friend.

Gedesal is the name of a small Sholaga village standing at the head of what I call the 'bison range' in the forests of North Coimbatore district. A forest bungalow called by the same name borders the road as it reaches the top of the ascent on its southward journey from the town of Kollegal to the hamlet of Dimbum. This road runs down the side of a hill for five of the seven miles that separate Gedesal from Dimbum.

211

For those last two miles it rises again. Dimbum is at the edge of an escarpment. The road falls steeply, in a series of sharp hairpin bends, from Dimbum to the plains below it to the south, whence it pursues an almost level course to the large town of Satyamangalam.

Gedesal itself is flanked on the west by the towering range of the Biligirirangan Mountains, their slopes a scenic combination of frowning crags jutting out of a green background of lawn-like grass. In the folds of the hills, and along the beds of the myriad watercourses that tumble downhill, clumps of trees and matted jungle have sprung up. These are commonly called 'sholas', or isolated islands of forest, surrounded by open, grassy areas or outcrops of forbidding rock.

To the east lies another range of hills, much less in altitude, size and grandeur than the mountain range of the Biligirirangan to the west. These low hills are entirely covered by forest, consisting mainly of tiger-grass that grows to a height of ten feet, interspersed with thousands upon thousands of the stunted wild date palms. Towards the middle of the year these palms bear long clusters of the yellow wild dates at the ends of drooping stems—dry, tasteless fruit, indeed, but much favoured by birds and animals alike.

Thus the topography, the vegetation and the dates combine to make the area a favourite haunt for bison, sambar and bear.

A long valley runs from north to south between the flanking ranges of mountains and hills, and along the side of this valley the road from Kollegal to Dimbum wends its lonely, southward way, passing between Gedesal hamlet itself and the forest bungalow of the same name.

This building is exceptionally large for a forest bungalow, and has a long line of outhouses at its rear for the occupation of the menials working for the Forestry department. Moreover it has a big compound, where some nice specimens of the wild hill-rose grow, the flowers of which bloom in large clusters, resembling small bouquets.

Just south of the bungalow is a low-lying stretch of land, holding a small pond and some marshy ground. Because of the tender shoots of green grass that grow there—entirely different from the coarse tiger-grass in the surrounding area—a small herd of spotted deer is almost always in residence. When I saw them last they were sired and led by quite a sizeable stag with a good head of antlers, his dark brown shoulders being almost black, against which the dappled white spots contrasted markedly.

I hope that no hunter, human or animal, has brought him down, and that he still roams at the head of his harem in that deeply green and refreshingly moist, cool glen—lordly and free as the jungle to which he belongs.

The low range of hills to the east of the road and the deep valley running along the base of the mountains to the west offer wide browsing opportunities to the many separate bison herds that inhabit the area. A perennial stream of considerable size flows down the length of this valley, the road being crossed every now and again by the various tributaries that feed it. A never-failing water supply, even during the hottest summer season, is thereby assured, which is the main factor that contributes towards keeping these animals permanently in residence.

These bison herds number from twenty to forty or even more, the majority being cows and calves of different ages, with perhaps about half-a-dozen sizeable bulls to each herd. The oldest and most mature bull automatically gains supremacy over his younger rivals and becomes the lord and master of that herd until such time as he in turn is overthrown by some younger and more vigorous male, or meets his end in some fashion that accords with the laws of the jungle. Occasionally a big bull will break away from the rest of the herd and pursue his own solitary existence.

Bison suffer severely from diseases such as 'rinderpest', which frequently attack the herds of domestic cattle belonging to the Sholagas, living in the forest or adjacent cattle *patties.* The cattle are let out to graze in the jungle and spread the infection to the bison. It is quite common to come across bison affected by the 'foot-and-mouth' disease which is so fatal to cattle, or to be led by the sight of vultures to the carcass of one that has succumbed to this most deadly of cattle scourges.

The big bull of which my story tells was the leader of a herd of at least thirty animals. Very frequently have I seen him early in the morning when droplets of dew glittered in the rising sun, and sometimes round about 5.30 in the evening, grazing within sight of the road between the 39th and 41st milestones. It was easy to identify him by his crumpled left horn, which was clearly deformed and turned inwards and forwards.

Perhaps the old bull owes his long life to this deformity, as it renders his head worthless as a trophy, though the right horn is beautifully shaped. True it is that some hunter and collector of oddities might value his head as an unusual specimen, but he has been lucky in that such a curiosity-monger does not so far appear to have met up with him. In battle his deformed horn has proved an invaluable weapon, as I am about to relate. He has the natural advantages that would be those of a unicorn, if this legendary animal actually existed, in that he could transfix an opponent in a frontal attack or badly slash him with a toss of his head.

I have often motored along that road on a dark night, shining the sealed-beam spotlight on my car from side to side, to see what I could see and just for the fun of it. Twice or thrice on such occasions the widely-separated blue eyes of a bison have reflected the lamp's rays and upon closer inspection I have found them to be the eyes of the old bull.

My attention was first attracted to this veteran some years ago when I was out for a walk on the lower slopes of the Biligirirangan range. There is a road running through the forest from the western side of the main road. It skirts Gedesal village, crosses the stream, and then starts to climb over the foothills of the mountain range to disappear eventually over a saddleback and descend a valley on the other side. Finally it leads to a beautiful forest lodge, the private property of Mr Randolph Morris who is one of southern India's biggest and most influential coffee planters. He is also an authority on *shikar* and a hunter of renown, having contributed many valuable articles on the habits of big game and on big game hunting. He was the honorary game warden of the area, well known to the Viceroys and former Governors of British India, and the owner of some of the most beautiful and well-planned coffee estates in the south.

Long before this road makes its way over the saddleback there is a prefabricated shed, the property of the Forestry department, which has been erected for the convenience of its officers on tour and for the use of licensed sportsmen on *shikar*. Some thoughtful soul has made, or caused to make, a ladder of stout twisted vines, which is kept in this lodge and comes in very handy for climbing up to and down from *machan*s erected on trees, to those who are not naturally gifted or adapted to this arboreal art.

That morning I had passed this lodge and was walking along a ridge overlooking a bowl-like shallow valley when I heard a clashing and thudding sound, interrupted with snorts of rage. The evidence pointed to a bison fight, and I hurried along, taking what cover was available, in the direction of the sounds. Very soon I saw in the valley below me, but quite three hundred yards away, two large bull bison locked in fierce combat. With horns entangled and foreheads pressed together, they were pushing against each other with might and main, the outstretched taut legs of each animal indicating the tremendous effort he was making to push his opponent back. At intervals one or other would momentarily disengage his horns and head from his rival to deliver a short quick jab before interlocking again, and before the opposing animal could score a similar thrust.

Then I noticed that one of them had a peculiar horn that gave him a distinct advantage over his antagonist which was bleeding profusely from wounds in his neck, shoulders and side.

The fight raged for the next twenty minutes or so with unabated fury, till the gasps that took the place of the snorts of rage that I had first heard, and the glistening sides of the two bulls, soaked in sweat and blood that was clearly visible even at that range, showed that the gruelling pace and strain of the fight was beginning to tell. Froth drooled from the mouths of the bulls and splattered their bodies, falling in splashes to the ground.

I had never witnessed a bison fight before and was very curious to know how it would end. Fortunately I had come alone. Moreover, the breeze blew in my direction. Therefore the combatants were quite unaware of my presence and fought their fight under natural conditions.

The bull with the crumpled horn seemed to be getting the better of things, and his opponent gave ground, becoming reddened by the gore that flowed from the many wounds in his body. Of course, he had also inflicted some telling jabs on his enemy, but the crumpled horn was obviously giving

216

its owner a decided superiority. After another ten minutes the severely injured animal began to falter. He fell to his knees several times, and at each opportunity that unicorn-like horn embedded itself in some part of the unfortunate animal. Eventually he broke, turned and ran at a staggering trot, the victor following up his advantage by pursuing him and butting his hindquarters. The two animals passed out of sight at a point where the bowl of the valley merged with the surrounding jungle.

Out of curiosity I walked down to the site of the recent combat. The ground had been torn up by the straining hooves of the two contestants and was flecked with blood and foam in a rough circle some twenty yards in diameter.

It was a considerable time after that when I saw my bull again. The second occasion was on another walk one evening on my way to visit a water hole situated on the eastern side of the road about a quarter of a mile from and almost level with the 41st milestone. A tiger had killed a couple of head of cattle belonging to the Sholagas of Gedesal village. They told me they had seen it on several occasions in the evenings, walking along—or crossing—the fire-line that leads past this pool and thereafter cuts across the road.

I went to the water hole at about 4.30 p.m. that day, and walked around its edge to discover what animals had been visiting it. There were the usual tracks of elephant, bison, sambar, spotted deer and of a few wild pigs. The tiger had also drunk there on about three separate occasions so far as I could judge by the age of his pug-marks, although the last time had been at least three days earlier than my visit.

Among the bison tracks were the pointed hoof-marks of what must have been a truly massive bull. The weight of his body had been so great that he sank almost a foot into the mire that bordered the pond. His tracks were also visible in many places in the vicinity, indicating that he was a frequent visitor to this pool. This was rather strange in view of the fact that he had the river, which I have already mentioned, at which to quench his thirst.

I asked the Sholaga who had told me about the tiger, and who had accompanied me, if he knew anything about this bull. He replied in the affirmative and told me that he and all the villagers had seen him many times, and that he had a deformed horn—the left one—which thrust forwards. Immediately my mind flew back to the scene I had witnessed in that memorable fight, in which a bull with a crumpled horn had completely routed his opponent. I wondered if this could be the same animal and thought it must be so, as such a deformity is extremely rare.

The Sholaga told me the bull frequented the pond, as he kept the herd under his care in that locality; probably because of the exceptionally fine grazing to be had on the low land around the water hole. Then he went on to say that if I cared to take a walk with him, we might be lucky enough to see this animal for ourselves, or even come across the tiger.

At that time the tiger was my immediate quarry and I was not very interested in the bull, so more with that objective in mind I consented. In any case, stalking a bison in broad daylight is a tricky business and depends upon the direction in which the wind is blowing, the cover available, and of course the lie of the land.

We set off on an aimless walk, following cattle trails and game *paths* and crisscrossing the fire-line several times. I remember we were ambling along a narrow track when quite suddenly the long grass parted before us, hardly thirty yards away, to reveal the head and shoulders of a massive bull bison which regarded us complacently and obviously without much concern. It was my friend, the bison with the crumpled horn.

He showed no signs of fear, but just stood looking at us. We advanced another ten yards; then, with a loud swish of the reedy grass, he turned around and disappeared. After that day, as I have said, I saw him on other occasions, and then came the memorable event which drew him to me.

An unidentified hunter, who was also poacher, came along the road one night and shot a cow bison. Before he knew where he was, a bull attacked his jeep and with a toss of his head tumbled the vehicle down a khud that bordered the road into one of the dry tributaries of the river. Fortunately the bison did not follow up its attack, so the poacher suffered only an injured leg and a smashed rifle. The Sholaga who was with him, and was sitting at the side of the jeep on which the assault was launched, had clearly seen the bull and avowed it was the animal with the deformed left horn.

I heard about the incident some months later, on a subsequent visit, and felt pleased that the old bull had acquitted himself so creditably. No doubt the fact that he had tossed the jeep down the khud had caused him to think, in his own bovine mind, that he had disposed of his foe. Had the khud not been there he would probably have followed up his initial attack with another, found the men inside and eliminated them altogether.

It was some time later, in November, 1953, that I was visiting Dimbum. I had not intended to halt at Gedesal and was motoring along the road when I espied a lone figure walking. Drawing level, I recognised the Sholaga, whose name was Rachen, whom I always employ when I camp at that bungalow. Stopping the car and returning his greeting, I asked him in Tamil: '*Yenna Sungadhi*'—which means: 'What news'?

Rachen replied that just two nights ago the villagers had heard the sounds of a terrific fight in the jungle, not very far from the village, between a tiger and some other animal. From the violence and duration of the combat, which appeared to last for hours, they decided that the tiger's opponent could not be a wild boar, which is the only wild creature of medium-size that fights back against a tiger, and thought it might be an elephant. But then again, had it been an elephant they felt sure they would have heard the trumpeting and screaming which an elephant invariably makes when in trouble or when fighting, or when otherwise excited.

Later in the night the sounds had gradually died away, but they had noticed before that time, from the great noise the tiger had been making, that it had been badly hurt.

Early next morning, impelled by curiosity, the Sholagas had gone to see what had happened and had come upon the scene of the marathon struggle they had heard the night before. The undergrowth had been torn up and trodden down by the combatants, and to one side of this arena lay the carcass of a tiger that had been repeatedly gored and trampled by a bison.

The Sholagas had then promptly removed the skin from the tiger and taken it to the village.

It was about noon when I heard this tale and, having time to spare, felt interested in visiting the spot myself. Seating Rachen beside me, I drove down the narrow track leading to Gedesal village and found the tiger's skin already pegged out on the ground to dry. The raw side was uppermost and had been liberally covered with dry ashes, which is the only preservative known to the Sholagas, salt not being available.

The tiger had been quite a large animal but, judging from the underside of the skin, it had been badly mangled and gored by the bison. There were no less than five distinct holes where the powerful horns had penetrated, and one of them, on the left side, showed where a fateful thrust had pierced the tiger's heart.

I was now more interested than ever and expressed a keen desire to visit the spot where the fight had taken place. Leaving my car, and accompanied by a crowd of Sholagas, I set forth. Less than half a mile away we reached the site of the incident.

'Arena' is the best word I can find to describe it, for indeed there had been a titanic struggle. Great gouts of gore were sprayed on the surrounding grass and bushes in all directions, which had been flattened by the weight of the contestants and were red with dried blood. The Sholagas pointed out the spot where the dead tiger had been lying.

It was obvious from the quantity of blood that the bison had also been severely injured. On a whim I decided I would like to follow him up if possible, to see if he was dead or dying somewhere in the jungle. In either case, I guessed he could not have moved very far from the scene of the fight in his present condition.

Even an entire novice would have been able to follow that trail, as the bison had left a wide *path* of blood through the jungle. He had passed downhill, heading towards the stream, and I felt certain I would find him there, very likely dead, beside the water.

We forged ahead, not troubling to keep silent. An hour and a half's quick walking along that tremendous blood trail brought us to the stream, and to the bison standing in shallow water and resting himself against the bole of a large tree that was partly submerged. Due to the noise made by the water as it rushed over the rocks, he had not heard us at first, and we were well out of cover before he turned around to face us.

It was the big bull bison of Gedesal, the bull with the crumpled horn.

From where we stood, with the breadth of the stream separating us, we could clearly see the awful wounds that had

221

been inflicted by the teeth and the talons of the tiger on his face, neck, sides and rump. Even his belly was badly lacerated, and something red protruded from it and hung into the water. Perhaps it was a portion of his bowel, perhaps a piece of torn skin; I could not see clearly into the shadows where he stood.

But his eyes were clear and fearless, although pain-wracked, as he stood and faced us. Then he turned and staggered away into the jungle.

I had thought of shooting him to put him out of his agony, but somehow could not find it in my heart to do so after the gallant victory he had won at such frightful cost. In any case, I never expected to see him again.

But very recently I visited Gedesal, and great was my surprise and pleasure when one evening I happened to see him, surrounded by his beloved herd, browsing contentedly on the long grass that borders the water hole on the eastern side of the road not far from the 41st milestone—his favourite haunt.

Long may he live in the jungle to which he belongs.

Eight

The Maned Tiger of Chordi

THIS IS THE STORY OF A VERY BIG TIGER THAT GAVE GREAT TROUBLE to the area in which he lived—or rather to the human inhabitants of the area—and was very troublesome to pursue and finally bring to bag.

In telling hunting stories, it is the purpose of the teller to keep his hearers interested. To do that he has to relate the efforts that ended successfully in the killing of his quarry. Perforce he has to leave out many of the failures and disappointments he encounters, for if he were to describe them all his listeners would soon be bored. But to mention only the successes is to give the impression that efforts to kill a man-eater, whether tiger or panther, are nearly always crowned with success, nearly always easy, and can nearly always be accomplished within a comparatively short space of time—a few days, at most.

In reality, all three of these impressions are very far indeed from the truth, and actual circumstances are invariably quite the opposite. Failures are very many and conditions—physical, mental and nervous—are most arduous; and frequently the animal takes months and even years to catch up with. Sometimes he is never shot.

So in this story I am going to tell of a pursuit that began in a casual way and took almost five long and tedious years to bring to a conclusion. Of course it was not a continuous hunt, but a series of sporadic attempts. Between my own efforts there were other hunters from Bangalore and Bombay, not to speak of the local nimrods, who all attempted to bring about the downfall of this wily creature. And we all failed— until those five years had passed.

He was known as the 'maned tiger' because he had an outstanding ruff of hair around his neck, behind his ears and covering his throat and chin. Naturally this outcrop of hair greatly increased the apparent size of his head, which was always described as being 'that big', the witness stretching out his hands sideways, with fingertips inwardly curved, though very few persons had seen him and lived to tell the tale.

His original habitat was known to be around Chordi, because that was the name of the village where he was first seen and near to which he made his first human kill.

Chordi is a small roadside hamlet, surrounded by jungle, about four miles from the little town of Kumsi, which itself is sixteen miles from Shimoga, the capital town of the district bearing the same name, in the state of Mysore. Shimoga is just 172 miles by a good road from Bangalore. Nearly seventy miles of this road, at the Bangalore end, is of concrete and the rest is tarred, so that a motorist can generally and safely— with the exception of a few nasty, unexpected bends—make quite good time to Shimoga.

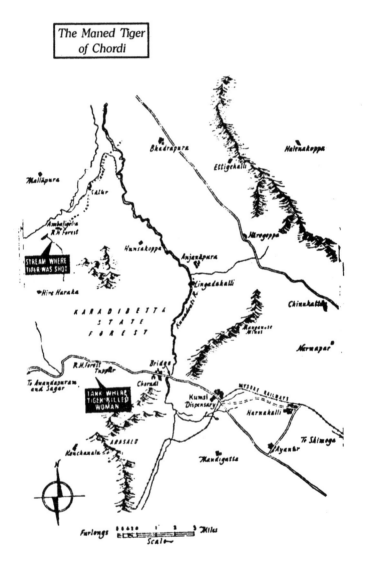

The Maned Tiger
of Chordi

From there the road goes on to Kumsi and Chordi, then to the village of Anandapuram about nine miles further on, then eleven miles to the town of Sagar, and thence about sixteen miles, past another village named Talaguppa, to the famous Gersoppa waterfalls, sometimes known as the Jog falls, where the waters of the Sharavati river descend 950 feet in four separate cascades. That is a sight to be remembered and one that has inspired feelings of awe and reverence in the hearts of the most callous and materialistic of men.

There are two Travellers' Bungalows at the head of the falls. The one on the southern bank of the Sharavati river, which is by far the more modern building, falls within the boundary of Mysore state and is appropriately called the 'Mysore Bungalow'. The opposite bungalow, across the river and on its northern bank, comes under the jurisdiction of Bombay state. It is an older building, very isolated and seldom occupied—for which reason I much prefer it. It is known, of course, as the 'Bombay Bungalow'.

It is rather unusual—and amusing—to find the visitors' books in both bungalows crammed with efforts to write poetry by the various people who have stayed in them from time to time. Undoubtedly the grandeur of the falls has been the cause of awakening this latent desire to wax poetical in minds that perhaps have hitherto remained indifferent. Some of their efforts are really laudable and inspiring; but for the rest I feel it would be difficult anywhere else to assemble such a pile of drivel in one place.

The depredations of the tiger accorded very closely with the pattern of events usually associated with the careers of man-eaters. From being a hunter of the natural game-animals that live in the jungle, he gradually became a cattle-lifter, tempted no doubt by the presence of the thousands of fat kine that are grazed in the reserved forests all over the Shimoga

226

district. Their presence, and the ease with which he could stalk and kill them, in contrast with the difficulties of creeping up on other wild animals, was the first step that changed him from being an inoffensive game-killer into an exceedingly destructive menace to the herdsmen around Chordi.

Attack followed attack as cattle were killed by the maned tiger, till the normal lethargy of the keepers was sufficiently ruffled to decide to do something about it. Matters came to a head when a more enterprising cattle-owner carried his loaded shotgun into the forest with him when he took his animals there for grazing, although it was against the Forestry department's regulations for him to enter the reserve with a weapon but without a game-shooting licence.

However, he did just that, and as luck would have it, the maned tiger chose that very day to attack and bring down one of his animals. From a position behind the trunk of a tree he let fly with his shotgun, and the L.G. pellets badly injured the tiger along his right flank. He disappeared from the vicinity of Chordi for the time being, and all the cattle-men were grateful to the owner of the shotgun for ridding them of such a menace.

Then the maned one reappeared a few miles away, in the shrub jungle that borders Anandapuram. But he still clung to his habit of attacking cattle grazing in the reserve. He had not yet been spoiled—had not yet become a man-eater—because the wound in his side had not incapacitated him in any way.

Once again his unwelcome presence forced itself upon the attention of the cattle-grazers, and once more he was wounded. This time in his right foreleg, and from a *machan* as he was approaching the carcass of a cow he had killed the previous day. He vanished for the second time. Once more false hopes were raised that his departure was permanent, and once again he reappeared.

However, there was a difference with his second return. No longer was he the obnoxious but nevertheless inoffensive tiger that had been so destructive to cattle, but harmless to their attendants. This time it was the other way round; the cattle were comparatively safe but the herdsmen were in danger—in very great and real danger—because he had become that greatest scourge and terror that any jungle can produce: a man-eating tiger.

The ball that had entered his right foreleg had smashed a bone. Nature had healed the bone, but the limb had become shortened and twisted. No longer could he stalk his prey silently and effectively, no longer could he leap upon them and bring them crashing to earth with broken necks. His approach was noisy, his attack clumsy. His ability to hold his prey was greatly hampered by his deformed limb, and very often they escaped. Even the dull cattle heard his approach and eluded him, or shook him from their backs when he attacked.

Because of his disability he became thin and emaciated, and he was faced with starvation. He—the big maned tiger—was forced to try to catch the rats that ran in the bamboo trees, and even they escaped him.

The only living things that were not too fast for him were the slimy frogs in the pools of scum-covered water stagnating here and there in the jungle, and the sharp-shelled crabs by the water's edge—and men. Sheer necessity, and nothing else, drove him to this new diet of human flesh.

These are the facts about this tiger as I gathered them from time to time. The nature of his wound I only discovered for myself when years later I examined him after I had shot him.

Thus one day a man alighted at Anandapuram bus-stand and began a jungle journey to a tiny hamlet three miles away. He had left the previous morning to go to Shimoga town, and had told his wife to keep his midday meal ready for him the next day, as he would be back in time. The meal was prepared accordingly, but he did not appear. This caused no untoward alarm in the little household because the settlement of business affairs in India, particularly in the lesser towns, is often protracted. Time is of little or no consequence in the East.

Even that evening he did not turn up, nor during the whole of the following day. On the third day his eldest son, a grown lad, was sent to Shimoga to find out what had delayed his father. There he was told that the transaction had been completed three days earlier and that his father had left to return to his home.

Still no untoward anxiety was felt, as it was thought he might have gone to Sagar, which is beyond Anandapuram, in connection with the same affair.

Five days thus passed without a sign, when the family became really anxious and alarmed. The consensus of opinion was that he had been set upon and robbed by *badmashes* or dacoits on his way home through the jungle and probably killed. The police were informed and a search was made, which brought to light a slipper lying among the bushes beside the track to the hamlet where he lived.

The old slipper was identified by the household as belonging to the missing man, and that gave further credence to the dacoit theory. Several known depredators (K.D.s) living in Anandapuram were taken to the police station and questioned. They avowed their innocence.

A closer and wider search was then made. Shreds of clothing and dried blood-marks were discovered on thorns and bushes, and across the dry bed of a *nullah* the pug-marks of a tiger. Thereafter, no traces were apparent.

Tigers are—or rather were in those years—quite common in those areas, and as there was no direct evidence to connect the pug-marks with the missing man, there was only a very vague suspicion that a tiger might have had anything to do with his disappearance. The presence of the pug-marks might have been purely coincidental.

The mystery was never solved.

A fortnight later a lone cyclist was pedalling the four miles from Kumsi to Chordi. Half a mile from his destination the road crosses the river by a bridge. A parapet of limestone—or *chunam* as it is called—flanks the road. Looking over as he was riding along, the cyclist saw a tiger drinking almost below him. He was at a safe distance from the animal so, applying his brakes, he sat in his saddle with one foot on the parapet and watched the tiger.

The tiger finished drinking, turned and began to reclimb the bank. In a couple of seconds he would disappear in the undergrowth, so for the fun of it the cyclist shouted 'Shoo-shoo'. The tiger stopped, looked backwards over his shoulder and up at the cyclist, snarled and growled loudly.

Very hastily, the man removed his foot from the parapet, applied it to the pedal, and rode as fast as he could to Chordi, where he told his friends that along the road he had met a very nasty tiger indeed which had tried to attack him. Only by God's grace had he escaped.

There was a lull for the next month or so, and then occurred the first authenticated human killing. This happened at a place called Tuppur, which is almost midway between Chordi and Anandapuram. It is a little roadside hamlet, and one of the women had taken her buffalo down to the stream behind the village so that it might take its morning bath. It appears that the buffalo was lying in the water with only its head above the surface, as is the usual habit with buffaloes, when a tiger attacked the woman who was sitting on the bank watching her protégé. Another woman from the village had just drawn water from the stream and had spoken a few words to the woman sitting beside her buffalo and was passing on. She had scarcely gone a hundred yards when she heard a piercing shriek and looked back in time to see a tiger walking off with her erstwhile companion in his mouth.

Tiger and victim vanished into the jungle while the other woman threw down her water-pot and raced for the huts.

What happened was usual with most incidents of this kind. Considerable time elapsed in collecting a sufficient number of men brave enough to go out to look for the woman. Eventually this was done and they found her, or rather what was left of her.

That was the beginning, and thereafter followed a sequence of human victims, whose deaths took place as far away as the road leading to the Bombay Bungalow near the Jog Falls on the further side of the Sharavati river.

Officialdom moves slowly, and it was a considerable time before the reserved forests in these regions were thrown open to the public for shooting this beast.

A number of enthusiasts turned up and the Bombay Presidency was well represented amongst them. They tried hard and diligently, but luck did not come their way. This particular tiger did not seem to be tempted by the cattle and buffaloes tied up as live bait. Meanwhile the human killings continued.

A friend of mine named Jack Haughton, who went by the nickname of 'Lofty' for the very reason that he was about six foot four inches tall and proportionately broad made up his mind to have a try at shooting this animal and asked me to accompany him. As far as I can remember, this trip was undertaken about one year after the tiger had turned man-eater.

It so transpired that for some reason or the other—most probably because I had already used the leave due to me—

I went with him for only a week, telling him I would have to return after that time. We travelled in his 1931 'A' Model Ford car, and the arrangement was that I should return to Bangalore by train after the week had expired, while he would remain for a full month or so.

We motored from Bangalore to Shimoga and stopped there for half a day in order to visit the district Forest Officer, Sagar Forest Range, where these killings had been taking place, to find out the names of the different places where people had been attacked and the exact dates of those attacks, in order to establish, if possible, by studying the sequence of the attacks, the precise 'beat' being followed by this tiger.

I have already explained that man-eating tigers generally pursue a definite course or itinerary when they become man-eaters. By noting the names of the villages or localities where they kill on a map, with the date of each incident, it is frequently possible to work out the beat for oneself, and forecast roughly in which direction or area the tiger may be at about the time one undertakes to try and bag him.

Our study of events on a map indicated very clearly that this tiger kept within a few miles of the roadside and operated up and down between Kumsi and the further bank of the Sharavati river, as far as the Bombay Bungalow.

This is a very densely forested region with many scattered hamlets, whose occupants are almost entirely devoted to grazing big herds of cattle. A large number of these animals are always killed in these areas each month by both tigers and panthers, so this fact made it difficult to find out whether our man-eater also killed cattle or not. We felt that it was almost certain he did so, as the human kills were too few and far between for him to have subsisted only on a human diet. Our opinion was quite contrary to the local one, which was that he would not touch any domestic animals.

Lofty chose to make his camp at a small forest bungalow situated half a mile from the Tuppur hamlet. It is a picturesque little lodge, standing in the jungle about two hundred yards from the roadside, and the forest in the vicinity is crammed with game, particularly spotted deer. In that year some of the stags carried magnificent heads and we came across quite a few outstanding specimens.

Lofty started operations in the routine fashion by buying three animals for bait. Two of them were young buffaloes, and the other a very old and decrepit bull. One buffalo was tied near the stream where the cyclist had seen the tiger. The aged bull was tied at about the spot where the woman of Tuppur had been carried off. The remaining buffalo we had taken and tied near Anandapuram along the same *path* that the man who had disappeared had been following on his way home.

Having completed these arrangements, we motored on to Jog and arranged two baits there—both buffaloes—tying one of them half a mile or so from the Bombay bungalow and the other on the southern bank of the Sharavati, near the spot where the river is crossed by a ferry plying between the bungalow on the Mysore bank and the Bombay bungalow. This ferry crosses the river about a mile above the waterfalls.

Lofty had therefore five baits in all, and I remember they cost him quite a bit of money. The plan was that we should spend alternate nights at the Tuppur forest lodge and the Bombay bungalow, checking the baits closest to the place where we had spent the previous night before setting out by car for the bungalow where we would spend the next night.

My calculations, made by the method of checking the dates of the human kills, which were now nine in number, seemed to indicate that this tiger might be somewhere in the middle of this region between Sagar and Anandapuram.

So on the third day I bought a buffalo myself, which I then tied up about halfway between these two places and within a furlong of the main road. We tied this animal about two in the afternoon on our way from the Tuppur bungalow to Jog.

Very early next morning we looked up the two baits tied in the vicinity of the waterfalls. Both were alive. So we set out for Tuppur, halting en route to visit the buffalo I had tied up the previous afternoon. It had been killed by a tiger.

Lofty, being a good sportsman and considering the fact that I had paid for this buffalo, insisted that I should take the shot. But I knew how keen he was and so quite an argument arose. Finally we tossed for it, and Lofty won.

Leaving him up a tree, sitting uncomfortably perched in a fork, I drove to Tuppur lodge to fetch his *machan*, which we had both most thoughtlessly forgotten to take with us on that important day. Lofty's contraption was nothing more than a square bamboo frame about four feet each way, interlaced with broad navaree tape. At each of the four corners was a loop of stout rope which helped when tying the affair to a tree. I also brought three men from Tuppur hamlet along with me to assist in putting up this *machan*.

We ate a cold lunch by the roadside while the men made a good job of fixing the *machan* and camouflaging it with branches. Lofty then had a nap in the back seat of the car till four o'clock, while I chatted with the three men. This was because, being close to the road, we knew the tiger would not put in an appearance before nightfall.

At four I woke him up and he climbed into the *machan* with all his equipment. His weapon was a 8 mm Mauser rifle—a really neat and well-balanced job—which Lofty affectionately calls 'Shorty Bill'. Wishing him good luck and saying I would be back by dawn, I drove to Tuppur, where

I left the three men and then returned part of the way to spend the night at the small dak bungalow at Anandapuram, which was closer to where I had left Lofty over the dead buffalo.

By break of day next morning I had reached the spot on the road opposite where he was sitting and tooted the horn of the car. He coo-eed back to me, which was the signal we had agreed upon before parting to signify that all was well.

I set out for his tree and met him halfway, walking towards the car. He told me the good news that he had shot the tiger, which had turned up much earlier the previous evening than we had expected, arriving just after dark.

I was very happy at his success, while Lofty himself was in raptures and simply bubbling over with joy and excitement. I went with him to see the tiger, which was a beautiful large male in the prime of life and handsomely marked with bold, dark stripes.

But I noticed that the he was a very normal tiger. He certainly did not possess the distinctive mane which the official government notification had said was the outstanding characteristic of the man-eater. I was surprised to find that in his enthusiasm over his own success Lofty had apparently quite overlooked this fact and I just did not have the heart to tell him.

I congratulated him very heartily on his success and tried my best to appear sincere. Then leaving him to guard his precious trophy, I motored back to Tuppur to bring four men and a bamboo pole for lifting the carcass.

Returning with the men, we tied the feet of the tiger to the pole and carried him upside down to the car. As Lofty had no proper carrier at the back that was strong enough to support the weight, we spread-eagled the carcass across the bonnet of the car, not only bending the metal in the process, but making it very difficult to drive as, in spite of his height,

Lofty could not see the road ahead for some yards because of the body on the bonnet.

In driving through Anandapuram, Lofty stopped to exhibit his prize to the townsfolk who crowded around, and it was then that disillusionment very cruelly came to him. For, no sooner did the people look at the tiger than they exclaimed: 'But, *Sahib*, this is not the man-eater.' 'Of course it is,' replied Lofty indignantly. 'What other tiger can it be? And in any case, how are you so sure it is not the man-eater?' 'Where is the mane?' they asked in justification.

'The mane?' Lofty looked blank at first. Then understanding crept into his eyes. Finally he looked at me accusingly. 'I forgot all about the mane,' he admitted. 'I have shot the wrong tiger. You knew all the time?'

'Yes, Lofty, I knew,' I admitted. 'But you were so happy when I met you this morning and you told me you had bagged the man-eater, that I just did not have the heart to disillusion you. The mane was the first thing I looked for. Of course, there was nothing else you could have done but shoot.' And then, to make it seem more convincing, I hastily added: 'After all, the tiger came when it was dark, and you could not look for a mane even by torch-light. In any case, it is a magnificent specimen and a trophy to be proud of; so cheer up, old chap.'

But Lofty was not so easily consoled. We drove to Tuppur, where I found him so disheartened as not to be in the least interested in supervising the skinning of the tiger, which he left entirely to me. I watched the men at work while Lofty lay moping in an armchair. Several times I tried to buck him up by drawing his attention to the large teeth and claws of the animal, its dark markings and other aspects, but he was not at all interested and refused to be drawn into conversation. He just said: 'Had I known it was not the man-eater I would not have shot the poor brute.'

Instead of throwing off his gloom, Lofty got more gloomy as the day wore on. Then he announced that, if no kills had taken place by next morning, he would like to return to Bangalore.

We were up early next day, but the three baits at our end of the line were all unharmed. Accordingly, we resold them to their previous owners, as already arranged, at about a quarter of the price which Lofty had paid for them. Then we drove to the Jog end of the beat, but both buffaloes were alive there also. We made the same deal with their owners as we had done at Tuppur, and late afternoon saw us in the 'A' Model on our way back to Bangalore.

For some time after this I did not come across any news of this tiger. It was over a year later, I think, that I read in the papers that a charcoal-burner had been killed and wholly eaten by a tiger quite near to Kumsi town and almost by the roadside.

So I wrote to the district Forest Officer (D.F.O.) at Shimoga, requesting him to keep me informed about future kills by telegram if possible.

The forests of Shimoga district, unlike those to the south-west of Mysore state, and in the Madras and Chittoor districts, are heavily sprinkled with villages and hamlets, and widely interspersed with cultivation, particularly great stretches of paddy-fields. The roads are also far more used, both by vehicular and pedestrian traffic. Because of all this, not only may a tiger be anywhere at all and difficult to locate, but tracking is left to the individual hunter's own skill. It is a strange fact that no aboriginal forest tribes inhabit this area, unlike the other jungles of India. The only people who go into the forests are coolies, of Malayalee origin, hired in large numbers from the West Coast of India. Next to them in number are the Lambanis. These last are the 'gypsy tribe' of

India, who strangely resemble their Romany cousins in the western world. But only the women are distinctive in appearance. They are lighter in colour than the local people and dress picturesquely, with many ornaments, big, white bone bangles, necklaces of beads of all colours, shapes and sizes, noserings, earrings and rings on their fingers and rings on their toes. They do not wear the saree in the same fashion as the other women of India, but a distinctive costume, made up of a very widely-skirted sort of petticoat, covered by a very tightly-fitting backless jacket, often displaying an ill-restrained bosom, over which a large shawl-like cloth is draped that covers the head and shoulders. The two halves of their jackets are held together by strings at the back.

The Lambani men, on the other hand, are darker than the women and dress very ordinarily. In fact, almost exactly like the rest of the local villagers, who are Kanarese. They wear rather nondescript loose turbans, and very ordinary or dirty-white cotton shirts, covering short pants or a loin-cloth tied high about their waists. Their knees and calves are generally uncovered, but rough leather sandals protect their feet against thorns.

A curious fact is that the men and women among the gypsies of southern India do not resemble each other in either facial or other physical appearances. Most of the women are as graceful and handsome in features as the men are ungraceful and plain.

They are an outstanding tribe of people and have preserved their individuality very strongly throughout the centuries. I am myself surprised at this, as the laziness of the men is such that one would have expected their tribal distinctiveness to have died away generations ago. It is entirely to the women that must go the praise for prizing their own traditions, and their picturesque dress and appearance, keeping the tribe and its customs so well-defined throughout the years.

These Lambanis, as a whole, are nomads and do not stay in one place for long. They prefer their own encampments of small grass huts in cleared spaces to life in the regular villages. As a rule they are not of much worth and they certainly do not excel as trackers. At the same time, the credit must be accorded to them of being far more cooperative than the local Kanarese.

Among the Lambanis, both men and women are hard drinkers, distilling their own very potent liquor from the bark of the *babul* tree; or from rice, bananas and brown sugar combined; or from the *jamun* fruit after it has been soaked in sugar; or, for that matter, from almost any material they can find—and they are most ingenious at discovering sources.

They will work more willingly in return for wages in kind—mainly food and drink—than for money, which in any case will be mostly spent in purchasing liquor, if they are unable to make it for themselves. However, they are a nice people, and one of India's finest exhibits among the very many interesting races and tribes of curious and distinctive appearance.

The coffee plantations and orange estates in western Mysore owe much to the Lambanis, particularly the women, who form the bulk of the labour employed by them. The remainder of the labour comes from the West Coast—from people of Malayalam and Moplah stock. These west-coast coolies have one trait in common. They are bound by unbreakable bonds to their homes among the coconut trees, lagoons, rivers and breakers that tumble on the western shores. It is indeed a beautiful country, and I can well understand their fondness for it. Lack of industry and lack of work of any definite sort drives them into the interior in search of employment. But no sooner have they earned and saved some more—for, unlike the Lambanis, they are very thrifty—then back they go to their homeland to enjoy some months of lazy comfort. This universal characteristic makes them rather unreliable as plantation coolies, because one cannot be sure of their regular attendance unless a portion of their pay is held back as a sort of bond. The law forbids this practice to estate-owners, while on the other hand the usual system is to grant advances to the coolies to enable them to buy stocks of gram and other foodstuffs, blankets and odds and ends. As can well be imagined, this is welcomed by the Malayalee coolies, who draw their pay and whatever advances they can collect and then disappear on French leave to their coast-land areas.

And so the planters encourage, and have come to rely upon, the humble and picturesque Lambani gypsy as a mainstay on the estates. For them he has become almost a 'must'.

My personal interest in this state of affairs lay only in the fact that I would have to rely almost solely on my own initiative if and when I went after this tiger. As good as they are as estate-workers, Lambanis are not on a par with the other aboriginal jungle tribes—like the Poojarees, Sholagas, Karumbas and Chenchus—in tracking and general jungle lore. I only wished this tiger was operating in one of the other forest districts where I had willing and experienced helpers to rely upon.

A month or so after writing to the D.F.O. at Shimoga I received from him a letter of thanks and the news that the tiger had attacked and killed a woman who had been gathering leaves from the teak trees that grew by the roadside about midway between Kumsi and Chordi.

For the benefit of those who have not seen the teak tree or its leaves, I should tell you that the latter are large in size and tough in fibre. They do not tear easily. Hence they are much favoured for the manufacture of leaf-plates, on which meals, particularly rice, are served in Indian hotels. Some four or five teak leaves go to make one such plate, which is an enormous affair by all Western standards. They are joined together at the edges, either by being stitched with a needle and thread, or more frequently by being pinned together with two-inch-long bits of 'broom-grass'. These plates are required in hundreds of thousands to supply the demands of the many eating-houses in Mysore state. Hence their manufacture forms quite an industry in some of the localities where teak trees grow in abundance. The Forest department sells the right of plucking these leaves to contractors, who bid at an auction for that right. The contractors in turn employ female labour and pay the women a certain sum of money per thousand good leaves plucked. Women are hired for this work rather than men as they ask only about half the rate.

The D.F.O. concluded his long missive with a statement expressing his hope that I would come to Kumsi to try and kill the man-eater.

The extent of the area in which the tiger operated, and even more the other conditions I have already explained at some length, made me feel that the quest was pretty hopeless at this stage. Also the question of leave was a great problem. Searching for a tiger under such circumstances might take several weeks, if not some months.

So I set myself the task of writing a very diplomatic reply. While profusely thanking the Forest Officer for his letter, I endeavoured to convince him of the time factor involved in trying to locate or pin down the man-eater in any particular locality. I explained that I did not have the time to spare just then to undertake a prolonged trip. I also suggested that he inform all forest stations and police stations in the area to warn the inhabitants to beware of the man-eater, and to move in daylight only and in groups, keeping to the main roads; also that grazers and contractors' coolies should temporarily cease operation. Should another human kill occur, I suggested he ask the police, as well as his own subordinates, to urge the relatives of the unfortunate victim to leave his or her remains untouched and send me a telegram. I also suggested that the Forestry department might materially help by sanctioning the purchase of half-a-dozen buffaloes, and to tie them out at intervals along the area where the tiger operated. I promised to come, upon receiving telegraphic news of a fresh victim, be it animal or human, on the condition that the body of the victim had been allowed to remain where the tiger last left it.

Back came the response to this letter on the third day. It deeply regretted that I had been unable to come, and added that it would be impossible to ensure that all the villagers living in such a wide area followed the precautions I had suggested. Further, relatives would not consent to the body of the loved one being left out in the jungle as a bait to entice the man-eater to return. They would demand that they should remove and cremate it at once. Lastly, he said that there was no provision under the rules whereby the Forestry department could undertake the expense of buying six live buffaloes for tiger-bait.

Of course, I had anticipated the replies I would receive to these two suggestions. As a matter of fact, I had merely made them to bring home indirectly the problem I was up against in looking for the tiger, which was like searching for a needle in a haystack. That first letter, asking me to come to Kumsi at once, gave the impression that the writer had perhaps overlooked some of the snags involved, and I wanted him to appreciate my side of the picture.

Nothing more happened for the next few weeks and then the man-eater struck again, this time making a double-kill between Chordi and Tuppur. News of this tragedy came to me in a telegram from the D.F.O.—quite a long one—which stated that the tiger had attacked a woodcutter and his son on the high road opposite the Karadibetta Tiger Preserve near Chordi. He had killed the man and carried off the son. Would I please come at once?

The Karadibetta Tiger Preserve borders the northern side of the road here. It is a large block of teak and mixed jungle, set aside by the order of His Highness the Maharaja of Mysore and the state Forestry department to provide a Sanctuary, where shooting is not allowed.

The enlightened ruler of this state, with the advice and cooperation of his far-sighted and equally enlightened chief conservator, has allocated forest blocks in different districts of Mysore state as game sanctuaries for the preservation of wild life. In such places, shooting is strictly forbidden. This advanced policy of Mysore state was a brilliant example to the rest of India of how a far-sighted ruler and his able assistant have pioneered in game-preservation. Such initiative may well be emulated throughout the subcontinent, where wild life of every kind is being rapidly shot out.

In this particular case perhaps, the man-eater had broken the rules of the game by taking refuge in the Sanctuary, intended to be the home of well-behaved normal tigers. I thought I would go and see for myself, as it was significant that the majority of human kills had occurred between Kumsi and Anandapuram. The Karadibetta Sanctuary is almost at the hub of this area.

I left Bangalore very early in the morning next day, after getting together the necessary kit for a ten-day stay in the jungle, which was the longest I could afford to be absent from town. Owing to large sections of the road being under construction for concreting, it was two o'clock in the afternoon

243

before I could reach the D.F.O. at Shimoga, where I halted briefly to thank him for his communications.

He was good enough to afford me still further assistance by handing me two letters addressed to his subordinates, the Forest Range Officers stationed at Kumsi and at Chordi. One directed them to render me all possible help, particularly in purchasing live baits, which is sometimes a bit difficult in Mysore state, while the other ordered them to permit me to go armed into the game sanctuary at Karadibetta in pursuit of the man-eater.

Once more I thanked him and then hastened on to drive the sixteen miles to Kumsi. The range officer there, after reading his superior's letter, assured me of the utmost cooperation and said he would come along in the car with me to Chordi to meet his brother officer, the ranger stationed at that place.

We covered the next few miles in a short time. The range officer at Chordi was a Mangalore Christian; that is to say, he came from the town of Mangalore on the West Coast, one of the earliest seats of Christianity in India. He was most enthusiastic about helping me, and called his subordinates at once and asked them to summon the other woodcutters who had witnessed the incident in order that I might talk to them.

These men arrived after a few minutes and related the following story.

A contractor at Shimoga had recently purchased the right to fell trees in a certain sector of the forest, a mile from Tuppur for charcoal-burning. He engaged the services of both of them, as well as of the woodcutter who had been killed and his seventeen-year-old son. They all had their homes in Shimoga, but had decided to live temporarily at Chordi village while the felling operations in the area lasted.

They had risen early in the morning of the day when the killing had taken place—which was now two days earlier—and had set forth to walk the three miles to where the felling was being done. They were passing by the Karadibetta block, which was on their right-hand side, when the son asked his father for a 'pan' leaf to chew.

I would like to interrupt my story here for a minute or two, for the benefit of those who do not know what the 'pan' leaf is. It is the longish heart-shaped leaf of the betelvine creeper and is a great favourite among all classes of people in southern India, more particularly among the labourers. It is made into what is known as a 'beeda'. On the outspread leaf some 'chunam' or white lime is placed, together with three to four tiny pieces of the areca-nut, which is called 'supari', perhaps a few shreds of coconut and some sugar. The betel—or 'pan-leaf', as it is called—is then wrapped around the ingredients and well chewed. The white lime and the 'supari' causes saliva to flow copiously and colours it blood red. As they walk along chewing, these peopole expectorate freely, leaving blood-red marks from their saliva on walls, pavements, and indeed everywhere. Europeans, who are newcomers to India and see traces of these marks everywhere, are generally thunderstruck at what they sometimes think to be the large number of cases of advanced tuberculosis in the country.

Returning to our story. The father stopped to hand the leaf to his son. To do so, he first had to remove it from the corner of his *loincloth* where it had been kept tied up in a knot. Meanwhile, the other two men had walked on. They heard a roar and looked back to see the son lying on the road with a tiger on top of him, while the amazed father stood by, his hand still extended in the act of offering the pan to his son.

They then saw the father perform a magnificent art—which was to be the last of his life and the supreme sacrifice. The old man rushed forward, waving his arms about, shouting at the tiger to frighten it off. What happened next was very quick.

The tiger left the boy for a moment and whisked around on the father, leaping upon him and biting fearfully and audibly at the man's throat and chest. Blood gushed like a fountain from the father's gaping wounds. Then leaving him lying on the road, the tiger leaped back upon the son, who was sitting up dazedly watching his father being done to death.

At that juncture the spell was broken and the two men turned tail and ran as fast as they could to Tuppur, nor did they once look back to see what had happened to the boy or his father after the last scene they had witnessed.

Tuppur, as I related, is quite a small hamlet. Besides, nobody there possessed a firearm. So a dozen men set forth to Anandapuram to tell the police and call someone with a gun.

It chanced that on the way they met a lorry going towards Chordi to collect sand from the stream where it passed under the bridge, at the spot where the cyclist had seen a tiger some time previously.

The men stopped the lorry and asked the driver to turn around and take them quickly to Anandapuram so that they could report what had happened. But the driver was an exceptionally bold individual, or at least appeared to be so. If they would all get into his lorry, he would drive down the road to the spot where this 'fairy-tale'—as he openly described it—had taken place. Then they would all see what they would see. 'What about the tiger?' somebody had asked. 'You have an open truck. Supposing it jumps in amongst us and kills some of us?' 'Brother,' the driver had announced, stoutly, 'I am here; so you have nothing and no one to fear. Do you think I shall be idle, waiting for the tiger to jump? I shall run my truck over the brute in a jiffy.'

Thus encouraged by the brave words of the driver, the twelve men had climbed on to the lorry. Very soon they had reached the spot. I was told the driver was really surprised when he saw the father lying on the road in a great pool of his own blood—quite dead by that time. He had thought the whole story had been concocted from beginning to end.

Of the son there was absolutely no trace.

The driver had lost a good deal of his self-confidence by this time. The thirteen men stopped long enough to put the dead body of the elder woodcutter into the lorry. Then they had driven to Chordi at top speed. There they had picked up the range officer and driven on to Kumsi where, after some slight delay, they were reinforced by the Kumsi range officer and the sub-inspector of police. The whole party had proceeded in the lorry to Shimoga where detailed reports were made to the police and to the Forestry department. A perfunctory post-mortem, for the sake of formalities, was held on the woodcutter and his body was handed over to his relatives late that night.

Next day a party of armed police returned in the same truck to look for the son. It was said that a blood trail could be seen, and a drag-mark where the man-eater had carried his victim through the bushes and into the game sanctuary. After that, nobody appeared to be competent enough in woodcraft to follow the trail, so that the police party returned to Shimoga that evening to report that they had failed to recover the body of the son.

And that, as far as I could see, was the complete story of the Tiger's latest exploit, as I was able to gather the details from the two woodcutters who had been eye-witnesses to the whole episode and the subsequent events.

The Chordi range officer served coffee, after which he and his colleague who had accompanied me from Kumsi, together with the two woodcutters and myself, set out for the scene of the attack on the roadside opposite the Karadibetta Tiger Preserve.

I had often travelled along this road before, and this was the second occasion on which a tiger I was after had taken refuge within this game sanctuary. The first time had been when a wounded animal from the village of Gowja had made for the sanctuary, and I was able to bag it just before it had entered within the boundary, which story I have related elsewhere.*

The range officers had visited the place already and were able to point to the exact spot where the tiger had made his attack on the father and son. Traffic had been considerable and all traces of blood had been obliterated during the intervening three days under the wheels of the many buses, trucks, private cars and bullock-carts that had traversed the road.

The sanctuary itself starts a few yards from the road in the form of a teak plantation. The trees at that time were of nearly uniform height, about twenty feet tall, having been planted in straight lines by the Mysore Forestry department some ten to fifteen years previously. The plantation extended thickly into the sanctuary for about two furlongs before it gave way abruptly to the natural jungle.

Tracking beneath the teak trees, for traces of a wounded animal leaving a distinct blood trail, is next to impossible. The ground is carpeted with fallen and dried leaves which take or leave no impression. In this case, the boy the man-eater had carried had apparently bled but little. Although the

---

* See *Nine Man-eaters and One Rogue* (Allen & Unwin, London).

woodcutters pointed out the exact spot where the beast and its victim had disappeared, we were able with diligent searching to find only three places where blood had dripped on to the teak leaves. It was not worth wastig time on a further search.

I knew the sanctuary extended northwards to a stream and cart-track that connected the village of Gowja on the west with another village named Amligola to the east. The cart-track and stream formed the northern boundaries of the sanctuary proper, although the jungle itself extended for many more miles. A wise plan appeared to be to tie four live-baits on the four boundaries of the sanctuary, and another at its centre, as I had obtained special permission to shoot this tiger within this hallowed area if occasion arose.

I told the two range officers (R.O.) that I would need their cooperation in procuring these five baits, as past experience in this area made me rather sceptical of being able to get as many as five animals because the people opposed the sacrifice of cattle as baits and would not cooperate. They told me not to worry and that they would have the baits sent to me by nine o'clock the following morning.

At Kumsi is a forest lodge—the one at which the emergency operation had been performed to amputate the arm of the Reverend Jervis after being mauled by a tiger. I decided to camp at this bungalow, and asked the Kumsi R.O. to let me see the baits he could get before having them driven to Chordi to join the others which his counterpart at Chordi had undertaken to procure. I did this because I am quite particular about the live-baits I use. Very sick or aged cattle, already close to death's door, are often palmed off to a *sahib* as bait. He then wonders why the tiger does not readily kill them. But the tiger is a *shikari* and a gentleman, like the *sahib* himself, and not a jackal to be satisfied with a diseased bag of bones.

My companions had been very fidgety while I had been talking about the baits, for it was six o'clock and the shades of night were fast approaching. I had not been unduly nervous, however, as I knew we were safe as long as the five of us kept close together. We threaded our way through that dense teak plantation in a very closely-knit bunch, I can assure you, till we regained the car standing on the road. It did not take long to drop the Chordi officer and the two woodcutters at the former's residence, and we were back at Kumsi in less than fifteen minutes.

I slept soundly at the forest lodge that night and went across early next morning to the R.O.'s quarters to see how he was getting along with the job of buying the baits. Despite his confidence of the evening before, I felt that with all his influence as a local forest officer, he had underestimated the difficulties he faced. It was as well I went there, for he had not yet started on the job.

To cut a long story short, it was past 10 a.m. before he had got three animals together. One was a buffalo-calf. The two others were scraggy old bulls. I did not at all approve of the latter, but the R.O. said it was the best he could do. Moreover, they cost me quite a lot of money.

We assigned three men to do the task of driving them along the four-mile stretch of road to Chordi and set off for that place in my car at eleven, reaching our destination just ahead of the three animals.

The Chordi R.O. had procured a half-grown bull—quite a nice animal, brown in colour—and said the second bait in the quota that he was to fill had been sent for that morning and was coming soon. It took an hour to arrive, and it was twelve-thirty before we had all five animals together. Half the day had already been wasted.

As a result, we were able to tie out only three of them that day. The best, the half-grown brown bull, I tied in approximately the centre of the sanctuary. The buffalo-calf was tied a few yards inside from the road to the south, where the attack had been made. The bait on the eastern flank of the sanctuary, which was incidentally about five miles north of Chordi, was one of the old white bulls.

Again it was sunset by the time we had finished, and I left the remaining two animals at Chordi, saying I would return very early the next morning to select the places to tie them out, which you remember were to be the remaining two sides of the rough rectangle formed by the sanctuary, on its northern and western flanks.

Before dawn next day I was motoring back to Chordi along with my friend the Kumsi R.O., who had been up and ready, waiting for me. A large sambar stag ran across the road about halfway to our destination and he remarked that it was a lucky sign.

At Chordi, the R.O. there said he would accompany me to tie out the remaining two baits, and he instructed his subordinate, a forester, to take two forest guards and one of the men who had been with us the previous day, and so knew where they were located, to see if the baits to the east and the south of the sanctuary were alive. We ourselves would look up the third one, tied out in the centre of the sanctuary, as we would make a short cut through it before turning off to the western and northern boundaries. We all set out together, and it was over an hour and a half later that we came to the bull-calf I had tied near the middle of the sanctuary. It was alive and well.

You must not overlook the fact that in tying each live-bait, the question of feeding and watering it each day had to be considered also. To feed it is not much trouble as a bundle of hay or grass is sent along for its consumption each twenty-four hours, but watering often provides quite a problem. Of course a pot or a kerosene tin might be provided and refilled with water each day, but this method has its own snags. Invariably the animal knocks over the receptacle, or breaks it if it happens to be a pot, while the proximity of a kerosene tin often makes a tiger too suspicious to attack. So the best method is for the men who visit the bait each day to untie it and lead it to some pool or stream, water it there and then bring it back. Rarely, however, does such a pool or stream happen to be handy for the purpose, and frequently the beast has to be led for a mile or more to a suitable place. Villagers are mostly lazy and apathetic by nature, and they generally feel such a long walk is unnecessary. In their logic, the animal has been tied out to be killed, anyhow. So why worry about watering it? This is a point that all hunters who tie out live-baits in India should bear in mind. If they do not supervise these daily visits, or at least employ reliable men to do the work for them, and should a tiger or panther not make a kill, it is almost a certainty that the poor bait has spent a very parched and thirsty week, unless the place where they have tied him has water close by, or it has been provided in a container.

In the present case there was a stream half-a-mile away. We led the animal there, allowed it to drink its fill and then brought it back.

You may wonder if it is not easier to tie the bait beside a stream or pond to overcome this problem of watering it. Very often this is done, as the tigers themselves visit such spots to drink. But there are other factors, too, to be considered. *Nullahs,* game-trails, fire-lines and certain footpaths, cart-tracks and even sections of roads, along which tigers are known to walk frequently, are equally good places to tie up, and may have an added advantage of tiger pug-marks being noticed there regularly. The places at which these tracks intersect are even better. Tigers do not always

252

stroll along the banks of streams, especially where streams are many. We had tied this particular bait on a game trail along which tigers often walk, so the Chordi range officer had assured me the previous evening, when we had been searching for a likely place.

We secured the two animals we brought with us to the feet of convenient trees at suitable places on the western and northern boundaries of the sanctuary. But it was past noon before we had finished.

Of course you should not for a moment imagine that, by doing all this, we had completely ringed the tiger within the sanctuary. For the sanctuary extended for miles and it by no means followed that, wherever he came out, he would be confronted by one of my baits. I had only done what was possible under the prevailing conditions, and the rest was left to fate or luck, whichever name you prefer. And fate played a fickle game that day.

It was close on three p.m. and we were on our way back and close to Chordi, when a group of men tilling their fields on the outskirts of the clearing that lay around that hamlet informed us that the forest guards we had sent out that morning had found that the buffalo-calf, tied near the spot where the man-eater had killed the two men, had been killed by a tiger the night before. They said the guards had been unable to get word to us as they did not know exactly which way we had gone or how we would return. So they had told all passers-by to inform us if they happened to meet us on the way.

After hearing this news we hurried back to Chordi, where the two range officers roundly abused the guards for not coming to inform us of what had happened. They were hardly to blame, poor fellows, for we ourselves had been on the move the whole afternoon, and had they come to try and catch up with us they were very likely to have failed and caused still greater delay. In the circumstances, I felt they had done the wisest thing by remaining 'put' at Chordi and sending word by all who passed through the village. In any case, it was not too late to put up a *machan* if we hurried, and the news that they had taken the precaution to cover the kill with branches—against a visit by vultures—caused me to intercede on their behalf.

By 3.30 p.m. my Studebaker was standing on the road to the south, opposite the place at which we were to enter the teak plantation and walk the little distance to where we had tied up the buffalo-calf. In three minutes we had unroped my folding *charpoy* from the luggage-carrier at the back of the car. I had made this *charpoy* quite recently and it was an improvement on the old one, in that the frame was only a little more than half the normal length. It was therefore easy to transport on my luggage-carrier without overlapping the width of the car at either end. Wide khaki *navarre* tape, for comfort and for unobtrusive colouration, was what I sat upon, the bands of tape being interwoven in the manner of a mat. The ends of the tape were permanently looped around the bamboos that formed the rectangular frame. The four legs at the four corners were but a foot long, extending beyond the rectangular frame for about six inches above and below. This was to allow sufficient purchase by which to tie the *machan* to a tree. The whole structure was simple, light, very portable and most comfortable; above all it did not creak at the slightest movement, as did any normal *machan* put together with branches lopped from trees.

Although the average height of the teak trees here was about twenty feet, being comparatively young, there were a few of much greater age and therefore taller; I had tied the buffalo at the foot of one of these, in case the occasion should later arise for putting up a *machan*. There was no other choice in this instance, for there were no other trees than teak growing in that plantation, and as teak trees have their branches fairly high up, it meant that I had to sit at a greater height from the ground than usual.

That confounded tree gave me a devil of a lot of trouble to climb, as there were no branches for the first twelve feet, and I never excelled as a climber of perpendicular poles. However, I stood on the shoulders of one of the forest guards, when all willingly helped to push and shove my legs a little higher till I could get a grip on the first branch and haul myself up. Due to the large size of the teak leaves, it was a simple matter to hide the *machan* completely from view. Moreover, as they were the only leaves growing there, the camouflage arrangements we made were most efficient, in that the *machan* became inconspicuous and blended naturally with the surroundings. The fork of the tree where we had placed the *charpoy* was over twenty feet from the ground.

The calf's neck had been broken and half the beast had been eaten, but there was just about enough left to justify another visit by its killer.

Neither of the range officers could drive a motorcar, nor could the two forest guards, but as the two woodcutters had also come along with us, I told the six of them to push my car at least half-a-mile or more away in order not to alarm the tiger should he cross the road anywhere nearabouts. Actually I had not thought of this until we were unroping the *charpoy* from the car. In any case, the road was more or less level, and the six men should not have too much trouble in trundling my 'Stude' along.

It was just 5 p.m. when they left me on the teak tree, and I figured that in another twenty minutes or so they would have moved the car and the way would be clear for the tiger to cross the road, provided he came from that direction. Perhaps I was being unduly optimistic, and he would not come at all.

Well, he came all right; but it was only at about a quarter past eight, when it was quite dark He gave me quite a lot of time to know beforehand, or rather the herd of spotted deer with their shrill calls, and a barking deer, with his hoarse, guttural 'Khar-r-r Khar-r-r' bark, did this for him. They had announced his passing to all the denizens of the jungle for the last mile or so of his journey. No wonder tigers are reticent animals. The popularity—or is it unpopularity?—that is often forced upon them by the humbler inhabitants of the forest must indeed be embarrassing. On this occasion, I am sure that the tiger had felt more than embarrassed.

Anyway, he came without undue caution, and I could hear his heavy tread crunch the dry fallen teak leaves long before he stood over his kill.

I shone my flashlight and he looked up at me, full in the face. It took about three seconds for me to notice, even in torch-light, that he did not appear to have any distinctive 'mane'. But I could not take the chance and he dropped to a bullet through his heart.

I waited fifteen minutes, just to make sure he was dead. He did not stir and I was sure. So I descended, having to jump the last seven or eight feet down from that infernal tree. I am perhaps heavier than I should be, and the jolt with which I came to earth did not cause me to think kindly of the practice of leaping from trees. I approached the dead tiger and looked carefully. I muttered invectives then. As I had known, even as I fired, this was not the man-eater; for the dead beast had no ruffle of hair at his neck. Once more the culprit had escaped, and once again an inoffensive tiger had paid the penalty. Besides, I would have some explaining to do to the D.F.O. at Shimoga. He had given me special permission to shoot the man-eater in the tiger sanctuary—but definitely not a harmless beast.

Well, it was just too bad.

I regained the road and walked towards Chordi, expecting to come up with my car where the men had pushed and left it. But there was no car on the road.

Poor fellows, I thought. They had misunderstood me and pushed it all the way to Chordi, which was about two miles.

I came to Chordi and to the Ranger's quarters. Both officers were there. I announced that I had shot a tiger, but that I was almost sure it was the wrong tiger, as it had no mane.

It might be the man-eater after all, they argued. Perhaps he had dropped his mane in the last two years. Or perhaps he never had a mane from the very beginning and that the description was only a myth. That was a point, I conceded; but my hopes did not rise.

Then I asked them where they had left my car. Car? Why, sir, they explained, you left it pointing up the road, away from Chordi. We did not know how to turn it towards Chordi, while you had very definitely instructed us to push it away from that spot for at least half-a-mile. We did that, sir, but in the opposite direction.

Well, life is like that, I said under my breath. It has its ups and downs. Tonight was one of those in which the 'ups' predominated—or was it the 'downs'? I could not find the answer.

Some more coffee followed. Then a carrying party assembled with bamboos, lanterns and ropes, and we made our way back. While the men were securing the tiger to fetch it to the road, I walked in the opposite direction and found my car exactly four furlongs away.

We were back at Kumsi in a little over an hour.

Next morning I skinned the tiger, while the two range officers wrote out their official report to the D.F.O. at Shimoga. I had shot a tiger without a ruff, they wrote. It might not be the man-eater. The special permit I had in my possession enjoined that I should shoot the man-eater and nothing else within the boundaries of the Karadibetta Sanctuary. They closed their joint statement by leaving it to their superior officer to 'take such further and necessary actions you best deem fit'.

Then they apologised to me for having had to write such a report.

I waited till my leave was over, but none of the other baits was killed. The D.F.O. at Shimoga wrote to me officially that his rangers had reported I had shot a tiger within the sanctuary which was said not to be the man-eater, whereas the permit handed to me had been for the man-eater and no other animal. Would I please explain?

Now, I have lived all my life in India. As such, the 'redtapism' that goes with all government transactions was well known to me. But I did not get annoyed at receiving the D.F.O.'s comunication. I wrote back an official letter stating that I regretted he had been misinformed that the tiger I had shot was not the man-eater. I affirmed that it was the man-eater itself, and no other tiger, that I had shot within the sanctuary in accordance with the provisions of the special permit that had been so kindly granted to me for that purpose.

So what? Everybody was happy. Official decorum had been amply satisfied on all sides. All concerned had strictly and very properly performed their duties.

The time came for me to return to Bangalore. I thanked the two range officers for their help, sold the remaining four baits back to their owners for less than a quarter of the price I had paid for them, and set out on the homeward journey.

On the way I stopped at Shimoga to pay my respects to the D.F.O. He informed me that I had replied wisely to his letter asking for an explanation and apologised for having written it, saying he had to do so in face of the report that his two range officers had made to him. I told him not to worry and that I was accustomed to such things, adding that it was I who had told the ranger officers that I had shot the wrong tiger when I discovered it had no mane. We parted good friends.

A whole year went by. There had been no more kills since the old man and his son had fallen victims. That had been somewhere about the beginning of the previous year. Or it may have been a few months later—I really forget now. Everyone thought the story of the maned man-eater had been a fable and that I had shot the actual miscreant. I thought so, too, till disillusionment came.

A tiger killed a man on the outskirts of the town of Sagar, which, as I have said, was on the road beyond Kumsi and Anandapuram, before it reached the Jog Falls. A fortnight later he killed a second man near Anandapuram, and then within the next month another man and woman at the villages of Tagarthy and Gowja respectively. Both these places are within a ten-mile radius of Anandapuram. Early in August he carried off a Lambani boy in broad daylight. He had been grazing his cattle close to the main road on the outskirts of Kumsi town.

The man-eater had returned from wherever he had gone after killing the old woodcutter and his son beside the sanctuary, and now was killing in real earnest. Or if it was not him, he had been replaced by another of his kin who was taking human victims at a far faster rate.

I manipulated matters to get a week's leave, which was the most I could manage, and motored to Kumsi. The D.F.O. at Shimoga had been transferred and another officer, whom I did not know, had taken his place. But he wished me success. I enquired of him as to whether the two range officers at Kumsi and Chordi were the same that I had met there early the previous year, and was glad when he answered in the affirmative.

It was a meeting of old friends, therefore, that took place at Kumsi when I met the ranger again at his quarters, and the same a little later at Chordi, when I met his colleague. Both the officers were of the opinion that the present man-eater was quite a different animal, and that I had indeed killed the right tiger over a year previously within the sanctuary. Their reason for saying so was the fact that no human kills had taken place since that time, till within the last couple of months. If I had not shot the man-eater, then where had he been for all those months? Once a man-eater, always a man-eater. A tiger has never been known to give up the habit altogether. So wherever this tiger had strayed, he must have killed at least some human beings during that period and we would have heard of it.

I must say their argument appeared very sound, and I was convinced in spite of myself.

We held a conference over what to do next. This tiger had killed at Sagar, Anandapuram, Tagarthy, Gowja, and now at Kumsi. It was the same area as that over which the other man-eater—the so-called maned tiger, if there had ever been such an animal—had operated two years earlier and more. Where was I to tie my baits? Where should I begin? We could not quite make up our minds.

The matter was decided for us the next day. As luck would have it, the tiger took a herd-boy in broad daylight at Amligola, which you may remember was the terminal point of the northern boundary of the Karadibetta sanctuary at its eastern end. In other words, Amligola formed the northeastern corner of the rough rectangle that was the sanctuary. The forest guards there hastened to report the matter to their R.O. at Chordi headquarters, who came to Kumsi at once to tell me about it. It was 3 p.m. when he arrived.

To reach this place, Amligola, the two range officers and I had to make a detour and follow a very, very rough cart-track beyond Chordi. Amligola boasts a delightful little forest lodge, with the stream that forms the northern boundary of Karadibetta flowing close behind it. This stream empties itself into a large tank about two miles away. The boy had been grazing cattle by the side of that tank. The tiger had walked up the bed of the stream and had attacked the boy at about nine in the morning. He had not touched the cattle, although they were feeding all around the spot where the boy had been standing. After the killing, the tiger had walked back with his victim along this stream and into the jungle.

I was shown the pug-marks of the tiger as it had come towards the boy, and its tracks on the return journey, where a drag-mark, made probably by the boy's feet as they trailed along, could be clearly seen. There was hardly any blood along the trail.

It was late evening by the time we had seen all this, and it had become too dark to try to find the body of the poor youngster. This was a great pity. I chafed at the unfortunate circumstance that had brought the news to us at Kumsi so late. Although we had made every possible effort to arrive earlier, the bad cart-track leading to Amligola had wasted time, as I had not wanted to break a spring or an axle. Had I been able to find the remains that evening, I would have sat up over them for the tiger to return. I cursed my bad luck.

The range officers slept in one room of the forest lodge. I slept in the other. The two guards had gone to a godown which adjoined the kitchen, a separate building to the main bungalow, where they barricaded and bolted the door.

A tiger started calling shortly after midnight. He appeared to be within a mile of us. He called again and the range officers heard it. They tapped on the door that separated our rooms to attract my attention, in case I should be asleep. I opened the door and let them in, telling them that I had been listening to the calls myself.

I then opened the main door leading on to the narrow front verandah of the lodge. Moonlight poured down on the jungle around us, and shone in at one end of the verandah. Only in a tropical land can one ever hope and appreciate to the full the eerie thrill of a moonlit night in a forest. As I gazed outside, drinking in the wonder of it all, the tiger called again, this time much closer. Suddenly I realized that the beast was walking along the bank of the stream that flowed a few yards behind the bungalow and would probably pass within the next ten minutes. Was this the man-eater?

I decided to chance my luck.

It took only a couple of minutes to fix my flashlight on to its two clamps along my rifle barrel. I ran out of the bathroom door at the back of the lodge, brushed through the thin hedge of young casuarina trees that bordered the compound and ran down the slope at the rear that led to the bed of the small stream.

I could see the surface of the water glistening and twinkling in the moonlight, although it was very dark under the trees which grew by the bank on which I stood. I have told you that this stream formed the northern boundary of Karadibetta. The opposite bank was within the sanctuary. The forest lodge and the bank on which I was now standing were just outside its limits.

The tiger called again. It was fast approaching and hardly a quarter of a mile away. I would have to act quickly if I wanted to ambush him.

The all-important question was this: along which bank was he walking? If he was on the opposite or Kardibetta bank, I would have to get much closer to the water's edge if I wanted to see him in the moonlight and get in the shot. On the other hand, if he was coming along the same bank as the one on which I was standing, and if I went down to the edge of the stream, the tiger, when he passed, would have the advantage not only of seeing me silhouetted against the moonlight on the water, but of himself being on more elevated ground. That could be most dangerous and disadvantageous for me if he made a charge.

He called again—about a furlong away. There was no time whatever to lose. I decided to take a chance. Most probably he was on the opposite bank of the stream and within the sanctuary.

Meanwhile my eyes had been searching desperately for a place to hide. A clump of reedgrass grew about two feet from my bank, completely surrounded by water. I knew the stream was shallow, so I ran down to the edge and silently waded the two feet, taking care not to make any splashing noises. Then I squatted low in the grass. Two or three minutes passed in dead silence. I could not see into the deep shadows cast by the trees on either bank.

Then the tiger moaned again directly opposite me—and on the very bank on which I had just been standing. He was passing at that very instant.

I counted, one-two-three-four-five, so as not to have him completely level and above me. Then I pressed the switch on the flashlight. There, hardly fifteen yards away, was his striped form.

He halted in his tracks and turned around. He was facing right side on, so that I had to take the shot behind his right shoulder. He sprang into the air and fell backwards. I fired a second and third time.

Then he realized where I was and came for me, sliding and stumbling down the sloping bank. At a distance of barely five yards, my fourth bullet crashed through his skull.

Later, as I examined him, I marvelled at the unusual ruff of hair growing around his neck. It formed a regular mane.

Some jungle mysteries can never be solved, and one of them is why this tiger had a 'mane' at all.

Nine

Man-eater of Pegepalyam

THIS IS NOT A COMPLETE STORY OF THE EXPLOITS AND DOWNFALL OF a man-eating tiger because the tiger of which I write is very much alive at the moment of writing. There is an official record of it having killed and eaten fourteen persons, although unofficially its tally of victims is said to amount to thirty-seven men, women and children. Of this unofficial estimate about half had actually been wholly or partially eaten, the remainder being just mauled by the animal's claws. The official record considers only individuals killed and eaten, and not those mauled. This accounts for the discrepancy between the official and unofficial death-rolls.

The interesting feature of the story I am about to tell is that I believe this tiger to be the same animal of which I wrote in an earlier book in a story entitled the 'Mauler of Rajnagara'.*

* See *Man-eaters and Jungle Killers* (Alen & Unwin, London).

When writing that account, a tiger had taken up his abode at the foot of the Dimbum escarpment, in the district of North Coimbatore, in the scrub jungle bordering the foot of the hilly plateau and about midway between Dimbum to the north, at the top of the steep ghat road up the hill, and the town of Satyamangalam on the arid plains at the foot, to the south.

The nearest village to the scrub jungles at the foot of the hills bears the name of Rajnagara, and since the tiger began his exploits against the human race by persecuting the herdsmen from this village who led their cattle to pasture in these scrub jungles, he became well known as the tiger of Rajnagara. Moreover, he earned a particular reputation because of a peculiarity in his mode of attack—or at least it was so at the time I wrote that story. The peculiarity lay in the fact that he would rush out of cover and severely maul a herdsman by scratching him with his claws and then invariably carry off his own selection from the herd of cattle which would be milling around during the attack on the herdsman. At that time there was no authentic case of his having bitten any of the human beings he had attacked. One or two persons were listed as missing and it was presumed the tiger had devoured them, but there had been no definite evidence to corroborate that presumption. All that was known was that this tiger always mauled his victims by clawing them—not by biting.

This peculiar habit gave rise to a universal belief that he was an animal that had been wounded in the face or jaw in such a way as to prevent him from biting. At the same time it was found that he generally made a very hearty meal of the cattle he killed after mauling their herdsman, which proved that he could bite and eat perfectly well when he was so disposed. Altogether, it was a most unusual and peculiar case, which has never been satisfactorily explained or proved, although many were the ingenious explanations put forward to account for this habit.

I have related how I tried to shoot this tiger and how I failed. He was a most elusive animal. Finally I returned to my home in Bangalore, leaving the 'Mauler of Rajnagara' the undisputed winner of the first round of our encounter. I sincerely trusted the time would come when there would be an opportunity for staging a second round, when I hoped for better success.

A few friends and well-wishers have since written to me, inquiring if there is any sequel to that story. An old acquaintance of mine, Joe Kearney, went as far as to send me a cablegram from Los Angeles, California, stating he was looking forward to further developments regarding this particular tiger.

Alas, I could not satisfy the curiosity of any of them, for the 'Mauler of Rajnagara' stopped his mauling, and simply faded out shortly after my visit. We all hoped that he had become a reformed character and had perhaps turned over a new leaf with the new year. Or maybe he had just gone away to some distant jungle or even died a natural death. Time passed and the herdsmen of Rajnagara resumed their accustomed cattle grazing in the scrub jungle that surrounded their farmsteads and came home in the evenings, tired but unmauled.

And then, one evening about nine months later, the sun began to set behind the Biligirirangan range of mountains some fifty miles north of Rajnagara, as the crow flies. Its oblique rays cast elongated shadows to the eastern side of the few huts that comprised the little hamlet of Pegepalyam, set in a clearing of the jungle, with the mountain range to its west, and the road from Dimbum to Kollegal flanking it to the east, barely two miles way. It was the time that the cows come home, and within a few furlongs of the village the local herd was wending its way along the forest tracks that led to Pegepalyam; two herdsmen, a man and a boy, were bringing up their rear.

Ravines, densely wooded, intersected the country. In the rainy season they were rushing torrents of water draining away eastwards, after cascading down the mountain range to the west. But on that balmy evening they were bone-dry, and the twitter of *bulbuls* and the rustle of several groups of 'seven-sister' birds lent an air of peace and tranquillity to the scene.

The cattle crossed one of these dips in the terrain, the adult herdsman was halfway across and the boy was on the further bank as it sloped down to the bed of the ravine. A clump of young bamboos surrounded by nodding grass-stems barred his way, and the tracks made by the cattle herd just ahead passed around it, the dust raised by the many hooves as yet unsettled. The boy followed, engrossed in his own thoughts.

The adult herdsman ahead thought he heard a hollow sound, followed by a sort of gasp and turned around to find the cause. There was nothing to be seen. The track behind him led the way to the bamboo clump. Nothing and no one was on it. The herdsman resumed his course in the wake of the herd. No doubt, the boy would come along.

Finally they neared Pegepalyam. The herdsman looked back once more. Again there was no sign of the boy. He called him by name: 'Venkat, Venkat,' he called, but there was no answer. The herdsman hesitated a while and called again, but still there was no response. Meanwhile the cattle were forging ahead towards the village, and as he did not want to leave them alone he followed them into the village. Then only did it become evident that the herdsboy had not turned up.

No serious notice was taken, as there might have been a hundred reasons for the boy's delay. But after an hour or so had passed and the boy had not appeared, the herdsman recollected that he had missed him after the track had circumvented the clump of bamboos. He also remembered the hollow gasping sound he had heard and came to the conclusion that something had happened to the boy. Perhaps he had been bitten by a snake. The thought of a man-eating tiger or panther never entered the herdsman's mind, as such a menace had never yet been heard of in the tranquil vicinity of Pegepalyam.

So he turned back and hastened to the bamboo clump. He circumvented the bend in the track, and there, clearly and boldly superimposed over the hoof-marks of the herd of cattle and his own footprints, were the pug-marks of a tiger, the signs of a brief struggle, and a drag-mark where the killer had hauled away his victim.

And thus the man-eater of Pegepalyam came to public knowledge.

Time passed and desultory human kills were reported from scattered places, southwestwards as far as Talvadi and Talaimalai, perhaps thirty miles away; eastwards at the base of Ponnachimalai hill, and another on the banks of the Cauvery river at Alambadi, over forty miles distant; and one more in a northerly direction, barely six miles from the big town of Kollegal. That one was the latest, being that of a fifteen-year-old boy who was boldly attacked and dragged off the field where he was working at about 10.30 a.m. in blazing sunlight.

A significant fact about this man-eater is the information that was brought in on the occasion of a kill that occurred some three miles from the spot where he had taken his first victim, the herdboy of Pegepalyam. Three men were traversing a cart track that led into the jungle and had formerly been used by carts for extracting felled bamboos from the forest. Because of the activities of the man-eater, such felling operations had been almost suspended, and when people entered the jungle they only did so if it was imperative; never alone and always in broad daylight. These three men had urgent business, which accounted for their presence, their number, and the time of day which was just before two in the afternoon. They had eaten their midday meal at Pegepalyam and had almost reached their destination. They expected to be back by 3.30 p.m. at the latest.

Suddenly and without warning, a tiger sprang on to the track just ahead of the leading man. The party came to a halt, transfixed with terror. Then the tiger attacked the leading man, standing up on his hind legs and clawing his face. His companions made for the nearest tree, which was fortunately close by, and scrambled up it. Meanwhile, with commendable presence of mind and great courage, the man who had been attacked swung blindly at the tiger's head with the knife that all Sholagas carry for lopping wood or clearing a *path* through the undergrowth. The blow caught the animal on the side of its head and glanced off. The tiger roared with pain at this unexpected retaliation, and the natural cowardice with which all man-eaters appear to be imbued caused it to leave its victim and spring back into cover.

Meanwhile the other two men had succeeded in scrambling to the topmost branches of the nearby tree, whence they looked down in terror on the scene below them. Blood poured from the face and chest of their companion, welling from the deep wounds that had been inflicted by the tiger's claws. He was sitting dazedly on the ground, numbed with shock. The men in the tree called to him: 'Brother, come and climb this tree quickly. It is unsafe to remain on the ground. The man-eater may return.'

The wounded man heard them, clambered to his feet and taking the turban from his head, began to mop up the blood that poured from the many scratches he had received. Again the men on the tree called to him, and he turned to walk towards its base with the intention of climbing. But fate had decreed that his days on this earth had run out. The man-eater's momentary cowardice had been supplanted by rage, probably caused by pain from the wound where the brave man's knife had cut through the skin on the side of his head. With a rush it was upon him, and this time a mighty blow of his foreleg across the back of the man's head broke the neck. Hardly had his body fallen to the ground than the tiger picked him up in his jaws and walked into the jungle in full view of the two men in the tree.

I visited Kollegal and Pegepalyam soon after this incident and spoke to both these men. Their accounts were unusually consistent with each other's and clear in detail. They both agreed that on both occasions when the tiger had attacked, he had done so primarily with his claws and not with his teeth.

Memory rushed back to me. Could this be that elusive tiger, the 'Mauler of Rajnagara', that had beaten me at the first encounter, grown bolder with the passage of time and become a confirmed man-eater, to appear now as the 'Man-Eater of Pegepalyam'? The evidence of the two men appeared to indicate the likelihood that this tiger was the same animal.

I took a lot of trouble in pursuing my inquiries on these lines, not only at Pegepalyam itself but at one or two of the nearer hamlets where this animal had claimed his victims, and also with the Forest department at Kollegal. A number of the human victims had been recovered before the tiger had completely eaten them. All had been clawed, but they had also been bitten. There was no conclusive evidence that the tiger killed only by clawing, as had been the method of attack by the 'Mauler'; and in any case, the actions of clawing and biting would both take place on any carcass in the normal process of a tiger eating it.

271

My first visit to Pegepalyam lasted only a week, but the man-eater did not touch any of the three live-baits I offered. Nor was there any news of him whatever during that period. Duty called and there was no excuse for extending my leave. I returned to Bangalore.

Since then, as I have indicated, the man-eater has killed again—a fifteen-year-old boy in broad daylight and in an open field, with the big town of Kollegal only six miles away. This time my son, Donald, is going after him and hopes to have more luck than I did.

We would both like to know very much if the man-eater is the mauler of which I have told you, although there seems no possible way of proving this point unless Donald succeeds in finding some reason for the quite unusual habit the mauler had of attacking with his claws rather than his teeth. If he succeeds, Donald will have certainly unravelled a most intriguing jungle mystery.

And as I think these thoughts, these pages and this handwriting once again fade from sight. In imagination I see the roaring flames of a camp-fire before me, from which cascades of sparks shower fitfully into the darkness, while a thick spiral of smoke curls upwards to the sky.

It is a clear night, but few of the myriad stars that spangle the sky are visible owing to the glow from the camp-fire.

With all its vigour, the flickering light is only able to dispel the shadows for about fifteen yards around me. Beyond is blackness—intense, silent and all-pervading, like some solid substance, covering and enveloping everything—the blackness of a jungle night, a blanket of velvety gloom.

Yet more smoke curls from the bowl of my pipe as I puff at it contentedly. The smoke rises to merge with the smoke from the flames and finally disappears in the flickering, fitful radiance from the fire, with its comforting though slightly oppressive heat.

Silence broods around me, broken only by the crackle and hiss of the flames.

Then I hear it. Over the hills and far away, but drawing nearer and nearer. 'O-o-o-n-o-o-n! A-oongh! A-oongh!' It is the call of a tiger!

I have heard it so often before, and the more I hear it the more I thrill to that awful yet wonderfully melodious sound.

'Ugha-ugh! Ugh! Aungh-ha! A-oongh! O-o-n-o-o-n!' There it is again! The tiger is drawing nearer, ever nearer.

And in my imagination I like to think this will be the 'Man-eater of Pegepalyam'.

Anderson, more famous for hunting man-eating tigers, find
in a wily panther a real challenger to his hunting acumen.
There are thrills, failures, disappointments, and at long las
the elusive success. He tells the real-life adventure story s
in the deep jungle, with snakes, bisons and of course tiger
with unique verve and colour which only he is capable of.

Kenneth Anderson (1910-74) hailed from a Scottish fam
settled in India for six generations. His love for the denize
of Indian jungle led him to big game hunting and eventua
to writing real-life adventure stories. His book are hailed
classics of jungle lore.

Cover Design: Arrt Creations

ISBN 81-7167-467-4

9 788171 674671

Lightning Source UK Ltd.
Milton Keynes UK
UKHW020701110321
380169UK00013B/1142

9 788171 674671